ENEMY CLOSER
THE SECOND EDITION

ANNA BOWMAN THRILLERS
BOOK ONE

This is a work of fiction. Names, characters, places, and incidents are the product of the author's imagination or are used fictitiously. Any resemblance to actual events, locales, or persons, living or dead, is purely coincidental.

Copyright © 2025 by AK Weller
Cover Copyright © by Westley Enterprises, LLC
Book Design by Westley Enterprises, LLC
Edited by Lisa McCoy Editing

All rights reserved. No part of this work may be used in any manner or reproduced or transmitted in any form or by any means, electronic or mechanical, including photocopying, recording, or by any information storage or retrieval system, without written permission of the copyright owner, except for the inclusion of brief quotations in a review.

NO AI TRAINING: Without in any way limiting the author's [and publisher's] exclusive rights under copyright, any use of this publication to "train" generative artificial intelligence (AI) technologies to generate text or images is expressly prohibited. The author reserves all rights to license uses of this work for generative AI training and development of machine learning language models.

Westley Enterprises Publishing
Helena, Montana
www.westleyenterprises.com

SECOND EDITION
ISBN 979-8-9916308-6-3 (Paperback)
ISBN 979-8-9916308-7-0 (eBook)

Dedicated to Cheyenne, for getting me right.

And still dedicated to my dear friend for his encouragement, criticism, and enthusiastic hatred of adverbs. I hope you'll always be out there somewhere, doing weird... stuff.

ALSO BY AK WELLER

Enemy Closer
House on Fire
Bigger Fish
No Port in a Storm
The Lost Portrait

CONTENTS

ENEMY
CLOSER

Introduction

"It's just a thriller, not an updated history textbook. Why do you need an introduction?"

I want readers to know what's different and why. If you read *Enemy Closer* when it was published in 2022, you may find as you're reading the second edition that nothing much has changed. You'd be right. Though I cleaned up some sloppy writing, it's the same story. The characters are the same, the plot is almost untouched, and certainly the "why" of the book is the same as it's always been.

The original Anna Bowman Thrillers were written during a difficult time, when I was so overwhelmed by life that I had to choose between going insane and pouring my heart, soul, and guts out onto the pages of a book or two or five. As a result, the graphic content in those original stories was more of an expression of my confusion and fear than of the sort of story I want to put my name on. While the originals would be rated R if they were movies, the second edition is firmly PG with occasional PG-13 scenes.

I don't want to alienate readers with graphic content, but there is still significant violence throughout the story. Sex and profanity are choices; violence is ever-present and as unavoidable as growing old. Violence helped create the original Anna Bowman Thrillers, and I've chosen to honor the peace in my life by cleaning up the sex and profanity. That makes perfect sense to me. If it's difficult for some readers to understand or appreciate, all I can tell you is, write your own darn books.

Seriously, write books. It's way better than going insane.

1

Saturday, June 20, 2020

I killed the engine and waited for a cloud of red dust to settle. In the passenger seat, Dude's desperation to get out of the pickup manifested itself in a barely audible whine. When I met his eyes, his ears stood at attention, eager to listen.

"I bet you need to go potty," I said. His answering bark was earsplitting in the close confines of the cab. I grabbed the last granola bar from my bag of snacks and climbed out, Dude bounding over the center console to follow me.

The air outside hit me like a blast from a campfire. I walked around the truck to get a better look at the cabin, the smoky odor of my pickup's overworked engine fading with the last of the dust it had kicked up. Shading my eyes against the sun hammering down on me from a cloudless, blue sky, I turned away from the unimpressive cabin to study the landscape. It wasn't at all what I'd expected.

The word 'Colorado' put me in mind of towering pine trees

on snowy slopes, shady trails through lush forests, and mild temperatures to which Texans like me fled in the summer when the South became unlivable. This cabin was in the middle of a desert, albeit with more trees and less sand than your typical desert.

Dude meandered off to explore the area. As his heavy paw-steps crunched away over gravel and dry pine needles, a silence unlike anything I'd ever known settled over me. Every *click-tick* of the cooling engine, every breath I took, even my own pulse seemed rudely loud. I wanted to open my granola bar and take a bite, but it didn't feel right to make such a racket.

I could feel my pale face and forearms burning as I stood there, though not a drop of answering sweat appeared on my skin. Spotting Dude roaming around behind the cabin, where thick trees blocked out some of the sun, I decided I better join him and get the lay of the land.

I grabbed one armful of stuff from the pickup and ducked into the cabin to drop it inside the door. I didn't waste time hunting for the key; I left the door unlocked. I'd seen all of three people since turning onto the unpaved road leading here, and the latest had been over half an hour ago. Hesperus, in rural southwest Colorado, was as far away from civilization as I'd ever been, for all the good and ill it would do me.

At least I had one friend, the only one I really needed. Bounding along beside me as I walked around the backyard enclosure and onto a path behind the cabin, Dude wagged his tail in luxurious, unhurried arcs. My two-year-old German Shepherd was a better companion that most humans I knew. *He* never lied to me. Tipping the scales at around 110 pounds, he would be more than a match for almost anything that tried to harm me. I alternated between eyeing the path ahead and watching my dog bask in an environment he'd never experienced before.

The crisp air smelled of pine and sage, an occasional warm breeze stirring the otherwise complete stillness. Though dry, the forest was a riot of life, desert shrubs rubbing shoulders with scrub oak, piñon pine, and cedar. Red earth, fallen pine needles, pinecones, and the eponymous rocks crunched under my feet.

Dude was ecstatic. I had to pause my uphill hike frequently so he could sniff everything twice, his furiously wagging tail only slowing when some particularly interesting scent caught his nose. His unencumbered joy made me so happy, I almost forgot why I was there.

A branch snapped ahead of us, crashing noisily to the ground, and I froze in place. For a couple seconds I couldn't breathe, but I relaxed when Dude gave the sound only cursory attention before carrying on. If he wasn't worried, I didn't have to be. Nevertheless, the happy feeling vanished, and I focused on the unpleasant task ahead of me.

Somewhere in these woods were answers that might get me killed, and it was only a matter of time before Philip tracked me down. I didn't even know where to start looking, and now that I'd gotten a taste of the vast emptiness around me, success seemed unlikely.

I caught up to Dude, and we hiked for a quarter hour more until I had to stop for a break. I was breathing hard after my first real exertion at this altitude. Disappointed in my own frailty, I told myself the thin air, not my leg muscles, were to blame. In a few days I'd be used to it and ready for anything.

We'd stopped in a grassy meadow bordered by trees to the north, east, and south, a sheer cliff face about twenty feet tall looming to the west. Above that, the mountain continued to climb to a height of about twelve thousand feet—more of a hill, since we were already standing at eight thousand.

The woods were as dry as tinder, making me wonder what Dude and I would do in the all too likely event of a forest fire. Where would we go? Would we be able to make it out via the endless gravel road between here and the state highway, or would the woods burn too fast, trapping us within?

Unburdened by my dark thoughts, Dude trotted away through the tall grass. He had a job to do, and I smiled as I watched him establish his protective perimeter. As long as we stayed in this place, he would consider it his duty to guard this imaginary line against anything bigger than a mouse.

I strolled to the center of the clearing, evaluating. A city girl to the core, I decided I loved the serene isolation and untouched beauty of these desert woods; but I was already bored. Dude finished his patrol and came back to me, plopping down a yard away to stare at me with an expectant expression. I pulled out my cell phone and checked to see how many bars I had. The top left-hand corner of the screen said 'No Service.'

"Fantastic," I sighed, slipping the useless object back into my pocket. I looked down at Dude and asked, "How about some target practice, then?"

All those months behind a desk could not have improved my marksmanship, and it was about time I got in some practice with my Glock 29. Though my dad had gifted the subcompact handgun to me well over a decade ago, it had been locked in my closet since I moved from Texas to Washington, DC a few years ago and was no longer allowed to carry it around. That had been an adjustment.

"I think I'll aim for that stump," I informed Dude, who'd never even heard gunfire. Something told me he wouldn't like it.

I drew, aimed, and fired three rounds. Even at ten yards, I missed twice before hearing the satisfying thump of lead striking the dense tree stump. Dude barked once.

"Sorry. That was loud."

I considered emptying the magazine, a mere eight more rounds, but I thought better of it. My spare magazine was in my backpack, in the cabin, and my compact 10mm wouldn't do much to defend me against predators if I turned it into a six hundred-dollar paperweight.

It was after six o'clock when we got back to the cabin, later than I'd guessed. I unpacked, showered, straightened up a little—needlessly—and avoided thoughts of dinner. There would be a few frozen meals for one in the freezer, courtesy of the cabin's owner, maybe even a bottle of wine in the pantry. Neither of those things was what I wanted.

I wanted to sit down in front of a huge flat screen television and order sushi on my phone while flipping through a mind numbing selection of movies and TV shows; I wanted to hear the constant rumble of city buses lumbering past on the street below my apartment on Dupont Circle; I wanted to have to turn the volume up to drown out my neighbor Dominque's "little get together." I wanted the city. *My* city.

Instead I had a combination VCR and 24-inch CRT TV and the endless peace of no less than fifteen miles of privately-owned land in every direction. I had a shooting range of sorts, a very big gymnasium for my own personal use that smelled of piñon pine instead of men's stinky socks, and even my dog; but if I wanted to hear city sounds, I'd have to pop the right movie into the VCR, close my eyes, and fake it. And I might as well forget about sushi.

Eventually I surrendered to the optimism required to go rooting around the tiny kitchen for this theoretical bottle of wine, and I was rewarded for my efforts by a relatively pricy bottle of merlot. Not knowing if I'd make it to the grocery store tomorrow, I allowed myself half a glass, then it was time for bed at 8:30. With no light pollution, it felt more like midnight.

Giving in to my better instincts, I ventured out into the pitch-dark night a few feet from the front door to look at the stars. I left Dude inside, the better to prevent a last-minute perimeter check that would have me waiting on the porch for an hour or more.

I craned my neck to look directly upward and gasped, hardly believing my eyes. There were so many stars, it seemed like every light in the universe was staring back at me. Some were so bright I couldn't look directly at them. For several minutes I enjoyed the breathtaking sight, but eventually I was distracted by a crick in my neck and thoughts of everything under those stars.

Bears, mountain lions, rattlesnakes, tarantulas, coyotes, all stalked these woods, and worse things I refused to think about.

As dry as it had been lately, most would be pretty hungry. I feared nothing, neither in the city nor the country, with Dude watching over me; but Dude was scratching at the door, wordlessly reminding me that all I had was my pistol and my wits to keep me safe out here. The latter sent me back inside with one last admiring look at the stars.

After feeding Dude, I scanned through the handful of books I'd lugged along, ignoring the new ones. I wanted familiarity, lines that would practically read themselves to me as I lost consciousness. I snuggled into the bed in the loft upstairs, cradling *The Scarlet Pimpernel* and all the hope of comfort it contained.

I made it to chapter two before a tickling sensation on my right shoulder wrenched me away from the story. Hoping it was my hair, I turned my head just enough to see a dime-sized brown body and eight horrible, spindly little legs on my bare skin.

The scream that exploded out of me was primal, a sound I could only make when under arachnid attack. Convulsing, I leapt from the bed and brushed myself off all over, twice. I combed through my hair, stripped naked and shook all my clothes out, and flipped through my book to check for any of the spider's friends. It wasn't like I'd ever encountered two spiders at once, but that didn't prevent me from compulsively looking every time one dared to cross my path.

The loft was out, obviously. I settled for the couch downstairs, cocooning myself in a thoroughly inspected blanket that prevented any contact with the untested upholstery.

2

Sunday, June 21, 2020

I rose with the sun, blinking back rays of light that pierced the thin curtains over the east-facing windows. First on my to-do list was a trip to the store for groceries, at least until I stood up. Naked as a baby, I remembered the spider episode from last night. I streaked into the bathroom, found the old clothes some previous guest had left in the linen closet, and threw on a men's extra-large t-shirt. Breakfast would have to wait until after I'd de-spidered the loft. I let Dude out to do his business and then had to face facts: There was a spider in the cabin.

"You knew this would happen, dummy," I mumbled to myself, rooting around in the kitchen for a weapon. "It's the wilderness."

Some kind soul had left a can of arachnid spray under the sink. I hesitated to pick it up, repulsed by the villainous-looking spider, tick, and scorpion on the label. Did Raid not know what kind of people resorted to chemical warfare just to kill a tiny bug?

I pushed past my discomfort and grabbed the can. Armed with this and a vacuum cleaner, I cleaned and sprayed the entire loft, stripped the bed, and dumped the linens in the washing machine. A part of me knew this was all pointless—the spider had probably hitched a ride in my braid from the hike yesterday—but I had to do it. I hated my kryptonite, my Achilles heel, this absurd arachnophobia; but it had turned me into one heck of a cleaner.

By the time I was satisfied the loft was inhabitable, it was already noon. I threw on the first clothes I found and jumped into my truck, absurdly eager to go grocery shopping. Breakfast on the way was Durango Joes, which was my only option unless I wanted wine for breakfast. I had to leave Dude in the cabin, and as soon as I got on the road, I felt a stab of lonely regret.

Like a lunatic, I had kept up a steady, one-sided conversation with Dude on the interminable drive from Washington, DC to Hesperus, Colorado. Aside from occasional wild-eyed glances from the passenger seat, he had ignored me in favor of watching the scenery race past the truck's windows, transforming from lush swamps to misty mountains, from dense forests to rolling hills to plains, and finally from fertile mountains to desert wilderness.

Dude had drawn so much out of me, fecklessly helping me piece together the disparate threads of my life into something I could cope with, mostly. Without my loyal pooch, I was just a 33-year-old, nominally unemployed, single woman in a black Dodge Ram, driving forty minutes one way to buy a month's worth of groceries. I didn't even know how many times I'd have to do this.

▼

I returned to the cabin at a quarter to three, a couple hundred dollars lighter and bearing enough food and other supplies to get Dude and me through more than a month of total isolation. The June day was deliciously warm, dry as the inside of an oven and perfectly, utterly still. I could scarcely stay inside long enough to put away the perishables before heading out again.

With Dude at my side and the basics in my backpack, I set out to explore the woods immediately around the cabin. I had to adjust my holster from my right hip to the front of my waistband because of the straps of the backpack, and as we hiked, I practiced my draw again and again until it felt good. Everything I missed while preoccupied with this task was thoroughly inspected by Dude, who guided me on a non-linear but generally upward path.

I let Dude lead me for an hour, long after I was satisfied I would be able to get my sights on target in under one second without accidentally clipping my femoral artery. Guessing we had about four hours of daylight left, I stopped and sat down on a fallen log. A minute later Dude realized I was no longer behind him and came trotting back, allowing me to serve him some water in his collapsible dog dish. I nursed my own bottle of water, munched on a granola bar, and contemplated my existence.

I had no real neighbors here. A retired couple named Ernest and Doreen Perkins, the cabin's owners, and their cows lived on the closest adjoining property. Their house was several miles away, and for the rest of June, they were in Ireland. My boss had rented the cabin from Doreen, who'd handled everything from Ireland.

Though my chances of running into any other people were low, the land had been settled in the early eighteen hundreds, so remnants of human habitation over the past two centuries were bound to crop up if I kept hiking and looking hard enough. Perhaps I would look, just to give myself someplace to start. But today, my dog was leading me toward the summit, and I was feeling brash enough to try to get there and back before dark.

"What are we, about halfway up?" I asked Dude, who cocked an ear at me. "Probably less, the way you hike."

I checked the altimeter on my watch and was dismayed to see we'd only gained 900 feet in elevation, leaving over 3,000 between us and the summit. Dude had been meandering more than I realized. I glared up at the sky, reevaluating. Maybe I would start again tomorrow and try to carve a more logical path from the cabin to the summit. I stood, stretched, and packed Dude's water dish into my backpack.

I met his eager, brown eyes and said firmly, "Haus."

He set off at once, confidently cutting an easterly, downhill course. Though it was instantly obvious we weren't returning by the way we'd come, I had no doubt his nose would get us back to the cabin.

After an hour and a half of hiking, however, I had to ask myself: Was Dude trying to get back to the cabin, or to Washington?

After another hour and a half, I had my answer. One look at the mountain ridge across the valley told me we were too far north and, very likely, already east of the cabin. Though I'd been fighting defeat for the better part of an hour, I groaned and sat down, calling Dude back to me.

"Well, this is perfect," I announced.

No sooner had the words left my mouth than I felt a long, low rumble to the north. A moment later I heard a rush of water nearby, a stone's throw to my right. I got up and edged toward the sound, pushing apart a thick clump of scrub oak to reveal a sharp drop on the other side. Roughly twenty feet below me, a deep creek bed had been transformed into a stream, which was quickly gaining volume and speed as rain from the north fed into it.

If I followed the creek south, chances were I'd come to the bridge I had crossed to get from the gravel road to the cabin. I had no idea how long that would take.

"Thanks a lot, Dude," I snarled.

I was hungry, tired, and furious at myself for being such a ridiculous city slicker. The sum of my supplies—phone, map, water bottle, fire starter, first aid kit, spare magazine, collapsible dog dish, flashlight, jacket, key to the cabin—fit in a backpack I'd had since high school. Would it have been so hard to put down a cairn or two on our way up, or to pack some real food? Why would I think Dude would suddenly consider the little cabin our home, when the apartment in Washington was the only home he'd ever known?

The rain came as the last rays of the sun disappeared from the tips of the highest trees across the valley. It was light but cold. As it fell, the surrounding woods began to emit the sweetest smell I'd ever smelled, so delicious I stopped to take it in. My anxiety about being lost in the woods started to slip away with each breath, until I realized I was actually glad to be outside, glad to be alone, even glad to be tired and dirty.

I closed my eyes, leaned back, and let the rain tickle my face until the sensation caused an involuntary shudder to rack my body. Laughing, I shook my head to get rid of the excess water. Dude, not to be left out, vigorously shook the water out of his fur and onto my clothes. The smell of wet dog broke through my lack of motivation and we set off south, following the creek.

As the light faded, the storm picked up until the sound of the stream rushing along at our left was nearly lost in the cacophony of raindrops. I fished the flashlight out of my backpack and clicked it on, and the last dregs of optimism finally drained away. It was fully dark, and we should have gotten to the bridge already. Even Dude had stopped wagging his tail and was merely plodding along at my side, huffing every time I paused to try to get my bearings.

"This isn't so bad," I reassured him with forced cheerfulness. "Just think how good it'll feel to curl up in front of the TV and watch a movie when we get home."

A piercing bark erupted from beside me and Dude shot off like a cannonball, crashing through the scrubby bushes ahead and vanishing into the darkness. I heard a few more barks, a splash, a growl, and then the sound of the rain took over again.

"Dude?"

Creeping forward, I directed the flashlight's beam from right to left and back again. Dude was nowhere to be seen. The bushes through which he had disappeared were dense and tall, and they stretched from the steep bank of the creek on the left as far as the light would shine on the right. I had to pocket the flashlight, lean forward, cover my head in my hands, and force my way through.

Scratched and somehow even wetter, I emerged on the other side. Knowing I'd just plunged through uncounted spiderwebs, I forced my breathing into a slow, predictable pattern and fumbled in my pocket to retrieve the flashlight. I clicked it on and panned around again.

"Dude? What the heck, man?"

The beam fell on the broad wooden planks of the bridge, and in the center of it lay my dog, tail wagging once more as he nosed joyously at something cat-sized between his front paws. It gave a plaintive quack and he barked in response, leaping up to bow to it in the universal doggy sign for, "Play with me!"

"You abandoned me for a *duck*?" I demanded. "You butthole!"

In answer, he gently picked the duck up by its neck and carried it over to where I stood, dropping it proudly at my feet. I watched it labor upright and then fall over again, disoriented but not sporting any obvious injuries.

"I'm not hungry."

Dude sat down, front paws astride the bewildered bird, and gave one pointed bark.

"Come on," I sighed. "Let's go home already. No, leave it. *Leave it.*"

Another half hour brought us within sight of the cabin,

warm light flooding through the windows and onto the gravel driveway. Dude, his duck offering forgotten, dashed ahead and began pawing at the door. Though I was as eager as he was to get inside, I stopped at the door and faced him.

"Sitz. Bleib."

He sat at once, eyes gleaming, and stayed put while I walked back down the driveway. I stopped several yards away before turning to face him again. Standing with my back to the dark woods was no picnic, but I ignored the impulse to look behind me.

"Komm!"

He bounded toward me, the cozy cabin all but forgotten.

"So, there is a brain in there!" I said by way of praise. "Now. Haus."

Watching him struggle to work it out was almost more than my severe façade could take. He glanced down the driveway, straight northeast as though guided by a compass; then with a whine he looked up at me, back down the driveway, back to me, then once at the pickup next to us before finally he made up his mind and returned to the cabin.

"Good boy, good dog!"

Halfway back to the door myself, I heard something behind me and whirled around, running the beam of light over my pickup and the trees that grew up to the edge of the driveway behind it. Warm pressure on my right thigh told me Dude had come to lean against me. I felt a deep, silent growl building in his chest as he gazed toward a spot to the left of the pickup.

"Hel—hello?" I stammered.

The growl rose in pitch, and Dude took one half-step forward. With a thrill of genuine fear, I saw his hackles were bristling, his teeth bared. My right hand drifted toward my Glock, but something told me retreat would be wiser than a show of force. I grabbed Dude's collar, turned us both around, and marched toward the cabin at double-time, too frightened to look at anything but the doorknob getting closer and closer.

The door, unlocked, gave way before my trembling hand and I stumbled inside, slamming it closed behind us. The *thunk* of the deadbolt sliding home was music to my ears. Dude stalked to the nearest window at once, pressed his nose to the glass, and froze.

"Duuuuuude, could you not?"

He answered with a low growl. Whatever was out there, he could still see it.

"Wine," I squeaked, manically chipper. "Wine is what we need."

I poured a generous glass, walked around the living room three times, took a sip, and then realized I was still wearing my backpack and hiking boots. Once I'd divested myself of both, I sank down onto the couch and took a second sip. My gaze was drawn inexorably to Dude, whose tail began to sweep from side to side as he continued to look through the window. Giving up on the wine, I joined him at the window and pressed my nose to the glass, too.

How long we sat staring at the rain-washed driveway I had no idea, only that I never saw anything. When my stomach gave such a mighty grumble that Dude's ears flicked unwillingly toward me, I tore myself away from the window and wandered to the kitchen for some dinner.

A hot dinner, warm shower, and the rest of the glass of wine later, I was drifting away on the couch with *Emma* keeping me company, feeling silly for getting lost and almost getting eaten by a mountain lion or whatever it was. Dude, who had resumed his post as soon as the last kibble of dinner had passed his lips, had long since curled into a ball in the chair next to the door. His long snout was propped on the arm of the chair, eyes darting toward the window every few seconds.

3

Monday, June 22, 2020

My eyes closed on that dark, rainy scene and opened onto a cabin transformed by morning. Through the east-facing windows, sunlight slanted sharply across the blank TV screen to bathe Dude in an ethereal halo of light. The great beast was snoozing peacefully in the exact position I'd last seen him, now blissfully ignorant of the threat in the woods. The cabin was chilly, but I was smothered in multiple blankets and had to throw them off to escape the heat.

I stood, stretched, and winced as a sore spot in my groin reminded me I'd never removed my holster last night. I readjusted it to the side and woefully rubbed the spot where a sharp edge had been digging into my skin while I slept.

This commotion roused Dude, who hopped down from the chair and began scratching at the door to go outside. I didn't think twice about opening the door; the freshly minted morning was the furthest thing imaginable from the horror movie scenario of the previous night. I let Dude out and, intending to follow him outside to get a better view of the sunrise, bumped right into his ample backside.

He was absorbed in something on the welcome mat, but as soon as I bumped him, he trotted off to do his business. I glanced down to see what was so interesting and saw a large, green and blue feather. Unimpressed, I tracked the dog as he cut across the driveway and into the trees behind my pickup, not to do his business, but to sniff eagerly around the spot as though looking for some trace of his new arch nemesis. I took another look at the feather.

Maybe it was the way it lay on the welcome mat, perfectly centered, quill pointing east, no other feathers in sight, that gave me a tingle of unease. I picked it up gingerly and twirled it between my thumb and forefinger. I was no expert, but it sure looked like a duck feather to me. I went to see what Dude had found, if anything, unconsciously slipping the feather into my pocket. Just inside the tree line, his nose was pressed to the ground inspecting what I assumed were paw prints. They were big and deep, confirming my worst fear: The tracks were made by a mountain lion or a bear, almost certainly the former considering how quiet it had been.

But as I pushed Dude away to look for claw marks, hoping to rule out mountain lion, I realized I wasn't looking at paw prints at all. Among the scuffs and general disarray caused by Dude's investigation, two distinct boot prints were plainly visible in the mud, toes directed toward my front door. Either the depressions had been protected from the rain last night, or the person who made them hadn't moved until the rain had let up—after I fell asleep.

They were large, at least size twelve, and so deep I had to marvel for a moment at the sheer size of the person wearing the shoes; or possibly I was only seeing what I wanted to see. He'd been mere feet from me in the darkness, and he'd done nothing.

A slow, disbelieving smile spread across my face, and I cast around the ground nearby for more prints. The tree cover was thickest over the footprints, and a step or two in any direction lay ground that would have been more exposed to the rain. There were no other prints in sight, and I concluded it had still been raining when he'd left.

"Go potty, Dude," I mumbled, still quite distracted by the questions and possibilities running through my head. It wasn't one of the fifteen core commands, but Dude knew what I meant. He picked his way deeper into the trees for some privacy, and I retreated to the driveway to gaze at the sunrise as originally intended.

The sun was just peeking over the top of the east ridge, dazzling me and warming the chilly morning air. I cupped a hand over my eyes and squinted down at the road, a mile or so away, which stretched twenty miles north-to-south and connected two remote Colorado state highways. A battered looking white Bronco was trundling north, kicking up a cloud of red dust in its wake. Last night's rain had already evaporated in the bone dry air. As I watched the Bronco disappear around a bend in the road, I was thinking of my view from home.

In two years, I'd only seen a road this deserted when the

president's motorcade was out and about, and a lone SUV had set out to scout the street in front of my apartment. The president's car hadn't even come that way. The scout had been one of dozens of SUVs sent out on every possible street they might've taken, but the whole block was shut down the entire day nonetheless. I wondered if the driver of the white Bronco even knew what the president looked like.

Once we got back inside, I decided to plot a course to the summit today. It seemed like a logical thing for a girl to do on her Colorado vacation. We struck out an hour after waking up, kitted out in more or less the same fashion as the day before. All I added to my gear was a poncho in my backpack, a second spare magazine, and some food, while Dude got to carry his doggy backpack laden with extra water, his own food, and a rain fly.

Dude was compelled to follow me this time, the better to forge a trail to the top that didn't double back on itself ninety-two times. I built a cairn where we left the gravel of the driveway, picked a spot uphill at the limit of my sight line, and climbed up to it to build another cairn. From the second cairn, I looked back to make sure I could still see the first. The unlikely arrangement of stacked rocks stood out surprisingly well against its disordered backdrop. I had no idea if this were the correct cairn-building procedure, but it seemed fairly idiot-proof to me.

The problem was that the higher up we got, the wilder the land became. Within a thousand feet of the cabin, the ground had been tamped down in a handful of fairly logical upward courses, all crisscrossing one another. After that, we were dealing with truly untouched woods. I lost count of how many cairns I built, only to trudge back and knock them over when the path ahead proved to be a dead end.

At 10:00, when I estimated we should have been halfway to the top, my altimeter read 9,301 feet. I couldn't believe it—three hours to hike less than 2,000 feet. Granted, we were stopping and backtracking frequently, but that was still dismal progress.

While I sat on a flat rock and mulled this over, Dude paced back and forth in front of me, eager to get moving again. By contrast, I was out of breath and slightly dizzy. I hadn't counted on feeling the altitude this much, another stupid mistake. My apartment was literally eighty feet above sea level. I gained five percent in elevation just by getting out of bed in the morning. My body was spoiled rotten with oxygen in Washington—not to mention moisture.

I forced down an energy bar and as much water as I could stomach before setting out again. If this was to be our pace, I couldn't waste any more time sitting around feeling puny.

Though my self-imposed task became more arduous with each cairn, Dude and I finally gained the summit just before 5:00. Exhausted as I was, the view from the top was worth every second of toil to get there.

We were about one hundred feet above the tree line, at the highest point for ten or twelve miles in any direction. The air was thin and cool, and thankfully no clouds had formed to threaten me with rain and lightning. Behind me, to the west, the slope of the mountain was significantly steeper. To the north and south, its spine rose and fell to form a number of false peaks, all below the tree line.

I stood on top of the world, surveying my domain, basking in the glow of conquest. The feeling was so heady I found myself laughing in disbelief, recalling with perfect clarity how the land had almost swallowed me up less than twenty-four hours ago.

Even with his boundless energy, Dude was tired, too. He lay down near my feet and rested his head on his paws, gazing out at the scene with what I imagined was satisfaction.

I gave him some water and wet dog food, his prize for sticking with me all the way to the top. For my own prize I forced down another disgusting protein bar and an entire bottle of water, chasing it with a pouch of energy supplement that was so sweet I nearly gagged. It wasn't much of a reward, but I'd need to really hoof it to get back to the cabin. Even if we started now and practically ran down the mountain, there was no chance we'd get back before it was fully dark outside. The prospect was uninviting to say the least, but the alternative—hunkering down, tentless, somewhere between the summit and the cabin and waiting for daylight—was worse.

Still, a few more minutes up here wouldn't make much difference, so I sat down and explored the eastern slope of the mountain with my eyes, comparing it to the satellite images I'd studied before leaving Washington.

I could pick out neither my cabin nor the meadow above it that I'd used as a shooting gallery. The denser, greener vegetation along the creek was my only point of reference. Beyond that, the scene compressed by my distance from it, the county road snaked its way along roughly the same course as the creek.

Turning to the south, I could barely discern a patch of bright blue nestled among the trees on the adjoining property: Ernest and Doreen Perkins, who I knew lived in a cabin with a blue metal roof. I turned north, wondering if I could spot any other structures, but the shoulders of the mountain were so high I couldn't see as far. There was something, though…

I stood up automatically, as though that would help me see better. Without binoculars, all I could do was cup a hand over my eyes and squint down at the tiny group of angles and straight lines that hinted at some kind of man-made structure. I couldn't tell how big it was or even what it was, but I knew it wasn't nothing.

I glanced back at the blue roof, then at the road, picking out a spot to the north of the roof and west of the road to approximate the location of my cabin. The mystery structure was about a mile to the northwest of my cabin, and it certainly had not appeared on the satellite images. Those images had been two years old, meaning either the structure was newer than that, or I had missed it when I was virtually exploring the area.

Dude stood, stretched languidly, and leaned against my thigh. I could feel his eagerness to get moving again, and it fueled my own. We had lingered long enough.

I extracted the paper map from my backpack and hastily marked down the location of the structure, or rather my best guess given the roughness of my estimates and lack of absolute points of reference. With that done, we began our descent.

The six hours it should have taken us to make the ascent were reduced to five on the way down, so much faster was our pace. My system of cairns worked beautifully, and I was impressed with myself. Nevertheless, the sun set when we were only halfway down, and darkness followed close on its heels. The last two hours of the trek were made by moonlight, aided occasionally by the beam of my flashlight. The otherwise gentle quiet became menacing in the near-total absence of light.

To distract myself from what would have been crippling fear, I put together a game plan for tomorrow. I'd sleep in for sure, as the hike in search of my mystery structure would be more of a stroll compared to today. I wouldn't need to carry much, and I'd have to conceal my handgun. I'd better leave Dude behind, too. On the off chance I found the man who made those footprints, the last thing I needed was for my massive guard dog to either scare him away or reveal himself to be a friendly, goofy people-pleaser.

Not until we'd entered the cabin and I'd closed the door behind us did I allow myself to feel the fear that had pursued me down the mountain.

"That was so stupid," I breathed, pressing my hands to the comforting, if insufficient, barrier of the locked door. "So, so, *so* stupid."

I could chide myself some more, but my heart wasn't in it. Now that we'd regained the relative safety of the cabin and the fear was just a memory, I was pleased with myself and proud of my furry friend. We had conquered the mountain.

I wasn't tired anymore, either. After a quick shower, I whipped up a calorie fest for dinner: fried chicken, mashed potatoes, green beans, and of course a glass of wine. I popped

Jurassic Park into the VHS player, gave Dude an extra-large dinner, and settled onto the couch; then I fell asleep with my dinner forgotten on the coffee table.

4

Tuesday, June 23 to
Wednesday, June 24, 2020

When I woke up, several minutes passed in utter disorientation while I tried to remember where I was and why. Never in my life had I slept such a deep, undisturbed sleep. A year, or perhaps only a few minutes had passed since I'd closed my eyes. My whole body ached in a good way, and my throat was as dry as though I'd polished off an entire bottle of wine rather than pouring and then forgetting a single glass of it.

I stumbled to the kitchen for water, which was Dude's signal to start scratching at the door.

"Please don't let me sleep on that couch again tonight," I implored him as I let him outside.

I made coffee and surveyed the disaster state in which I'd left the kitchen. Cleaning up my mess would take an hour or more, but I didn't feel like cleaning. I caught sight of my spotlessly clean plate on the coffee table and decided to let Dude clean up whatever else he could reach. Good thing I'd opted for boneless chicken.

As comforting as it would be to have Dude by my side, I couldn't take him with me today. On top of my wish not to scare away anyone I encountered, the danger to him was too great. What if said stranger was armed? I would just have to look after myself.

With this sobering thought, I abjured the kitchen cleanup and started getting ready for a much shorter hike than the day before. In addition to the usual hiking clothes, I fastened an oversized flannel shirt around my waist under which to hide the Glock holstered behind my right hip. The folds of plaid flannel made the bulge of the holster hard to see, but drawing a gun from such deep concealment would take at least twice as long as normal.

With my arms bare in the loose-fitting tank top I'd chosen, I paused in front of a mirror to study myself. I looked a bit leaner than when I'd left Washington, or I was imagining things. For a moment I turned this way and that, liking the way the shadows threw my hard-earned triceps and biceps into sharp definition, until my mother's half-teasing admonition popped into my head.

Stop admiring yourself in the mirror, young lady.

"Fine," I muttered, annoyed at the phantom intrusion. It wasn't as though all the rigorous training I'd put myself through had paid off in the end.

I reduced my backpack's contents to lessen the weight, opting for a bottle of water, my useless cell phone, a granola bar, and a can of bear spray. When I stepped outside around ten o'clock to begin my search for the mystery structure, I felt positively naked.

As I started down the driveway, Dude realized he was being left behind and began to howl frantically. I winced, hating myself for leaving him, as his howls grew sharper and louder. I knew he was hamming it up—as soon as I was out of sight, he'd probably get started cleaning the kitchen the same way he'd cleaned my plate last night—but it still made me feel like a jerk.

I made my way first to the bridge, then cut into the woods and began to retrace my steps from two nights ago. I planned to follow the creek north for one mile, then cut west uphill and begin a spiral search at 9,000 feet elevation. It could take an hour, or it could take several days, but I was determined to find that building. Even if it turned out to be no more than an abandoned remnant of early settlers, it was a place to start.

In the end, though I tramped through the woods for four solid hours, north then west then south then east then north again a dozen times, my prey eluded me. I was too hungry to search anymore and could think of nothing but food, so at the northwestern-most point of my search area I noted the elevation—9,715 feet—and headed straight east until I hit the creek. I built a cairn at the edge of the drop-off and walked south for an hour and a half to get back to the bridge. My methods might not have been the most scientific, but the last thing I needed was to get caught with the tools required to conduct a real, thoroughgoing search.

The rigamarole and exertion had gotten me through the day, but I'd never expected to find him that quickly. With one day's search under my belt, I returned to the cabin and let myself feel the fear I'd been successfully ignoring all day. Sooner or later, I *would* find him, and then I'd find out what kind of person he really was.

When Dude and I had gotten lost that first night, we might have passed right by the structure in the dark. I thought about the duck, and the boot prints, and that feather, and a chill settled around me in spite of the balmy June afternoon.

▼

Wednesday dawned a gloomy, cheerless gray. When I stepped outside to begin a new day's search, I was shocked to feel a chill in the air. It wasn't the briskness of a desert morning; it was genuinely cold. I ducked back inside to swap my tank top for a long-sleeved shirt, then set off at a quick pace to get my blood pumping as soon as possible.

A wiser woman would have grabbed an umbrella or rain jacket too, but I was only half-pretending to be a clueless city girl. It didn't occur to me that the cold might foreshadow rain until I heard again that rumble of thunder in the distance.

"Okay, I thought this was the *desert*," I complained to no one as I plopped down under a cedar to eat lunch.

No sooner had I gotten settled with my flannel as a picnic blanket than the sky let forth, fat rain drops making the dirt and pine needles dance outside the shelter of the cedar's thick branches. I ate my PBJ and apple with unhurried pleasure, still warm from the hike and wrapped again in that sweet, woodsy smell kicked up by the rain.

As the thunder grew louder, the lightning ever closer, I worried how Dude was coping with the rain in my absence. The mighty German Shepherd was a bit of a wuss when the sky started to fall, unless I was there to give him a reason to act brave.

How clearly I could recall the first thunderstorm after I'd moved to Washington. It was a pale shadow of the North Texas storms that made the house shake and the lights flicker, but it was a good one all the same. I'd sat at work and gazed out the window, my task of the moment forgotten as I watched all the important people caught outside, scurrying for cover in their fine suits and high heels. When I'd come home that night, my living room floor was covered in fluff from the throw pillows Dude had eviscerated in his unhinged panic.

Dude was the first dog I ever owned. I'd had no idea dogs were afraid of thunderstorms, and I'd felt so bad for leaving him alone that I'd given him the steak I brought home for dinner and eaten a disappointing salad instead.

I couldn't recall easing over to lay on my side, but that was how I woke up sometime later.

The rain still fell, though lightly now, and a chill had seeped through my shirt into my very bones. My arm shook as I raised my watch to my face. I'd been asleep for nearly an hour. I sat up, groaning.

Though the cedar had kept me mostly dry, the cold was a real problem. I was ill prepared for anything but sunny, warm weather, and I couldn't seem to stop shaking. As I dragged my flannel out from under me and shrugged into it, I weighed my options: Return to the cabin and admit defeat for the day, or suck it up and carry on?

I sipped some water to give myself time to think. I had a job to do, but Dude needed me. I needed to make some progress. I needed to not die of hypothermia. Tomorrow was another day, but today was barely half over. Choices, choices.

My dithering was interrupted by a faint shuffling sound that seemed to come from my right. I couldn't tell how close it was. My heart started to pound before I even realized I was scared, and I drew my Glock and held it half-concealed between my knees, pointed at the ground, as I squinted into the surrounding trees. Whatever was making that sound, it was either close and small, or far away and big. I prayed it was the former. The cedar hid me from the rain but not much else, and I wasn't exactly dressed in woodland camo.

As the sounds shuffled ever closer, they resolved themselves into so many light footsteps from not one but several small somethings. My pulse slowed, and I nearly laughed with relief when five wild turkeys materialized out of the trees. As birds went they were big, huge even, but a far cry from one of the many apex predators I'd feared.

I holstered my gun and watched, bemused, as they stalked past me. Their heads bobbed stupidly, occasionally darting down to peck at the ground, and they didn't seem to notice me at all. I wished they would gobble—there's nothing funnier than a turkey gobble—but they had nothing to say to me or to one another.

They passed the cedar and continued on their way. At the limit of my vision, they seemed to speed up as one. A few startled gobbles rang out, and then they were out of sight. I started to get up, thinking I'd carry on with my search after all, and stopped mid-movement at the faint but unmistakable sound of a panicked turkey fighting for its life. One last gobble—more of a shriek—cut through the rain, and then silence fell again.

My butt was practically glued to the ground for uncounted minutes. My ears started to work again, letting the light pitter patter of rain drops through. I had no idea what to do. If this was fight or flight, I'd chosen the lesser-known third option: freeze. It wasn't the first time.

Eventually I convinced myself to stand up, put on my backpack, and beat a quiet but quick retreat back to the cabin. Safely inside, I cuddled up to Dude for while, then spent the rest of that day berating myself. He could've been there, mere feet away, and I'd run home like a scared little girl. As I fell into an uneasy sleep that night, I promised myself it wouldn't happen again. The sooner I found him, the sooner the real work could begin.

5

Thursday, June 25, 2020

With an odd mixture of fear and frustration, I set out on Thursday to continue my search. After two evenings of practice at drawing my weapon from beneath the inconvenient folds of flannel that concealed it, I was getting reasonably fast. Dude had mostly forgiven me for this new habit of disappearing for hours each day without letting him tag along.

Though the bright dawn promised another warm day, yesterday's rain had continued through the night, and the ground was soft under my boots. My footprints were so easy to spot that an imbecile could have tracked me into the woods and, if the rhetorical imbecile cared to follow my prints for any length of time, he or she could probably also figure out I was searching for something or someone. I didn't care; I was going to find him today. I hiked straight to the cedar I'd napped under yesterday, and the search began anew from there.

I was headed west yet again when I finally stumbled across

it: a ramshackle wooden building tucked between two piñon pines, sitting ghostly and silent as though it had been waiting for me. I didn't see or hear anyone, and the building had a cold, empty feel to it.

It was about fifteen feet square and constructed of vertical wooden slats, most of which appeared to be severely old. A few brighter, straighter pieces of wood gave it away for someone else's discovery, and I recalled the lack of obvious buildings on the property in the two-year-old satellite footage I'd reviewed. I had to assume the structure had been built, or partially rebuilt, within the last two years. Scavenged-looking rectangles of corrugated metal made up the roof. There were no windows. The door, which faced east, had been painted green at some point in the distant past and still bore a few flecks of color. It was ajar.

With unhurried motions, I reached into my backpack and armed myself with the cell phone, the camera app open. I took a couple pictures of the front the building and then approached the door. I pushed it open, and an earsplitting creak shattered the stillness. I forced a laugh and stepped brazenly inside.

The shack was devoid of inhabitants, but it was far from empty. A twin-sized bed, card table, folding chair, cooler, and old-fashioned wardrobe had been packed into the tiny space. I couldn't believe my eyes, couldn't fathom my dumb luck. Someone was actually living here, and I'd not only spotted the shack from the summit but had found it, not terribly far from where I'd estimated its location on my paper map. I snapped several pictures of the interior and then inspected the contents of the little habitation more closely.

Under the table was a small hand crate full of canned food. The cooler held two gallon-sized jugs of water, a partially eaten summer sausage, most of a loaf of bread, and something that looked suspiciously like a roasted turkey leg. Within the wardrobe, the shack's resident had hung another plastic wardrobe protecting several men's shirts and pants, a heavy-duty coat, and a pile of socks and underwear at the bottom. The cell phone's camera captured it all. I closed everything up, made sure nothing looked out of place, and turned to go.

Just outside the door I froze, my heart leaping into my throat as the cell phone slipped from my nerveless hand.

He was standing several yards away in the deep shadows of a dying piñon, watching me. The shock was genuine, the subsequent combo of triumph and fear clumsily covered over by a shaky laugh.

"You scared me," I said weakly, stooping to pick up the cell phone. "I'm sorry—Is this your house? I didn't think…"

I got a good look at him when he stepped out of the shadows and came toward me, walking quickly enough to goad me into taking a step backward. My back bumped against the wooden exterior of the building.

He was well over six feet tall, broad shouldered and dark haired, wearing a deep scowl as he appraised me. I scowled back.

"Look, I said I was sorry. Jeez."

I started to walk away and he sidestepped, blocking my retreat. I threw up my hands, palms out, a universal sign of appeasement. He was just outside arms' reach, far too close. I stepped backward again.

"I don't want any trouble," I breathed.

"Who are you?" His voice was flat and forced, as though unused for weeks or even months.

I slid backward another step, and his eyes darted down to my feet. His scowl deepened, and I squeaked, "Nobody. I'm nobody. Please—I'll just go—"

"Who are you?" he repeated, closing the distance again.

Every bone in my body was howling with outrage that I was allowing him to advance unchallenged, but I'd seen his puzzlement when I'd slid rather than stepped backward like a normal person would. That was stupid, a mistake I couldn't afford to repeat.

"I'm—I'm Abigail," I stammered, adding with a brave attempt at friendliness, "What's your name?"

"Why are you here?"

"I'm not—I mean—I didn't mean—I was only exploring—Please stop!"

He took two more menacing steps toward me and I turned and fled, rounding the corner of the shack; but he was too fast. I felt myself jerked backward by the backpack straps around my shoulders, then a painful impact with the ground. As I started to rise, I was instead jerked upright by my upper arm and pushed against the exterior of the shack.

"Why are you here," he snarled, making each word its own individual demand.

Weighing the crushing grip strength of his hand around my arm with how close I'd just come to accidentally showing off my carefully concealed gun, I decided on balance to freeze, staring up at him in only partially feigned terror. A moment later I was ripped away from the wall and frog-marched back around the shack and through the door, where he hurled me toward the bed and stood, arms crossed, glaring down at me while I struggled with the straps of my backpack.

"I have money, okay, just take it," I sobbed, flinging the backpack on the floor between us.

He stared me down for half a beat and then picked up my backpack, tearing it open.

"Okay, I mean, I don't have any money with me now… but the bear spray was really expensive and I have some cash in my cabin and some credit cards and jewelry—"

"Shut up."

I sank down onto the bed as though slapped and watched as he rifled through the contents of my backpack. One by one the useless items within were tossed to the floor, followed by the backpack itself.

"How much money?"

"A lot," I said eagerly. "Like, two thousand dollars. I swear, it's yours, I don't even care. Just please don't hurt me."

"And the dog?"

"The… the dog?"

"You think I'm an idiot? I follow you back to that cabin, and you let your dog do the dirty work? I don't think so."

"How do you know I have a dog?" I breathed, feeling myself shrink as the atmosphere in the shack thickened. He closed the door with a snap, but there were enough gaps in the walls that the interior was dimly lit as though by a gas lamp.

"Should've brought him with you, huh?"

The mocking tone was too much and I bristled, standing back up. "I didn't know I was gonna run into a psycho jerk or I would have!"

"Sit down."

I complied, and as my eyes darted to the closed door, he surprised me by taking one deliberate step backward, as far away from me as he could get in the tiny shack. He knelt down to gather the scattered contents of my backpack back into it, and words seemed to explode from his mouth against his better judgment.

"Do you have any idea the world of hurt I'm in now? Do you have any clue?"

"I'm sorry."

He swore under his breath, then asked, "Who else knows you're out here?"

"What? I—everyone, like literally everyone I know, my parents, my boyfriend, my boss, all my girlfriends—" He studied me, clearly not sure whether to believe me, and I blundered on, "They're probably already at the cabin now, wondering where I am."

"Your boss?"

"Well—I mean, no, my parents. And—and my brothers."

"You're a terrible liar."

"I'm not lying."

"Lie."

Tears welled up in my eyes as I thought about Dude, and what would happen to him if I never came back to the cabin. I let a couple tumble down my cheeks before whining, "I won't tell anyone anything, I swear. I have money…"

"Yes, you said that. Now shut up, I need to think."

While he thought about whatever it was he needed to think about, his eyes never left me. I wrapped my arms around my torso and looked around the shack as though trying to pretend he wasn't there. The silence became unbearable, and I forced myself to look at him. His eyes narrowed, and he seemed to reach some kind of conclusion.

He said firmly, "Stand up."

"I—why?"

In answer he took two long strides across the small space and yanked me upright by the arm. To my horror, his hands were suddenly sliding down my torso—he was patting me down. I had about a second to prepare before his left hand brushed against my holster and he stopped, clearly surprised.

"Take your shirt off."

"No!"

"The shirt tied around your waist, take it off or I will."

"Fine!" I untied the knot with some difficulty and flung the shirt to the floor, snapping, "You can't have my gun."

"Give it to me."

Instinct and training overwhelmed conscious thought. The order had scarcely left his mouth before he reacted to the automatic movement of my hand toward the gun. He pinned my right hand to my side and caught my left wrist in his other hand. Inwardly seething, I allowed him to wrench the gun away and watched in defeat as he examined it. He ejected the magazine and inspected the round peeking out of the top, then slammed it home again. He press-checked the weapon and saw the round in the chamber, and his scowl grew impossibly more pronounced.

"Who are you?"

This time I didn't answer, instead staring at him and trying to figure out what his next move would be now that he hadn't shot me. I was glad he didn't want to kill me, at least not right away; but he couldn't let me go either. I had sorted that much out on my own, making his next words redundant.

"This may be hard for you to understand, but I can't let you leave. Not right now."

I stared at him.

"I'm not going to hurt you."

Still I stared, happy to believe my accusing gaze was making him uncomfortable.

"Turn around," he said.

"No."

He raised my weapon, directing it at my chest. The gun was closer to me than it was to him, and the temptation to make a grab for it was almost more than I could bear. I pressed my arms to my sides.

"Turn. Around."

I turned and was unsurprised to feel my wrists pinned together as he looped something around them. I forced a sob.

"Calm down. What is this?"

He pulled the cell phone from my back pocket, where I'd slipped it when he first pushed me against the wall. Darn it.

"You're really starting to annoy me," he grumbled.

That didn't seem to require an answer. With my hands tied behind my back, I offered no resistance as he led me out of the shack. It had been so dim inside that I was momentarily blinded by the daylight outside, recoiling. He pushed me forward roughly.

"Lead the way," he grunted.

I had no other option than to head toward the cabin, striking out directly south.

6

Thursday, June 25, 2020

I picked my way through the woods, unsure of how exactly to get back to my cabin. The man followed close behind, poking me between the shoulder blades with the barrel of my gun whenever I slowed down. He was really starting to annoy me, too. After half an hour, he wrenched me to a stop.

"You're going the wrong way."

"Well excuse me," I snapped back. "I'm lost."

He sighed, taking my word for it, and began leading me through the woods by the elbow. Belatedly I noticed he'd grabbed my backpack and was carrying it as though it belonged to him. Being dragged along by the arm was far from an easy way to hike, and I was grateful his course brought us to the cabin in far less time than mine would have. Despite being glad to see the familiar cabin, I was gripped with sudden, blinding panic as Dude caught sight of us through the windows and began to bark wildly.

"Please don't hurt him," I cried, "I'll do whatever you want just don't—"

My pleas were cut off as he spun me around. He untied my hands and pushed me toward the door. I turned, and he leveled the gun at me again. "So put him in the back yard. Try anything and you're both dead."

I was quite interested in why I wasn't dead already, but I didn't think it would be too smart to ask. I strode up to the front door and cracked it enough to let Dude see I was unharmed. Only great affection for my four-legged companion kept me from throwing the door wide and letting him loose. A horse-sized dog rushing at the stranger might distract him enough to grant me an opportunity to wrestle the gun away, but it would almost certainly cost Dude his life. Instead I wedged myself through the door, kneeing Dude away as he tried to get around me.

I closed the door behind me and turned to see the man with my gun had followed me to the door and was now at the window, motioning meaningfully with the weapon from me to the fence behind the house—the six-foot fence over which Dude could very easily leap.

Taking Dude by the collar, I dragged him, resisting all the way, through the cabin to the back door. My mind raced through my options, none of which was particularly appealing, but I had to establish control of this situation. Any obvious ploy by me would leave Dude vulnerable, so it had to be sly—and it had to be quick. Already I could hear the front door opening as I snapped the back door closed in Dude's face. So far he was only eager to sniff and greet the man, not realizing yet what was really going on.

A tiny keychain flashlight was hanging on a hook by the back door. Out of time, I snatched it from the hook, ripped off the chain, and made a fist around the flashlight, pressing my back to the door as the man came around the corner, gun first.

"Get away from the door."

I stepped forward stiffly, stopping halfway between him and the door to ask, "What are you going to do?"

"I don't know. Sit down at the kitchen table." As I walked past him to the table, both hands balled into fists, he barked, "What's in your hands?"

I froze. "Nothing."

"Open your hands."

I turned toward him and complied, and his eyes followed the flashlight as it tumbled from my right hand to the floor. By the time he realized his mistake, I was already moving. I cut to his right and slapped my left hand around his wrist and my right hand over the barrel of the gun as it went off. A searing burn against my palm confirmed the spent casing had failed to eject. Ears ringing, I experienced a fleeting stab of concern for Dude, who had started barking again; but I was distracted by the man's left hand arcing toward my face. I pushed forward, slamming the gun and both our hands against his chest, and crashed my forehead against his nose with all the force I could muster. He hardly paused, his left hand twisting into my hair and yanking me backward. I pushed off his chest, ripped the gun from his hand, and tried to use it as a bludgeon; but the blow missed his temple and hit his left bicep instead. We crashed to the floor, unbalanced by my attempt to relieve the pain in my scalp. I lost the coin toss, landing on the bottom. A rush of air escaped my lungs as he landed on my chest, and I relinquished my hold on the momentarily useless gun. He freed his right hand from my grip and wrapped both hands around my neck.

Immediately I was seeing stars, and I felt an errant impulse to stop fighting. Instead, I forced my hands between his arms and straight back, over my head. As his grip loosened, I bucked my hips and rolled us both over. He locked his ankles together behind my back, an alarming clue that I needed to get off the ground as soon as possible. I pummeled him in the groin two, three, four times; but instead of loosening, his legs constricted painfully against my ribs and I lashed out automatically at his face.

That did it. A mere two seconds later the fight was over. I was losing consciousness as my right arm and his right thigh tightened against either side of my neck. Gradually all light and sound slipped away, and the last thing I heard was the back door shaking as Dude crashed against it.

▼

"Wake up."

Something smacked against my right cheek, hard enough to make me flinch. My left cheek was pressed against something soft. My head felt ready to explode and I groaned, not wanting to open my eyes. Another smack.

"Hey. Wake up."

I forced my eyes open to behold exactly what I least wanted to see: the man's face a few inches from mine. Recoiling, I felt my head push against the back of the couch. I was on my side, my hands once again tied behind my back. I didn't hear any barking, and my heart broke into a sprint.

"My dog, he's—"

"Fine. Quieted down."

"How long was I...?"

"Less than a minute."

The pain in my head was already subsiding, making room for unwelcome thoughts. I tried to sit up, but he pushed me back down.

"No. Don't move."

I glared daggers as he stood and backed away, settling into the armchair next to the door. I noted with satisfaction that he was still catching his breath, but otherwise his expression was blank as he studied me. I held his eyes for as long as I could, then let my gaze drop. I focused on his left wrist where it rested on the arm of the chair. He had a really nice watch.

"Good fight," he said. "I'm impressed."

The defeat rankled, totally separate from the life-or-death concern, and I pushed my lips together to suppress a nasty retort.

"Where'd you pick up those moves?" When a few seconds passed and I obviously wasn't going to answer, he shrugged. "Should've thrown some jujitsu classes in there too, huh?"

The unsolicited criticism almost got a rise out of me. I took a breath and snarled, "Apparently."

In answer, he slowly retrieved my gun from the table next to him and made a show of clearing the malfunction I'd caused. He popped a round out of the magazine and studied it.

"Penetrators. These aren't cheap. Not easy to find, either. Normal hollow points aren't good enough for daddy's little girl, or are you that worried about bears?"

Evidently he'd chosen to believe, out of all my babbled lies earlier, that I had money. I filed that away. He pulled my cell phone from his pocket, the one I'd used to document the shack and its contents.

"What's the pin?" he asked.

"I forgot."

Ignoring me, he studied the touch screen, angling it this way and that in the light from the window.

He said, "Never mind."

No doubt following the smudges left by my finger, he guessed the too-simple unlock pattern after a couple of tries and began perusing the cell phone. I watched his brows push together and knew exactly what he was seeing: a stock background, no apps except the preloaded crapplets, no contacts, no calls or texts—nothing but a couple dozen photos. He tossed the phone to the floor, annoyed.

"Where's your real cell phone?"

"On the floor in front of you."

"Think I don't know a burner phone when I see one?"

"I didn't say it wasn't a burner phone."

"All right." He sat back, returned the gun to the table, and crossed his arms. "Talk."

"About what?"

"Who you are and what you're doing here."

"I'm nobody doing nothing. I'm on vacation, or I was before you attacked me."

"Try again."

"Look, what do you want me to say? My name is Abigail Breckenridge, which can't possibly mean anything to you, and I came here for some peace and quiet. Had I known you lived here, I would've gone to Puerto Rico instead and taken my chances with hurricane season. And yes, I'm very worried about bears."

He started to reply, only to be interrupted by one curious, forlorn bark from outside. He gazed thoughtfully toward the door for a moment. "Strange you'd bring your dog instead of your alleged boyfriend. On vacation. With your burner phone."

He stood, leaving the gun on the table, and walked toward the kitchen. As soon as he left my peripheral vision I closed my eyes, listening, trying to guess what he was seeing. He found nothing of interest in the kitchen, because there was nothing to find, so he went upstairs to the loft. I listened breathlessly as he rifled through the items on my bed, the things I'd removed from my backpack. I heard a rustle of paper as he unfolded the map, then deep silence. A minute later, he came back downstairs.

"X marks the spot?" he asked, holding the map in front of my face.

"I saw it from the summit a few days ago. I was curious. Sue me."

"I think litigation is the least of your worries right now."

He sat down again, and I saw he'd snagged a container of mixed nuts from the kitchen. He tossed a handful into his mouth, chewed thoughtfully, and resumed his study of me.

"Thing is, this isn't a vacation cabin. It's for hunters. That's all there is to do up here, hunt and trap. Since you're obviously not doing that, and you're not entertaining yourself by any other means I can figure, I'd really like to know—and please don't make me ask again—what are you doing up here?"

I let the silence simmer for a full ten seconds, then said quietly. "The same thing you are. Hiding."

"Oh?"

"That's why I went looking for your house—shack, cabin, whatever. I didn't think there was anyone else up here but those people to the south, the ones who own this cabin. They didn't ask nearly as many questions as you do."

"Hiding from who?"

"My ex-husband."

"Ah. There it is."

"If you tell him I'm here, he'll kill me," I said.

"Why would I tell him? Is this someone I know?"

"Only if you're into politics."

He shrugged. "I try to stay out of it. Who said I was hiding?"

"Seriously?"

He stood abruptly, grabbing the gun. I drew in a quick breath, noting with a tingle of fear that his demeanor changed in an instant. He tapped the barrel of the gun against his left hand and began pacing back and forth in front of the couch.

"Here's the thing," he finally said, his voice tight. "In about two months, it's not gonna matter that you know I'm here. You could plaster it all over the internet and it wouldn't make one bit of difference. Until then, though… I can't have you talking. To anyone."

"*Who* am I going to talk to?" I demanded. "Did you not listen to my story?"

"Can't risk it."

"I don't even know who you are, and I don't care."

"By my count, I've committed at least five individual felonies today, against you. I'm a criminal, what more do you need to know?"

"If I called the police, I'd have to file a report. That would be suicide."

"I know you've heard of confidentiality."

"Enough to know it doesn't mean anything. It wouldn't even slow him down."

"Doesn't matter. I can't risk it." He stopped pacing. "I can't let you out of my sight. It's that, or a bullet between the eyes. You choose."

He met my eyes and held them while I tried to look away, to think. What did he mean? What was I even choosing? I decided it didn't matter. Killing me in cold blood was obviously off the table, no matter what he wanted me to think.

"I choose the bullet, please."

"You think I'm kidding?" he demanded, incensed that I'd called his bluff. He stalked over to the couch and pressed the gun against my forehead. Right before I squeezed my eyes shut, I saw his finger slide into the trigger guard.

7

Thursday, June 25, 2020

My entire being seemed to revolve around the cold circle of steel pressed to my forehead. Maybe the man wasn't bluffing about shooting me, or maybe his finger would twitch and squeeze the trigger. The result would be the same. Seconds seemed to stretch into hours while I waited for the bang I knew I wouldn't hear, but it didn't come. The pressure of the barrel against my skin disappeared.

"Say I do. What do you think is gonna happen to Colonel Klink out there? Think I'm gonna feed him? Take him to the vet when he gets bitten by a rattlesnake?"

When I gave no response other than to stare blankly at the ceiling, he came back and bent over me.

"You came here. You found my cabin. This is on you. I'll give you some time to think."

He went back upstairs. I heard a creak of mattress springs and knew the real reason he'd retreated: He was the one who needed to think.

I eased into a sitting position and was able to see down the hall and through the window in the back door. Dude stood on his hind legs, his nose pressed to the glass. He barked once, as though to say, "I'm still out here. What's going on?"

I gazed at Dude, fatigued beyond words. Most of me still hurt from the fight, and I was thirsty. A part of me wanted to slip out of the poorly tied restraints, dash upstairs, and fight him again, to kill him or force him to kill me. That was my ego talking, though, and I ignored it. I leaned sideways against the couch cushions into a mostly comfortable position, said a quick prayer, and waited.

An hour passed, then two. I started to worry about Dude, not sure if the water bowl outside actually had any water in it. The June day would be heating up, but the sun was already far enough to the west that most of the enclosure was shady. I decided he was fine for now. Better than me, at least.

Had the man fallen asleep? What the heck did he have to think about, anyway?

"Hey," I called when three full hours had passed. "I have to pee. Hello?"

When he didn't answer, I stood up. The old couch creaked loudly in protest and I froze, looking up into the loft. Nothing.

I sat down on the floor and tried to work my arms underneath me so my hands were in front, but it was no good. Getting up from the floor was a challenge, too, but I managed it without attracting any notice from upstairs. I figured I might as well go for broke.

Creeping to the kitchen, I eased open the cutlery drawer and extracted a serrated steak knife. Gripping it gingerly by the blade, I crouched down and wedged the handle between the rubber heels of my hiking boots, blade up. After that it was just a matter of sawing at the thin cord without making too much noise, or cutting myself.

Once the improvised restraint, which turned out to be a shoelace, fell away, I replaced the knife and closed the drawer. A rustle of movement upstairs caught my attention and I stopped, holding my breath.

He swore again. It was just a whisper, but it carried easily from the loft to the kitchen.

He rushed to the banister and saw me standing in the kitchen, as motionless as a deer in headlights, the severed shoelace hanging from my left hand. I experienced a baffling impulse to explain myself, followed closely by an even stronger urge to run for it—to where, I had no idea.

I understood what was happening, but it didn't help. While my lizard brain tried and failed to decide whether to fight or flee, he had plenty of time to make his way slowly downstairs and join me in the kitchen.

He stopped a foot from me. "Didn't think you'd still be here."

"Yeah well… all my stuff is here. You can head out whenever, though, feel free."

Since I was looking at his shoes, I couldn't tell if his huff of air was a laugh or a sigh. I finally realized my hands needed to be up, just in case, and casually brought them together in front of me. He backed away. Aside from his apparent disinterest in punitive violence, this wasn't going well at all. I needed to change the tone.

"How do you feel about mutually assured destruction?" I asked.

"Sorry?"

"I mean, do you think it's a viable option here?" I looked up at him, checking his expression. He was studying my face as though trying to figure out if I were joking. He didn't answer. I pressed, "You told me to think about this. So… that's what I have. You don't want to be found, and neither do I. If I get found, you get found. You send nukes, I send nukes back. It's the Cold War. Get it?"

"That's… a terrible idea."

"Oh?"

"You want to start a cold war?"

"Is that analogy not good for you? Because the core concept—"

"I'm pretty sure I follow."

"I'm just trying to think of a solution here. I don't see you coming up with anything. And *you* started this."

"Maybe we got off on the wrong foot," he allowed.

"When you attacked me?"

"No, before that, when you were trespassing and snooping around."

"You overreacted."

"I thought you were—someone else." He frowned to himself, as though unsure whether he'd said too much. "If you knew my situation, you'd understand."

"I don't want to know your situation. And even though you seem incapable of getting this, I'll say it again: I don't care. I'm not going to talk to anyone—"

"You wouldn't have to. It could be something as simple as… as deviating from the norm. Acting in a way you otherwise wouldn't, because you found me here."

"I don't have a norm! I've been here less than a week! And if anyone were watching me closely enough to notice anything, I'd already be dead because he would've found me."

"Who, your ex? I think you're giving the guy too much credit."

"I think you're giving the—whatever you've got going on—too much credit, too."

"I'm just being cautious."

"Ugh." I looked up at the ceiling, looking for patience or some kind of distraction. Dude helpfully pitched in with a keening whine. "If you're not going, can I let my dog inside? He won't hurt you."

"Hm."

"He's trained. He won't attack you unless you attack me again."

He argued, "*You* attacked *me*."

"Whatever. I'm going to let him in. Are you going to freak out?"

"Only if he does."

Hoping it wouldn't come to that, I went to the back door and cracked it enough to talk through.

"Sitz."

Though he'd started crowding the door as soon as he saw me, Dude obediently plopped down and waited for my next demand.

"Bleib."

I swung the door open all the way and walked past the man (who for all his sudden civility had yet to tell me his name) and through the kitchen, sitting down on the couch.

After several seconds of tense silence, I said, "Komm."

Dude bounded inside, straight to the couch without giving the man a second glace. He sat down at my feet, then rested his head on my knees.

"Did you forget to close the door?" I asked.

His ears perked up.

"Schliess."

I turned to watch, feeling smug beneath the general feeling of discomfort and danger as Dude returned to the door, nudged it partially closed with his nose, and then rose to his hind legs to push it to with his front paws. From behind me, in the kitchen, I heard a muttered, "Wow."

"Good boy. Komm."

Dude took that as an invitation to curl up on the couch with his head in my lap, which was fine by me. As our unwanted guest came around the couch to resume his earlier seat, Dude's eyes followed him, but he remained otherwise motionless.

"You speak German?" he asked.

"I give him commands in German. It's how he was trained." If he noticed this wasn't an answer, he didn't press the issue. "I guess I could give you some credit for not killing me," I said by way of re-opening the dialogue. "You're obviously in a tight spot."

"Likewise."

"I vote for the Cold War. Still the only idea on the table."

"Thing is, someone else could send nukes, and you'd still blame me. And you could nuke me on accident. I don't like it."

"Come up with something better."

He shrugged, throwing his hands wide as though to say, "This is it."

"No way," I blurted. "You can't stay here."

"Let me ask you something: How'd you untie yourself earlier? While I was asleep?"

"Pass."

"Had to have been something sharp."

"If you insist."

"Why didn't you use it on me?"

"Because you woke up."

"Do you still have it on you?"

I frowned into abstraction, thinking; but by the time I answered, "No," he already knew.

"So you put it away to use later," he suggested.

"I heard you wake up."

"Uh huh."

"Look, what are you getting at?" I demanded. "You already kicked my butt, now you're mocking me for failing to kill you?"

"No, I'm making a point."

Apparently there was more point to make, because he then

withdrew my gun from his waistband and, to my open astonishment, handed it to me, grip-first. I didn't move.

"Take it," he demanded, leaning across the space between us and nearly forcing it into my hands. I held it loosely, the barrel directed more or less at his knees. I could tell by the weight that the magazine was still nearly full. I press checked it, confirming I was a mere six pounds of pressure away from firing at him.

"I don't get it," I admitted.

"You've got the gun. You've got Colonel Klink—"

"His name is Dude."

"—So now I'm significantly less of a threat to you than you are to me."

I just blinked at him.

"All I want is to make sure you don't do anything to mess up my plans. Please."

The word surprised me. I stared at him for a few more seconds, then I stood. He tensed, possibly wondering if he'd misjudged me. I jammed the gun into my holster and stalked back to the kitchen, Dude at my heels.

"Are you hungry?" I asked bluntly.

"Uh… yeah."

I began pulling ingredients out of the pantry and refrigerator, feeling his eyes on me the whole time. He waited until I'd turned to face him again before standing up and edging toward the kitchen, clearly not wanting to spook me.

"That was a quick one-eighty," he said.

"Whatever. You could've killed me like nine times and you haven't. Having you lurking around out there would be just as unnerving as you being here."

"Thanks, I guess."

"What am I supposed to call you?" I asked.

"Um."

I watched his gaze wander around the interior of the tiny cabin and almost laughed out loud. It couldn't have been clearer that he was looking for something to inspire a fake name.

After a complete, visual circuit of the cabin, he concluded, "Alan."

My eye was drawn at once to the empty *Jurassic Park* VHS box on top of the TV. "Okay."

He shot back, "It's not like you gave me your real name."

I pressed my lips together, focusing on opening the box of spaghetti in my hands.

"Wait... Abigail is your real name?"

"It didn't occur to me to lie."

"Well now I almost feel bad. Can I give you a hand with that?"

"No, just—Can you just leave me alone?"

He shrugged again, then disappeared into the bathroom. A moment later, I heard the shower turn on.

"Make yourself at home," I mumbled.

8

Thursday, June 25, 2020

Alan—for lack of his real name—still had my cell phone, and I knew he'd be using the privacy in the bathroom to go through it more thoroughly. Fortunately, there was nothing to find. My laptop, comparably a Rosetta Stone of information, was safely hidden under the passenger seat of the pickup. I hadn't even touched it since before I left Washington, much less turned it on. The worst he could do was Google my name, and I already knew what he'd find: bland, private social media profiles with my face over the name Abigail Breckenridge, the website of a Sydney-based photographer who clearly wasn't me, and a few other obvious dead ends.

Alan took significantly longer to shower than I did to make dinner. I was sitting on the couch, picking up where I'd left off with *Lost World* and enjoying my second bowl of spaghetti, when I heard the bathroom door open.

"Where are those clothes that were in the closet?" he asked

69

through the cracked door.

Studiously fixing my eyes on the TV screen, I answered, "In the dresser upstairs, where clothes—wait." *I'd* worn the clothes that were in the closet. I looked over my shoulder. "Those were yours?"

Rather than answering, he asked, "Could you… um… maybe go grab them for me?"

I turned back around, huffing, "I'm not your servant."

Focused again on the TV screen, I heard the slap of bare feet on the wooden floor as he went upstairs. Dude, who'd been feigning sleep in his favorite chair by the door, jumped up to follow.

Alan came back downstairs, helped himself to the rest of the spaghetti, and sat down, not in the chair by the door, but on the other end of the couch. I glowered at the TV, trying to ignore him, but it was useless. As Dude descended from the loft, evidently assured all was in order up there, I gave up and retreated into the bathroom for my own alone time.

Though I locked the door behind me, the feeble barrier of hollow wood veneer did nothing to ease my mind. I leaned against the sink, facing the door, and for a good half hour simply listened and waited. Gradually boredom replaced nervousness, and I got in the shower.

The hot water lasted about three minutes. Cursing the inconsiderate hot water hog all the while, I endured the freezing cold water as long as I could—about another three minutes— and then gave up. When I turned off the tap, I froze, listening again.

The movie was still playing, but it sounded like he'd turned down the volume. I checked my watch: half-past five. Shivering violently, I threw on a bathrobe and started blow drying my hair, partially for the warmth and also for something to pass the time. I hadn't been able to think in the shower, so as my hair slowly dried I tried again to focus my thoughts and assess the situation.

Circumstances were far from ideal, but I decided they could have been worse. Philip hadn't found me yet, which put me in the lead. The man calling himself Alan was either a paranoid schizophrenic or actually involved in something momentous, but either way he was as committed to keeping a low profile as I was. If he was who I believed he was, he was a dangerous person—a bad guy—but he'd intentionally shifted the balance of power to me to prove a point. He was essentially my guest now, uninvited though he was, and I could make him leave—or shoot him—whenever I wanted.

I wondered what he would do if I grabbed my pickup keys and left, announcing my intention to drive to the nearest police station and file a report. What could he do?

A new, unnerving thought popped into my head. I grabbed my Glock, cleared the chamber, stripped the magazine, and flipped it over, inspecting the underside of the slide. The striker assembly was in place, at least the part that was visible without further disassembling the weapon. I briefly considered stripping it down entirely, just to banish that last whisper of doubt that he'd tampered with it somehow; but this would be relatively time-consuming, I had no tools to speak of, and maybe I was being crazy. What was I thinking, that he'd somehow removed or disabled the firing pin? Why bother, when he didn't have to give me the gun back at all? I *was* being crazy. I put the weapon back together and steeled myself for a dash through the living room to the loft.

I took a deep breath, let it out slowly, and opened the door.

Not sure what I'd been expecting to see, I was mildly surprised to find Alan sitting on the floor between the TV and the couch, rubbing Dude's belly. The magnificent beast heaved himself over as soon as he saw me, trying to act all casual like he hadn't just been getting belly rubs from the person who'd choked me out a few hours ago—not that Dude witnessed that part. I spared 'Alan' one disdainful look before whisking past them both and up the stairs as quickly as I could without losing too much dignity.

Once upstairs, I heard the kitchen tap come on and a clatter of pots and pans as Alan began doing the dishes. The kitchen sink, almost directly below the loft, was one of the poorer vantage points for anyone trying to see from the first floor into the loft. Alan seemed to be going out of his way not to make me uncomfortable. Or maybe I was riding a mental pendulum—overly suspicious one minute, overly generous the next, back and forth until eventually I'd stop somewhere in the middle. I hoped.

In any case, I had to hedge my bets a little. The usual contents of my backpack, which Alan had dumped in a pile on the dresser, contained one of two spare magazines. I squirreled it away in the same place I'd hidden my shotgun, other spare magazine, and small stash of ammo: the crawl space behind the bed, the entrance to which was hidden by the bed itself.

A few minutes later, I stopped at the foot of the stairs, dressed for a hike. Dude sprang up at once, tail working madly. He was intent on not being left behind this time. Out of the corner of my eye, I saw Alan stand up, too. I ignored him as best as I could, opening the door so Dude could dash outside.

As I started to follow, Alan asked, "Where are you going?"

Drawing my gun as I turned, I held it loosely in one hand and snarled, "Wherever I want, I guess."

"Okay." He held up his hands, clearly unimpressed. "Just don't…"

"Don't what?" I gave him a few seconds to not answer, then went on, "Or better yet: What are you going to do about it?"

"… Can I tag along?"

"No."

"I need to get some stuff from the other cabin."

"Be my guest." I gestured vaguely toward the south. "I'm going that way."

Again I turned to leave, but he moved so quickly I barely had time to react. Yanked backward by the back of my shirt, I was spun around as he slammed the door closed. His left hand pinned my right wrist to the door, taking the gun out of the equation for now. As soon as my left elbow arced toward his jaw, that too was pinned to the door.

He glanced down at my feet, then back at me, shaking his head. "Don't start that again. I don't want to hurt you."

"Let me go."

The door shook slightly as Dude jumped up, standing on his hind legs to peer through the window. I turned my head to lock eyes with him. For now, he seemed more curious than defensive.

"Are you going to the neighbors?" Alan asked.

"They're not even home."

"They have a phone."

"Well, I don't have a key."

"Right, a locked door is going to stand in your way."

"I'm not going to call the police!" I sighed, irritation overshadowing my fear of him. "You dummy, I keep telling you I don't want anyone to know I'm here!"

"Thing is, you already lied to me about why you're here, so I'm having trouble believing the rest of it."

"I didn't lie about anything."

"Lie."

Too angry to even attempt a response, I settled for glaring at him as the silence condensed in the too-small space between us. Up until now I'd managed to observe very little about Alan in the way of physical details, reflexively shying away from even looking in his direction more often than was absolutely necessary. At this distance, however, certain details simply couldn't be ignored any longer: dark blue eyes, thick brown hair, a faint smell of pine needles. I frowned, annoyed, and managed to block out anything else by simply closing my eyes.

"If you think it's time for round two, I'm game," he said. "But you'll have to put the gun down."

"I just want to get out of this cabin."

"Fine. But I'm not letting you out of my sight. And you can't be trusted with this, obviously."

He twisted the gun out of my hand, stepping backward so he was well out of reach. He stripped the magazine and tossed it to me, then removed the round from the chamber. After slipping the unloaded Glock into his pocket, he came back and pressed the last round into my free hand.

"There. Now we're both half-armed."

I yanked my hand away—his hands were freakishly large—and crossed my arms. "Great. Now all you have to do is find some ammo." No need to mention the tiny arsenal hidden upstairs, not if he thought we were on an equal playing field now.

"I'd still only have one shot. Based on my experience, that won't be enough."

"It won't be."

One sharp, impatient bark cut across his retort. Outside, Dude jumped up to press his nose to the window again, probably wondering why the hike hadn't started. I stuffed the magazine and loose round into my pocket and opened the door.

"I guess we're going back to that tiny crack house, Dude," I informed him. He responded by turning in several tight circles on the spot, overcome with enthusiasm.

"It's not a crack house," Alan defended.

"It's a wreck."

"Well, I wouldn't have been cooped up in there if you hadn't showed up."

He took the lead as we started down the driveway. I glanced over my shoulder at the cabin, seeing it in a new, unflattering light. "You *live* here?"

"Normally."

"Oh." That explained why Dude was so comfortable with Alan. The man's scent was all over the cabin, marking it as his own. I hurried to catch up to his long, quick strides and asked, "Did you leave that duck feather on the welcome mat?"

"I don't know what you're talking about."

"You did! You were creeping around the other night, when Dude and I got back after dark."

"Nope."

We walked in silence for a few minutes while I mulled this over. His denials were so poorly delivered that he'd basically confirmed my suspicions. When we got to the bridge and cut left to follow the creek, I asked, "Were you trying to scare me away?"

To my surprise, he answered promptly, "It's worked before. I had to give it a shot."

"How long have you been up here, then?"

"That's enough chit chat."

That was fine by me. I let him get a few yards ahead, so once we'd pressed into the thicker foliage away from the bridge, I could almost pretend it was just Dude and me out for a hike. We still had about two and a half hours of daylight left, and it took less than an hour to get to the other cabin with Alan leading the way.

While he ducked inside to get whatever it was he needed, I waited in the clearing. Dude waited with me for about two seconds, then decided he needed to see the inside of the cabin. For a few more seconds, I glared toward the doorway through which he'd disappeared, then gave up and followed him inside.

9

Thursday, June 25 to Friday, June 26, 2020

Since there wasn't much room inside the little shack, I leaned against the door frame to see what was going on. With practiced speed, Alan was piling clothes into a duffel bag I hadn't noticed on my initial search of the cabin.

He glanced up at me. "Got somewhere to be?"

I shrugged. "Don't forget your toothbrush."

After a mumbled, "Uh huh, thanks," he proceeded to ignore me.

I ducked back outside, stifled by the close confines. I didn't envy anyone who had to spend a single night there, let alone several. I walked around the outside, studying the highly permeable walls and unstable-looking roof. When I got back to the front, Alan was waiting outside.

"You done?" he asked, tossing me a bundle of something. I caught it on reflex and realized it was my flannel shirt.

"You know what I think?" I shot back, feeling ornery and awkward all of a sudden. Not waiting for him, I answered myself, "You want to stay in the cabin, and since you couldn't scare me away, you've cooked up this whole insane story about needing to stay hidden from someone or something just to make me think you're in some kind of danger so I don't run off to the police and have you hauled away for trespassing."

"Brilliant," he said. "Totally wrong, but brilliant."

"I wasn't asking for confirmation."

"You're assuming I gave up on the Scooby Doo act pretty much immediately."

"You had to give up when I found your hideout."

"Ah. So you've got it all worked out, then."

"Yes, I have."

"So what's my end game, genius?" he asked.

"What?"

"What is the logical conclusion of my master plan to have a snarky, paranoid, violent, lying roommate?"

"Don't hold back."

"I'm genuinely curious how you think this is supposed to end."

I crossed my arms, dithering for half a second. "I guess… it can't end well for me. That's a given."

"That's a bleak outlook."

"It's the simplest answer."

"Well on August thirty-first, when I leave and you've got this place all to yourself, you're going to feel pretty foolish. And you'll definitely still be alive."

With that he brushed past me, slinging the duffel bag over his shoulder, and started back toward the cabin. Dude trotted along behind him, happy as a clam, and I grudgingly brought up the rear.

Twilight was starting to settle when we got back, and the cabin's interior was noticeably murkier than when we'd left. I hurried to flip on as many lights as I could, but the thought of bedtime had already occurred to me, so I couldn't feign surprise when he brought it up.

"Guess I'll take the couch," he offered.

I met his eyes, looked away immediately, and found I had no answer for this.

"I'm not going to bother you," he insisted. "You won't even know I'm here."

I met his eyes again, forcing myself not to look away. "Dude will."

"Consider me warned."

"Good."

I departed for the loft, measuring my steps so it didn't look too much like a hasty retreat.

I stretched out on the bed, not bothering to take off my hiking boots, and faced the top of the stairs. It wasn't 8:00 yet, but with two hikes under my belt, one knock-down-drag-out scuffle, and all the adrenaline and stress associated with having a scary roommate foisted upon me, I felt my eyelids drooping almost as soon as I'd settled into the position in which I intended to pass the entire night in hawklike wakefulness. Several times I caught myself nodding forward and jerked back upright, becoming more uncomfortable each time.

It was Dude who saved the day: Right at nine, when I was losing the will to stay awake, he trotted noisily up the stairs and rested his big face on the bed. He stared at me, his brown eyes beseeching, for a good minute before I realized what he wanted.

"Oh! It's dinner time, isn't it?"

At the word "dinner," Dude erupted in ear-splitting barks, his way of saying, "Yes, please!" He preceded me back downstairs, tail held high, pleased with himself for making the human understand and comply.

A quick, surreptitious glance confirmed Alan was still awake. He was stretched out on the couch, totally at ease, reading one of *my* books. I scoffed audibly but let it go.

Dude's dinner routine usually included a series of tricks that were guaranteed to please an audience, on the rare occasion he had one. I didn't much feel like putting on a show, but one look at Dude's perfect, statuesque sit and his eager eyes convinced me we couldn't skip it.

"Platz," I said, trying to speak just loudly enough for only Dude to hear me. He dutifully lay down, paws stretched toward me, tailing wagging slowly as though he had no control over it.

"Namaste."

He pushed his big, fluffy rear end in the air, rested his chin on his front paws, and froze. Perfect downward dog. I couldn't resist a grin. He was so darn clever.

"Sitz."

He returned to a normal sitting position, and I pointed a finger gun at him.

"Bang."

For his final act, he lay down, rolled over, and became as still as a statue—at least until his tail started wagging again. His part of the show thus complete, I filled his bowl and watched indulgently as he went to work.

"That could be German Shepherd for all you know."

He crunched happily at the kibbles, ignoring me in favor of the singular delight that was the same dry dog food he'd eaten every day for his entire life. I glanced toward Alan again, wondering if he'd caught the show, and saw his eyes dart back down to the book in his hands. I wasn't sure why, but an intense urge to be rude to him suddenly overwhelmed me.

"I don't remember inviting you to use my library."

He looked up, eyebrows raised. "I don't remember inviting you to rearrange my stuff."

A derisive laugh was the only response I could manage. The sleepiness that had plagued me minutes before had vanished, replaced by restlessness. I almost wanted to go for another hike, but I knew Alan would defeat the purpose by insisting on coming with me. A full understanding of how little there was to do up here, and how long I'd be stuck here with little to do, settled over me like a raincloud. I was going to have to think of something to keep me busy and sane.

In the meantime, I had an ample supply of wine. It wasn't the wisest course of action by any stretch of the imagination, but I went ahead and poured myself a generous glass of merlot for something to do. I carried it over to the bookshelf, which forced me to walk past the couch, and made quite a meal of picking out a book to read. I would much rather have watched a movie, but that would require me to remain in close proximity to Alan.

Eventually I decided *The Hobbit* was the book for me, and I carried my wine and my fiction back upstairs with a totally un-deserved sense of accomplishment.

For about half an hour I read and sipped, mostly relaxed; but my hiking boots, belt, holster, and jeans seemed to grow more uncomfortable with each passing minute. Still, I refused to put on pajamas or even more comfortable clothes. Besides, the mounting discomfort was helping me stay awake. At least, I thought it was.

▼

My eyes snapped open to find the cabin aglow with the dawn. I was freezing.

Bemoaning my stupidity, I rose quietly to my feet and crept to the banister. Alan was still stretched out on the couch, either asleep or faking it. Dude was unwinding himself from his chair, ready to go outside now that he knew I was awake. I slipped off my hiking boots, the better to creep noiselessly down the stairs. I let Dude out the front door, then returned to the loft without drawing any notice from Alan.

The cold was too much. I burrowed under the covers, in-tending to warm up while I waited for Dude to scratch at the door to be let back in. Instead, I fell asleep immediately.

I could tell by the light when I woke up again that at least a couple more hours had passed. Sitting up too fast, I groaned as the edge of my empty holster dug cruelly into my hip. I yearned to reach a place in life where I no longer occasionally fell asleep strapped for battle.

Thinking Dude was still outside, I forced myself out of bed to go rescue him. To my surprise, he bounded up the stairs to receive some morning pets. Alan must have let him back in. Or he'd figured out how to open doors.

"Who's my good boy?" I cooed. In answer, he jumped up onto the bed and laid his head in my lap. My heart melted. "What would I do without you, you big lump?"

I sat on the bed for at least ten minutes, stroking Dude's comfortingly soft fur and contemplating my next move. I had to pee, and I needed food, but to meet either need I'd have to venture downstairs. While I mentally rehearsed this, I heard the toilet flush followed by the sound of running water as Alan presumably washed his hands. He left the bathroom, walked into the kitchen, and got something out of a cabinet. I heard the telltale sound of the coffee machine clicking off, then a tantalizing pour. He carried his coffee to the living room, sat down on the couch, and fell silent. All this I gathered from listening, safely out of sight on the bed. He probably didn't know I was awake.

I could smell the coffee. It weakened my resolve to hide all day, which in any case would have been defeated soon by all the water sounds to which I'd just been subjected.

Since I had no reason to believe I'd be getting my gun back anytime soon, I finally gave in to the temptation to ditch the jeans, belt, and holster in favor of a loose pair of sweatpants. Still a little chilly, I threw on a hooded sweater and thick socks to complete the ensemble. Nearly silent in my socked feet, I finally crept down the stairs.

Though I knew it was impossible not to be seen, at least peripherally, by anyone sitting on the couch, I carefully avoided looking in that direction and headed straight for the bathroom without a word. I could feel Alan's eyes on me, but he said nothing, not even to ask why I hadn't made my escape last night while he slept.

Once the urgent business was done, I felt plenty calm enough to whisk into the kitchen, grab a bottle of water, a package of Pop-Tarts, and a cup of coffee, and retreat back upstairs.

I went downstairs in the early afternoon to pee again, let Dude out, and grab lunch (a can of soup). I finished *The Hobbit* at dusk, having successfully passed the day without even acknowledging Alan's existence; but I was murderously bored, aching with hunger, and unable to take my mind off the rest of that bottle of wine. My unwanted guest had been as unobtrusive as I'd endeavored to be, though with access to the kitchen and TV he had certainly passed the day in greater comfort than I had.

The thought of spending one more day, let alone many, the same way made me want to scream. I went back downstairs at eight o'clock, grabbed the wine bottle, and took it to the shower with me.

The Pop-Tarts and cold soup were no match for the wine, which hit me like a ton of bricks after only two swallows. I took my time in the shower, making sure all the hot water was gone before I got out and got dressed. I was still nursing my wine when I emerged to find Dude sitting outside the bathroom door. Was I going crazy, or was he wearing a disapproving expression? I peered at him.

"Got something to say, dog face?"

He cocked an ear at me.

"Oh right. Dinner."

We went through the routine again, and then I let Dude outside for his nightly perimeter check. I watched through the window as he disappeared into the darkness, then turned to face the living room, expecting to see Alan on the couch; but it was empty. I heard the fridge open. Another look at the couch revealed my cell phone sitting on the arm, just a few feet away from where I stood. Ignored for the moment, I crept over to the couch, slipped the phone into the pocket of my sweatpants, and headed for the stairs.

I was halfway up when I heard, "Hey—crap—Abigail!"

"What?" I asked, hoping I sounded innocent. With the wine muddling my senses, I couldn't be sure. I turned to see him standing at the foot of the stairs.

"Bring it back," he said, so perfectly deadpan that he could have been mad, amused, or anything in between.

"The wine? No chance, get your own." I continued up the stairs. He followed. I stopped at the top of the stairs, crying, "You leave me alone!"

"I don't want any trouble, just the cell phone."

"I don't have it!"

"Abigail, I can see it in your pocket."

"Ugh—fine." I pulled it out and, rather than tossing it to him, I threw it over the banister.

As it clattered to the floor, a tinkling sound confirming I had broken it, I met his eyes and felt a jolt of fear. I'd really managed to make him mad with that one. He stared at the spot where the phone had hit the floor, then slowly continued up the stairs. I froze, torn between apologizing and kicking him in the face. I failed to make up my mind in time and he stopped one stair below me, eye-to-eye with me.

"Excuse me."

I stepped to the side, gripping the edge of the banister for support, and watched on tenterhooks as he crossed the room, grabbed a spare blanket from the chair next to the dresser, came back toward me, and brushed right past me to return downstairs. I realized I'd been holding my breath and let it out slowly. A minute later, scratches at the door announced Dude had returned from his patrol. While I was still frozen in indecision, Alan let him inside.

There was nothing else to do but curl up in bed, shut my eyes, and pray tomorrow would be just a little bit better.

10

Saturday, June 27, 2020

I woke up much later the next morning, no doubt thanks to the bottle of merlot I'd so unwisely finished off. It was immature and irresponsible, and I was mad at myself for following the impulse. My sleep had been restless, plagued by dreams I forgot as soon as my eyes opened. As the last tendrils of sleep evaporated, I finally registered a delicious smell that seemed to be floating up from the kitchen. Unless my nose deceived me, pancakes were in the works.

I trudged downstairs, more or less ready to face another day.

A stack of pancakes was already waiting on a plate on the kitchen island. I approached them warily, not sure what to make of the scene: Alan at the stove, busily flipping more pancakes, Dude sitting at attention next to him, gazing unwaveringly up at him in the hopes of scoring some breakfast. The pancakes looked very fluffy, and I was very, *very* hungry; but I couldn't quite convince myself to take one.

While I deliberated, Alan finished another couple of pancakes and turned around to add them to the stack. He jumped at the sight of me, nearly dropping the pan.

He gasped, "How long have you been standing there?"

"Like a minute. Sorry, I thought you heard me."

His eyes raked me from head to foot and back. "Feeling better?"

Ignoring this, I asked, "Why are you making pancakes?"

"To fatten you up, obviously."

"That's not funny."

"Oh, lighten up. It's an olive branch, okay? You could've run off by now, but you haven't, which tells me you really are stuck here. I want to get along. I even made some for Dude, without salt or sugar. That's safe for him to eat, right?"

He presented a smaller plate of three tiny pancakes. I stared at them, stomach knotting into a ball, and concluded, "You're freaking me out."

"Whatever," he said with a shrug. "More for me."

Scowling, I grabbed one of the non-dog pancakes and took it to the couch. Failing to take the hint, Alan joined me a minute later with a plateful of pancakes for himself. He also brought the plate of doggy pancakes and set them on the couch between us. Dude, sensing they were meant for him, sat down with his nose two inches from the plate and stared at me.

"I think he's waiting for permission from you," Alan hinted.

"What's the secret ingredient, rat poison?"

"What kind of monster do you think I am?" he asked. He seemed sincerely offended. Grabbing one of the sugar-and-salt-free pancakes, he took a bite and looked at me as though to say, "There, happy?"

"Ugh. Fine. Dude, hol."

The dog pancakes were gone within seconds. I cradled my own, uneaten pancake in awkward silence, watching Dude lick the plate long after there was any trace of food left on it. After a good five minutes, he gave up and curled into his favorite chair. Alan took both empty plates back to the kitchen, returned to the couch, and sat down. Rather than facing the TV like a civilized human, he turned toward me.

"Jury still out on that olive branch?"

After a beat, I realized he was talking about the pancake. I still hadn't taken a bite. For half a second I considered tossing it on the floor just to be ornery, but I was too hungry. Without returning his gaze, I took one bite. As soon as it hit my stomach, I felt my crankiness slipping away.

I turned toward him, mirroring his posture, and asked, "How do you get them so fluffy?"

"Wow, that's a really personal question."

I laughed, the first real expression of mirth I'd managed since discovering I wasn't alone up here. Alan couldn't possibly know how personal the questions were going to get, but I was in no hurry to go there—yet.

In short order the rest of the pancake was gone, and I got up for seconds. I stood at the counter and plowed through a couple more, then brought the plate back to the couch to finish them off.

"There is syrup, you know," he said.

"Don't like it."

"Honey? Butter? Peanut butter?"

He was asking me what I liked on my pancakes. What a quantum leap forward! Forcing back a smile, I said, "I don't really like sweet stuff, especially not if it's sticky. This is easier to eat."

"Weird."

I shrugged. Down to the last pancake, I decided to try a little niceness and offered it to him.

He shook his head. "Go for it."

"Thanks."

As soon as the plate was empty, I returned to the kitchen to make coffee and clean up the mess he'd made. Olive branches and quantum leaps notwithstanding, I wasn't thrilled about hanging out on the couch with him.

While I got to work, he sidled up to stand on the other side of the kitchen island.

At length he asked, "Getting along seems to be the best option, don't you think?"

"Depends on what 'getting along' means to you," I answered without looking at him.

"Well… we've got two problems to sort out, and if we can do that, we'll be getting along. Living in peace."

"What problems?"

"One, we know nothing about each other, so we don't trust each other."

"No argument there."

"And two, there's nothing to do up here. Thanks to wine-o

Abigail, I can't even play Candy Crush anymore."

"Uh… sorry. Won't happen again. What do you normally do?"

"Patrol. Explore. Make sure no one gets too close. When hunters come up, I hide in a cave up near the summit. It's uncomfortable, but they never stay long. A couple times some tourists have come around, so scaring them off is actually pretty fun. Other than that, I just… wait."

"For what?"

"Something I have to do."

"On August thirty-first?" I asked.

"… Yeah."

"Do the Perkinses know you're up here?"

"The owners? Nah. They never come to the cabin, and they don't even do the cleaning themselves. Right before someone rents it out, they call a cleaning company to get it ready, and I bug out when I see them coming. I think the cleaners think they're cleaning up after someone, not the other way around. At least I don't think anyone's figured it out yet. I thought maybe you were here to clean the cabin, until I heard gunshots."

"That's a pretty blasé attitude, compared to how you're treating me being here."

"Up 'til now, no one else has ever even seen me."

"Lucky me."

"Why'd you come snooping around the cabin anyway?"

I sighed. "I told you, I saw it from the summit. I was curious."

"Why were you packing heat?"

"Wouldn't you?"

When he failed to answer, I turned around. He was studying me with a strange expression, as though unsure exactly what he was looking at. I decided to press my luck.

"Earlier you said you thought I was someone else, or something like that. Like someone is looking for you."

"And?"

"Do you think someone sent me here to find you?"

His expression hardened.

"I only ask because you talked about trusting each other. That really won't be possible if you think I came all the way up here just to mess up whatever it is you've got planned for August."

Still he said nothing.

"As long as you're not gonna kill anyone, I still don't care what you're planning to do."

Having said my piece, I forced myself to meet his eyes, to evaluate the effect of my little diatribe. For a fleeting moment, he looked so threatening I almost reached for the knife drawer; but as soon as I'd seen it, it was gone. I was still shaken from that brief moment of terror when he finally spoke.

"You probably won't understand this… but I have no choice but to assume the worst about you."

"Well that's stupid. Why'd you even bring up trust, then?" I asked.

"To get you to talk. About yourself."

"What do I have to tell you to convince you I'm not some… spy or assassin or some nonsense?"

"I don't know, Abigail. I'll know it when I hear it."

"Meanwhile I'm supposed to trust you, when the only thing I know about you is that your name isn't Alan."

That got me half a smile. He said, "Maybe we should focus on something to do. Let the other stuff happen organically."

"Let's see." I started counting on my fingers, "We've got hiking, eating, sleeping, drinking, fighting, reading, and watching TV. Where do you want to start?"

"Hm." He crossed his arms, regarding me appraisingly. "I wouldn't mind learning a few of those Krav moves. And you need some ground skills."

I flared up at once, snarling, "I *have* ground skills! I just made a mistake. It won't happen again."

"All right, all right… Wow."

More calmly, I said, "I have no interest in teaching you to more effectively terrorize me."

"Who's terrorizing? I made you breakfast!"

"Well I have a request for lunch: Go away."

"You're mean, you know that?"

I saw the corner of his mouth twitch, as though he were holding back laughter. For a moment I was so angry I couldn't speak, but after a deep breath I said slowly, "I would like to take a break from this conversation."

He held up his hands palms first, giving no other answer. I dashed upstairs and lay down on the bed, covering my eyes with my arm. I was incapable of rational thought when I was mad, and he seemed to have picked up on the fact that nothing angered me more than losing a fight.

"You can't let him get to you like that," I whispered.

If I'd learned one thing from the morning's discussion, it was that Alan remained as suspicious of me as ever. How or why he was convinced I'd lied about my reasons for coming here, it was obvious he'd made up his mind. He'd probably given me back the gun to see what I would do, and my purported attempt to use the Perkinses' telephone, followed by my botched cell phone heist, had been all the answer he needed.

I couldn't keep bouncing back and forth from grudging compliance to feeble rebellion without provoking more suspicion, and I couldn't afford to keep stupefying myself with alcohol.

I had to get him to trust me.

11

Saturday, June 27, 2020

Ten minutes later, I descended from the loft, dressed for a hike and prepared to not be quite so mean. Dude reacted to my appearance in the predictable way, bounding around the cabin and barking joyously. Alan was nowhere to be seen at first, but soon enough he emerged from the bathroom, looking puzzled by my change of clothes.

"You said you've explored the area," I said, in answer to his unasked question.

"Yeah, I've been around."

"Anything interesting you can show me?"

"Uh… sure."

He got dressed while I crammed some snacks and water into my backpack. When we set out a few minutes later, Dude launching himself uphill as soon as he realized we were hiking that direction, I could sense Alan's suspicion waxing rather than waning.

Sure enough, he started in almost immediately by accusing, "You're giving me whiplash."

"Come again?" I asked his back, as he was leading the way to whatever destination he'd picked. I hadn't even asked.

"Your mood swings. It's hard to keep up."

So he'd noticed the pendulum effect, too.

"Yeah, well—" I started to answer, tripped on a rock, and caught myself on a tree. I stopped to pick bits of bark off my palm, inspecting a minor scratch, and finished, "It's hard to suppress the survival instinct. It comes and goes."

He stopped too and turned around. "Why are you suppressing your survival instinct?"

I could hear in his voice that my words had somehow managed to put him on guard. Hoping to gloss over the moment, I shrugged and asked, "What other option do I have?"

"You could've shot me. Could've set Dude on me. You could've jumped in your truck and made a break for it while I was asleep last night."

"Dude's not really an attack dog. And where would I go? This is kind of my last stand, you know?"

"Fine, and the first thing?"

"You really want to know why I didn't shoot you?" I asked.

"Let's hear it."

For something else to look at besides his openly dubious expression, I watched Dude snuffling around under a pine tree. "I felt sorry for you. I thought you were a—I thought you were crazy. I'm not sure I could even kill a non-crazy person, let alone—well, you wanted to know," I finished lamely.

He crossed his arms, and the movement made me tear my eyes away from Dude to rest on Alan again.

"Thought?" he asked. "As in, past tense?"

"I guess. I think maybe… there's a chance you're not crazy. You don't seem crazy. But yeah, fight or flight still crops up every couple of hours."

He studied me for a moment, and then his gaze wandered to a point over my right shoulder. Finally he asked, "You have that magazine on you?"

"Sure. Why?"

"If we run into anything dangerous, I'm gonna need it."

"I'll toss it to you. If we do."

"Fair enough."

We got moving again. As my thoughts began to wander to what sorts of dangers we might encounter, I started to feel deeply uncomfortable about going unarmed. I asked Alan's back, "Are you a good shot?"

"Decent. Are you?"

"Um… no, not really. I miss a lot."

"Is that why you carry a hand cannon?"

I sniffed disdainfully. "It was a gift."

"From someone who'd seen you shoot, I assume."

"Rude."

"I'm just trying to figure something out. You've got a big, powerful truck, a massive dog, and you're carrying around this ten millimeter that probably kicks like a mule, when most people are happy enough with nine. I'm thinking you've either got a massive inferiority complex, or you're from Texas."

A laugh burst out of me. Despite his insulting tone, I was flattered. I asked, "Which one do you think it is?"

"Texas. But you don't have an accent, so I'm guessing you moved away at least a few years ago. Somewhere on the east coast? New England?"

Alan was leading us uphill, but not directly toward the summit. We passed my third cairn and then turned northwest, still gradually gaining altitude.

I swallowed a lump in my throat. His guess was a little too close for comfort. I argued, "You watch too many movies. Not all Texans have accents."

"Hm," he hummed, again not challenging my non-answer.

Feeling very much out of my depth, I fell silent and focused on putting one foot in front of the other. Alan didn't talk anymore either, but eventually I could hear him breathing heavily from exertion. After forty-five very quiet minutes, we reached a derelict barbed-wire fence.

"I assume you have no objection to trespassing," he quipped.

"Oh that's rich," I shot back. I stepped on the lowest wire and pulled up on the middle one, creating a decent-sized gap in the fence. "After you."

He ducked under, then held the barbed wire open for me. Dude had already army-crawled under the fence and was waiting for us at the edge of a steep gully that ran parallel to it. We followed the gully straight uphill at a punishing grade that had me out of breath within minutes. As I refused to ask Alan to slow down, I was gasping for air when we finally came to a stop fifteen minutes later. Abandoning pretense, I plopped down on the ground to catch my breath. I was getting angry with myself. I was acclimated to the altitude, and I was in incredible physical shape—or so I thought—so why was this still so taxing?

"This part's tricky," Alan explained. "The gully keeps going for miles before it's narrow enough to jump across. This deadfall is the closest thing to a bridge we've got."

He was looking appraisingly at a piñon that had fallen across the gap, its dying crown clinging to the soil on our side of the gully.

"Have you ever crossed it?" I asked warily. The tree wasn't very sturdy looking, and its roots were clinging to the very edge of the gully on the other side.

"Yeah. It'll hold, but if you're not a fan of heights…"

I leaned over the edge of the gully to see what he meant. My stomach squirmed with discomfort. It was significantly deeper than I'd guessed. I glanced east, then west, confirming it stretched as far as the eye could see in either direction.

"Uh… is the thing we're hiking to worth this?" I asked.

"One way to find out."

"Okay… well… you first."

He climbed onto the tree and started across the twelve-foot gap, going carefully but otherwise outwardly unaffected by the possibility of plunging to his death. The tree didn't move at all, which was a good sign. I pegged him at 230 pounds easily, making me 100 pounds lighter (give or take a few pounds). Alan gained the other side and turned to me.

"Is this the part where you run away?" he asked.

"I should, shouldn't I?"

"Afraid I'll catch you?"

"Not before someone else does. Be as scary as you want, I'm still safer here with you than I am out there." Turning away from his bewildered expression, I looked down at Dude. "Sitz. Bleib," I told him. He sat, wriggling a little with impatience.

I climbed onto the tree, and two small steps forward brought me away from solid ground with nothing but the bottom of the gully to catch me. It was at least twenty feet deep. I paused, took a deep breath, and moved forward two more steps.

"Don't look down, dummy," Alan chided from the other side.

"I'm not!"

"You were."

"Shut up."

A few more steps, and I was across. I scrambled over the roots, and as my boots finally hit solid ground on the other side I felt, or imagined I felt, the ground shift ever so slightly under my feet. My stomach squirmed again, more insistent this time; but if I hadn't brought down the tree bridge, Dude wouldn't.

"Komm!" I called.

Dude loped gracefully across the log, leaping over the roots to land behind me. I crept toward the lip of the gully again, glaring suspiciously at where the roots were twisted into the earth. When Dude had jumped, it had definitely moved.

"What?" Alan asked, coming up behind me. "Something down there?"

"No, I just thought—"

The distinct sound of a large rock tumbling down into the

gully cut across my words. With a deep groan, the root end of the tree slipped, tearing the earth all around with it. Closest to the tree, I felt myself sinking as the soil slid into the gully, dragging me with it.

12

Saturday, June 27 to Sunday, June 28, 2020

Alan grabbed me around the waist and hauled me backward. I twisted out of his arms immediately and backed several paces away from the gully. The tree hadn't slipped far, only a few feet, before the sloping edge of the gully caught it again. I wouldn't have been injured, obviously, but the adrenaline rush was real all the same.

I laughed shakily. "That was a thing. Think we can still get across?"

"Probably. Let's cross that bridge when we come to it."

I laughed again, enjoying the sensation of panic subsiding. "I see what you did there."

"Yeah. Sorry for…"

"No, it's fine," I said in a rush, eager to dismiss the moment. "Let's see what's at the end of this trail, already."

Another hour's hike straight north brought us to our destination. Tucked into the side of a steep slope, mostly obscured by trees and tumbled rocks, sat another wooden building even more dilapidated and neglected-looking than Alan's shack. Its roof was formed by long, wooden beams driven into the hill, supported by a frame of vertical logs. Whether it had never had walls, or they had simply rotted away, I couldn't tell.

Peering into the interior of the structure, I saw it extended deep into the side of the hill. The back of the building was lost in shadow. I found my flashlight and shined it inside, gasping. The interior wended away at least fifty feet into the side of the mountain, its terminus lost around a sharp turn.

"How far does it go?" I whispered.

"I don't know. I haven't gone too far inside. It doesn't seem very stable. But look." He ducked under the roof, which was no more than five feet high, and crouched down next to a pile of rusted metal. "I think this was a still. There are broken bottles everywhere."

"Bootleggers?"

"Yeah, I bet. This building is at least a hundred years old."

"Cool."

"Worth it?"

"Yeah."

I ducked inside too, toeing curiously at the detritus. Dude paced back and forth in front of the building, unwilling to venture inside. I stood with my back to the tunnel-like interior for about four seconds before some instinct forced me to turn around and shine my light into it again. It was undeniably creepy, the way the light sputtered out, the tunnel still receding, its depths unknowable.

Did something live down there? Was it asleep?

I asked, "Do you think… maybe bears live back there?"

"Maybe," he said, unconcerned.

It occurred me that as unnerved as I was by the tunnel and the possible bears, I was totally at ease with Alan. I watched him picking through the remains of the still, wondering why, and recalled something I'd once read in a book about fear and intuition: Dogs were credited with being better judges of character than humans, but the author posited that they merely reflected their owners' unacknowledged intuition. If a stranger creeped me out, Dude would sense my emotion and behave accordingly. I'd notice his dislike of the person before I was able to acknowledge my own. I wasn't wary of Alan because Dude wasn't, because I wasn't. It didn't really explain much.

"Is this where you go when hunters come?" I asked.

"No way. Too easy to find, and I'd never be able to sleep with that behind me," he jerked his thumb toward the tunnel. "There's a real cave, farther up the mountain."

"Can I see it?"

"Maybe tomorrow. What do you think this is?"

He passed me a long, rusted tube of metal. It was about ten inches long and slightly bigger around than my thumb. One end was flakes of rust, the other a neat if entirely rust-covered embrasure. I pointed it at him.

"It's a rifle barrel. Twenty-two. Nice." I passed it back to him. "I wonder where the rest of it is."

We both started looking, but we gave up after a few minutes.

There was too much organic matter—leaves, pine needles, and loam—to hope to find anything. Alan sat back and studied the .22 barrel, obviously pleased with his find.

"I bet there was a shoot-out here," he mused.

"Come on, it was probably just for squirrels."

"Ugh," he frowned, "Squirrels. I hate them."

"As… food?"

"As anything. Did you bring anything to eat?"

We sat down outside the distillery to share a lunch of energy bars, jerky, and water. Though I sat with my back to the building, within a minute I pointedly moved so I was facing it.

"Pretty freaky, huh?" Alan asked, smirking.

"Yeah. I thought I could feel cold air coming out of there just now."

After lunch, rather than exploring farther into the distillery, we decided we'd had enough of the place. Alan led the way back to the gully, where we found to our dismay that the tree had slipped even farther into it. It was now plainly idiotic to attempt to cross that way, so after a brief debate we decided to follow the gully uphill until we found another deadfall or a point narrow enough to leap across.

Thanks to that detour, which added nearly three hours to our hike, we didn't get back to the cabin until just before sundown. Exhausted, cranky, and starving, I flopped down on the couch as soon as we got inside. Over the sounds of Dude noisily satiating his thirst at the water bowl, I heard the shower come on. I heaved myself off the couch and knocked on the bathroom door.

"What?" came the guarded response from inside.

"Leave some hot water this time, please."

"Oh—yeah, I'll make it quick."

I returned to the couch, intending to start a movie, and went out like a light.

▼

When I woke up, night had fallen. I glanced at my watch: 10:30. The movement caught Alan's attention at the same time he caught mine. Rather than dislodging me from the couch, he had chosen to sit on the floor to watch *Armageddon*. The movie was about halfway over.

"I made macaroni and cheese," he said, probably in answer to a very loud grumble from my empty stomach. "And I fed Dude. Didn't want to wake you."

I groaned a "thank you" and staggered upstairs to fetch my pajamas. One quick, very hot shower later, I felt up to cramming some food in my mouth. I carried the half-full pot of mac and cheese to the couch with a spoon and went to work, which was unfortunately timed to coincide with a vomit-inducing, tender love scene in the movie.

To drown out the dialog, I announced, "Know what we should do?"

He jumped a little, startled by my too-loud voice. "What?"

"We should take all the movies they have here and try to line them up in a chain. You know, Kevin Bacon style. I bet we can do it."

"Kevin Bacon style?"

"Sure, you know: Peter Stormare is in *The Lost World* and *Armageddon*. We've got *Con Air*, which also has Steve Buscemi, and *Gone in 60 Seconds* has Nick Cage... get it? Most of these movies are from the nineties. They all have the same supporting actors, so it can't be that hard to match them all up."

"Would that... be fun for you?" he asked, bemused.

Seeing that my babbling had gotten us through the love scene, I sat back and concluded, "It would be something to do."

"All right, I'm game."

He pulled the entire VHS library, which was substantial, out of the TV cabinet and laid each movie out on the living room rug. He lined up *Jurassic Park*, *The Lost World*, the empty *Armageddon* box, *Con Air*, and *Gone in 60 Seconds*.

"Okay, now what?"

I mused for a moment, then said, "Save Jolie for later. We'll need her for the newer movies. What about something with Malkovich or Cusack?"

After much re-shuffling, debate, and compromise, we had arranged thirty of the forty-six titles in an unbroken chain. Sorting through old movies, most of which came out when I was still a kid, made it seem natural to talk about myself: my parents' refusal to let me watch *Titanic*, my sister spoiling *The Sixth Sense* for me, etc. Alan didn't reciprocate, but he didn't seem bothered by my yammering. Around midnight when we were both too tired to carry on, I took myself upstairs with all three *Lord of the Rings* books and nodded off sometime after two in the morning.

▼

Thanks to the unplanned, five-hour nap, my Sunday morning started early. I stayed in bed for a half an hour, fighting it with all my might, but I couldn't get back to sleep.

There was nothing for it but to get up and get to work. After over a week at the cabin, I hadn't done any laundry or cleaned much since that first de-spidering. I started a load of laundry, then tackled the kitchen. At first I tiptoed around, trying not to wake Alan; but after I'd dropped the macaroni pan on the floor without waking him up, I figured there was no point in trying to be quiet. While I scrubbed the dishes, I mentally shuffled those last sixteen movies, absurdly enthusiastic about such a silly task.

I was up to thirty-seven, totally lost in thought, when someone knocked on the door.

Dude, who'd been asleep in his chair, exploded at once into earsplitting barks. Deeply asleep as he was, Alan had no hope of snoozing through that. I whirled around as he sat up, both of us looking automatically through the window in the door. Whoever it was stood to the side, only a shoulder visible. Dude got in the way as he bounded against the door, still sounding the alarm.

"Oh, no," I breathed. "No, don't hide," I added, seeing Alan shrinking toward the bookcase in the far corner. "They probably already saw you. Just walk to the bathroom like it's not a big deal."

"How do I walk like it's not a big deal?"

"Just go!"

I waited until he was out of sight, then banished Dude to

the back yard. In the interim, the person at the door had moved in front of the window, either spying inside or trying to identify herself. I opened the door on a tiny, white-haired old woman who looked both startled and abashed at the chaos she'd provoked. She gave me an uncertain smile.

"Abigail?" she asked.

"Yes—hi, are you Doreen? I didn't expect you for a few more days."

"Oh yes, we had to come back a little sooner than expected. I'm sorry to come so early, but I needed to speak with you as soon as possible. May I come in?"

I stood back, acutely aware of Dude still raising Cain in the back yard. "Of course. Do you want some coffee? Sorry about the mess, by the way. I just got started cleaning."

"Don't worry about it. I won't be long." She glanced at the couch, which she had almost certainly seen Alan vacate, and then at me, the question unspoken.

"Had a date," I said, nearly choking on the lie; but I couldn't think of any other way to explain the presence of a man in the cabin. "We met in Durango. Don't worry, I'll get him out of here soon."

"Oh. Um. Very good. Lovely… lovely town, Durango."

I could barely look at her and covered over the moment by saying, "Yes, it's—um—fun. What brought you back from Ireland early?"

"We have someone who's interested in seeing the cabin, actually."

"Oh." My smile faded at once. When my boss was renting

the cabin, Doreen had warned him that it was for sale; but she hadn't gotten any offers, or even any interest, in six months. I hadn't thought it was worth worrying about.

She looked apologetic, explaining, "I was as surprised as you are. Probably he won't want it—but he did want to come by for a viewing. Today."

"Oh! Wow… okay."

"I hate to ask, I really do… but he wanted to come at four. Could you…?"

"Beat it?" I asked, trying to make light of the situation. "No problem. That'll give me plenty of time to get the cabin sparkly clean again. How long should I be gone?"

"Just a couple of hours. I really do appreciate it so much. Like I said, I doubt he'll make an offer…"

She left the rest unsaid: But if he does, you've got to go. I forced a smile onto my face. "I understand. I'll leave it unlocked for y'all."

"Thank you, dear." Doreen started to go, paused, and glanced toward the back yard as though not quite sure of something.

"I'll take Dude with me, don't worry," I said.

"Oh, wonderful, thank you. Say hi to your friend for me."

"Will do."

I closed the door behind her, leaned against it, and stared into space. After a few minutes of silence, punctuated only by sporadic barks, Alan broke cover. He let Dude back inside, then cautiously approached the front door.

"Is she gone?"

I nodded.

"She saw me, didn't she?"

I was too worried to give any thought to how Alan might react to a second person daring to lay eyes on him. Dismissively, I explained, "Yes, but I told her we were on a date. I think she bought it. She wants me to leave at four so she can show the cabin to a prospective buyer."

Unsurprisingly, Alan was not too happy. He huffed in indignation and said, "I didn't even know the cabin was for sale! Since when? What if she says something to this prospective buyer about me being here?"

I waited for him to swear several times before asking calmly, "Why in the world would she tell him that?"

"I don't know—but she could. Why did you have to come here?"

"Hey, easy!" I defended, heating up at once. "It was your idea to babysit me. If we'd gone with my idea, she wouldn't have seen you."

"Yeah, yeah. Sorry."

"Whatever. If you're that worried about it, we'll have to listen in to their conversation. As long as she doesn't blab, there's nothing to freak out about, right?"

He gave me an evaluating look, asking, "How are we supposed to do that?"

Shooting him a haughty glare, I whisked past him to the little mud room next to the back door. A storage cabinet on the wall contained all the basics—toilet paper, tissues, laundry detergent, trash bags. I'd snooped through the cabinet my first day here and knew it also held four walkie-talkies in a charging stand that was plugged in to the wall. I saw an instruction manual next to the charger and grabbed it, leafing through it eagerly.

"You didn't know these were here?" I asked Alan, who had followed me, while I scanned the instructions.

"Sure, but what good are they? You have to hold down the button to talk."

"They all have voice recorders."

He grabbed one of the walkie-talkies, studying the buttons around the main screen. "Oh."

"This says with a full charge, they can record up to three hours of audio. We can hide them… Say, one under the couch, one upstairs, one in the kitchen, and one by the front door. Once they leave, we can listen to the recordings, and you can decide whether to keep freaking out."

"What if they go back to Doreen's house to talk? We won't be able to hear that. And they'll be talking on the phone, email-ing…"

"I know it's not a perfect solution, but it's better than noth-ing. Would you prefer I grill her about what she's told him? Talk about suspicious."

He seemed in agreement, at least for now. I plucked the walkie-talkie out of his hand and replaced it in the charger.

"We need to keep these charging for as long as possible. We can turn them on right before we leave, when we see his car coming up the road." I returned the instruction manual to its place and turned to Alan, all business now. "Are you going to help me clean this place up, or what?"

13

Sunday, June 28, 2020

Alan and I spent the next few hours making the cabin sparkle, neither of us talking much. Dude sensed the tension that filled the tiny cabin and curled up in his chair, watching us warily. With four hours left before the prospective buyer arrived, we sat down at the kitchen table to test the walkie-talkies and work out the finer points of our strategy.

At two o'clock, we piled into my truck and left the cabin. I drove four miles up the county road and, guided by Alan, turned west onto a tiny service road that snaked up the mountain and curved back south a couple of miles before dead-ending. We left the truck there and hiked back to the cabin.

The journey Alan had claimed would take no more than an hour ended up taking ninety minutes, which put us back at the cabin uncomfortably close to the prospective buyer's arrival. No sooner had we stepped inside than Alan spotted a car turning off the main road. I hastily turned on the walkie-talkies and then we booked it, following my cairns up the mountain to a point about a thousand feet up, from which we could see the cabin below.

By the time we got there, the view through Alan's binoculars confirmed they were already inside the cabin, barely visible through the windows we'd left open. In the driveway were two cars: a green Subaru I assumed was Doreen's, and a white Ford sedan with New Mexico license plates.

"They're in there," I mumbled, passing Alan the binoculars. "Hope they don't stay too long."

"How long could it take to look at a twelve hundred square foot cabin?" I glared down at the white car, just a bright speck without the binoculars. "Please, please don't let him buy it."

"Who are you talking to?"

"God."

"Don't worry. Even if he makes an offer, I've got tons of tricks to change his mind."

I laughed, momentarily reassured. "Who is this guy, anyway? Who makes a septuagenarian cut her vacation short just so he can look at a cabin in rural Colorado? He couldn't wait a few weeks?"

He shrugged, the binoculars still pressed to his face. "Some rich jerk from Texas or California, trying to start a cult probably."

"What?" I almost laughed. "Why a cult?"

"Seems like a good place for a cult, you know?"

We passed the time speculating about who this person was and what he wanted the cabin for, passing the binoculars back and forth every few minutes. I could tell Alan was getting antsy, probably imagining Doreen chatting the buyer up and divulging too many details about the cabin's current tenant and her new 'friend.'

I was about to distract him with more cult talk when he tensed up and announced, "They're coming out."

"Let me see," I whispered, as though they might hear us, and grabbed the binoculars from him.

They had paused in the driveway, still chatting. Doreen motioned toward the house, expounding, I assumed, on some rehearsed buying points. The man, partially hidden behind her, stepped backward and put his hands on his hips. While he listened to her spiel, I finally got a decent look at him. He was about five-ten and smartly dressed, a sheen of red-blonde hair catching the sunlight.

My pulse quickened, making my hands shake. I tried to adjust the focus and ended up dropping the binoculars. As I scrambled to retrieve them, Alan picked up on my change in demeanor.

"Something wrong?" he asked.

"No. No, no, no, no…"

"Is that a yes?"

"Oh no. No, no. Not good."

I pressed the eyepieces against my face so hard it hurt, fumbling to get the picture back in focus. I finally got it right and was treated to a very sharp, unmistakable image of the last man in the world I wanted to see.

"It's him," I breathed. "It's Philip. Philip Levin, my ex-husband."

"You're kidding me."

I handed the binoculars to him, lapsing into stunned silence.

Alan said, "He's leaving. I'm no body language expert, but it doesn't seem like they made a deal."

"Obviously, he doesn't really want to buy the cabin," I muttered, mostly to myself. "Let's get back. I want to hear what they said."

I was so distracted on the return hike that I tripped three times, thankfully avoiding anything worse than a scuffed palm. After the third fall, Alan grabbed my upper arm and practically dragged me the rest of the way. Too absorbed in my own thoughts, I made no attempt to shake him off.

Inside, Dude immediately sensed Philip's presence and began snuffling all over the cabin, seeming nearly as upset as I was. We gathered the radios together and started with the one by the front door.

The recording was silent for a few minutes, the radio emitting the odd crackle of static. As soon as I heard the crunch of tires on gravel coming through the speaker, the vise around my lungs loosened ever so slightly. It had worked. Brakes squealed, doors opened and closed, and finally, voices rose.

"Philip Levin?" Doreen asked. She sounded far away, but as the conversation moved on toward the cabin, the voices grew louder.

"Yes, nice to meet you, Missus Perkins. Thanks again for letting me come on such short notice."

I stiffened at the voice, my last thin shred of hope disappearing. It was definitely Philip. Smarmy, self-satisfied Philip.

The sound of his voice made me want to hurl the walkie-talkie through the window. Instead, I listened.

"Oh, my pleasure. You can call me Doreen. How was your flight? Did you get to see any of Albuquerque?"

"No, we were delayed leaving Dulles, so I had to come straight here from the airport. Lovely exterior. When did you say it was built?"

They went back and forth about the cabin for a couple of minutes, their voices rising to a crescendo as they passed the walkie-talkie hidden in the rosemary bush by the front door. The door closed, and the voices stopped. We switched to the next radio, the one that was under the couch, but before I could press play, Alan took it from me.

"Why?" I demanded, making a grab for it.

"I have an idea. Take the kitchen one, set it on the counter and turn the volume all the way up."

I complied with poor grace, not bothering to ask questions once I realized his intention. He set the second radio on the arm of the couch.

"Okay, press play on three…"

After a few false starts, we got the two recordings to sync up. Sitting between them at the kitchen table, the stereo effect was so perfect that if I closed my eyes, it was almost like Doreen and Philip were still there. It was not a pleasant sensation.

Doreen was audible first, asking, "What were you thinking as far as move-in date?"

"Oh, I haven't given it much thought yet. How soon could it be?"

"Well, I've got a tenant renting it now through the end of July. I might be able to make it the first of July, but I haven't discussed that with her yet."

After a pause so short I might have imagined it, Philip said, "Not much notice for her."

"Of course. I'm sure we'll be able to work something out."

"Sure, sure…"

As they carried on about the usual nonsense—appliances, well water, heating, yadda yadda—I could hear Philip opening and closing doors, cabinets, and drawers, snooping around as one does when viewing a house for sale. Doreen's voice stayed mostly still in the kitchen while he looked around, and then they both went upstairs. Soon, their voices were too muffled to hear.

"Want to switch?" Alan asked.

I shook my head. "We'll listen to that one last. I don't want to mess with the timing on these two."

Five or so minutes later, their conversation came back into focus.

"… get pretty cold up here in the winter, but the wood stove does a good job heating the whole cabin. No AC, of course. You'd never need it."

"That sounds pretty nice," Philip answered, the smile in his voice making my teeth grind together. "You wouldn't believe how hot it gets in DC."

I closed my eyes, willing him to shut up about where he lived, but Doreen was all too happy to engage him.

"Oh, I know. I've been a few times myself. Ernest and I just love to travel. Do you live in the city?"

"No, we live in Fairfax. DC's too expensive."

"You and your wife?"

"Yes. It was too bad she couldn't make it. Here, I can't resist showing her off…"

To my horror, the recording picked up a faint but distinct sound of paper slipping out of a wallet. *He was showing her a picture of me.* I held my breath, waiting for the fateful response: "But that's the young woman who's staying here!"

Instead, Doreen was silent for a moment, then said in a strangely sweet tone of voice, "My goodness, she's a doll. That beautiful red hair. Do you have any children?"

I didn't realize my mouth was hanging open until Alan tapped me under the chin. I looked at him, puzzled, having all but forgotten he was sitting next to me.

"She's got your back."

I nodded, at a complete loss for words. Had Philip believed her? They were talking about the cabin again, going down the familiar "room for children" road. They finally went outside, and we moved on to the fourth walkie-talkie. Only then did I realize it was off.

"Did you turn it off?" I asked Alan, who shook his head.

"It was on when I brought it downstairs."

"It must have died."

We plugged it in and let it charge, and in the interim we waited through half an hour of silence on the first radio until we heard Doreen and Philip come back outside.

Doreen was expounding, "…exposed logs when we built it, but we had it stuccoed a few years ago. There's a small enclosure in the back yard, good for smaller pets. You know we get all sorts of wildlife up here, bears, mountain lions, coyotes of course. I haven't seen any rattlesnakes this year, but there were several last year."

Over Philip's response, Alan whispered, "Is she trying to talk him out of it now?"

"I don't know, shush."

As they wrapped up the visit and said polite goodbyes, it was clear Alan's initial assessment had been right and Philip wasn't even feigning interest in the cabin anymore. Once the outside recording was over, we fetched the charging walkie-talkie and tried to play the last recording. Rather than hearing Philip exploring the upstairs, all we heard was silence. It wasn't the crackling silence of nothing happening, but the absolute emptiness of a failed recording. The timestamp claimed to be playing something back, but obviously nothing had been recorded. We let it play out, just to be sure.

"Perfect," I snarled. "He was up there touching all my stuff and I don't even get to hear it."

Though we listened to the other two recordings at full volume, not a word from the loft was discernable. I went through both several times, long after Alan had lost interest and started making dinner, but there was nothing to hear. Just for good measure, I went upstairs to see if anything was out of place.

It didn't take long to find. In my underwear drawer, tucked between the cups of a fancy bra I never wore, was a business card. On the front were Philip's name, title, office address, phone numbers, and email address, adorned by the embossed seal of the Federal Bureau of Investigation.

On the back, scrawled hastily in all caps, was the simple missive, "CALL ME."

14

Sunday, June 28, 2020

How Philip had managed to slip a business card into my underwear drawer without being seen was a mystery to me. Or maybe he hadn't; maybe Doreen had seen him pawing through my unmentionables and decided he wasn't on the level. Either way, there was no way I was going to let Alan see a business card boldly identifying Philip as a Supervisory Special Agent at the FBI. I slipped it back into my bra and decided if Alan found it there, we'd both be in deep trouble.

I returned downstairs, answering Alan's questioning glance with, "Everything looks okay up there. Just a dead horse's head tucked into the sheets."

"Okay, good." He peered at me, concerned by my attempt at humor. "Ready to go get the truck?"

"Oh, right. Sure."

We left Dude in the cabin, halfway hoping Philip would come back and get the business end of a German Shepherd.

All the way back to the truck, my mind was filled with Philip's two-word demand, trying to figure out why he would risk leaving his card in my dresser if he weren't sure I was there. Maybe something he'd seen had confirmed my presence: a book on the nightstand, a bottle of wine in the pantry, my shampoo, something. Maybe he had long since figured out what I was trying to do and found this place the exact same way I had.

Lost in thought, I tripped again. This time I stayed down. While I stared numbly at my right hand pressed into the loam, a quarter-sized, brown spider crawled across it at leisurely pace and disappeared. I didn't even flinch. After a while, Alan realized I wasn't behind him anymore and came back. He sat down on the ground next to me.

"Can we do this later?" he asked, not a trace of sympathy in his voice.

"Give me a break," I shot back, shutting my mouth as soon as I heard my own voice. I was actually getting choked up. I could feel hot, stinging tears starting to build, and I turned away so he wouldn't see. "Can you not wait like three seconds?"

In answer, he stood up, hauling me up with him. Though I pushed his hands away, he took me by the shoulders and waited for me to meet his eyes.

"This is not the end of the world," he said slowly.

"Oh, you're one to talk! I just—I needed more time," I argued, pushing his hands away again.

"What, are you pregnant or something?"

"No! I—it's hard to explain. Just drop it. And don't touch me. I'm serious."

"All right, take it easy. Can we get the truck?"

"Fine."

Back to the truck, down the service road, then the county road, and finally up the driveway and into the cabin, I remained totally silent, lost in thought. The simple fact was, I needed weeks, ideally months, with this man who was calling himself Alan; but now, thanks to Philip's hounding, I'd be lucky if I had days. One more surprise visit like that, and I had no doubt Alan would leave me to deal with my own problems and find somewhere else to hide.

I watched Alan as he milled around in the kitchen, finishing the dinner he'd started earlier. He was smarter than I'd given him credit for. Though I'd dyed my hair brown, he'd understood that Philip had showed Doreen a picture of me, and that she'd lied to put him off the scent. I had to admit, Alan had gone from my second greatest problem to a possible ally in a remarkably short span of time. What else might be possible?

Over a dinner of grilled cheese and tomato soup, our movie-chain plan forgotten, we watched *Con Air* and ignored each other. When Alan went to the kitchen for seconds, I followed him.

"Gah," he breathed when he turned around and saw me. "Please stop doing that."

"Sorry. What are you going to do now?"

"Finish off this soup, unless you want some." He held up the pan, and I shook my head.

I pressed, "I mean about Philip."

Rolling his eyes, he asked, "Oh, are we ready to talk about

that now?"

The patronizing tone was a bit much, but I bit back my anger. "I guess we should."

"Okay. Well. He found you, so you're about to try to convince me to let you leave, right?"

"No. Can you teach me jujitsu?"

Alan paused, a spoonful of soup in mid-bite. "Seriously?"

"Yes." I took a bracing breath. "You've obviously had some training. And I don't want to run from Philip anymore. If he really does know I'm here, and he wants to start trouble, I want to be ready for it."

"Aren't you?" he asked. I stared, not understanding, until he added, "You know Krav Maga, you have a guard dog, you've got that ridiculous boom stick—"

"*You* have my Glock."

"Well, you have me."

I blinked through my surprise, asking quietly, "I do?"

"I'm not going anywhere just because that little pipsqueak wants to hunt down his ex-wife. This is my spot."

The rush of triumph and satisfaction nearly made me laugh out loud. Maybe he trusted me, maybe he didn't, but for whatever reason he felt protective of me.

"Granted," he went on, cutting through my self-congratulations, "you've ruined a beautiful thing, bringing all your drama here."

"Sorry."

"I probably can't come back, but I think I'm good for now. All the attention seems to be on you."

"…Sorry. So, jujitsu?"

"It's a full-contact sport, Abigail," he said, brushing past me to return to the couch. "I seem to recall something about you not wanting to be touched?"

"I didn't mean… like that."

He didn't answer.

"I'll teach you Krav Maga," I offered.

"Malarky."

"No, it's not."

Finally turning to face me, he said, "If your plan is to kill the guy, I think the Glock is your best bet."

"I don't want to kill him. I just… don't want him to kill me."

"I doubt he'll come at you with Brazilian Jujitsu."

"I didn't expect you to, and you beat me."

"That's because I'm bigger than you."

"You know what, fine!" I spat. "Forget it."

He let me stew until the movie ended, then continued the conversation as though there had been no pause. "You're not going to like it."

"What, jujitsu?"

"It's very technical. It takes a long time to get good at it."

I shrugged that off with, "I have to start somewhere."

"We're gonna be rolling around on the floor. I'm going to be on top of you. A lot. Can you handle that?"

"I'm not afraid of you," I mumbled, avoiding his eyes.

"Good. We can get started tomorrow."

15

Monday, June 29, 2020

Dude woke me up the next morning by licking me right across the face. I sputtered into consciousness, wiping dog slobber off my cheek and pushing him away.

"Why?" I groaned.

He sat down primly and stared at me, tail wagging so fast it was just a blur. It didn't take long before the source of his hyperactive state became apparent: The whole cabin smelled like bacon. I could hear it sizzling downstairs. If I had a tail, it would've been wagging, too. I got dressed in loose-fitting workout clothes and paused halfway down the stairs.

The couch and kitchen table had been pushed back, leaving the area rug open in the center of the living room. Alan spotted me when I got to the bottom of the stairs.

"Ready?" was his greeting.

"Not really. I better put Dude in the back yard. He's not going to approve of any of this."

"That's what the bacon is for."

I goaded Dude outside. To prepay for good behavior, I gave him two full strips of bacon. I watched through the window as he carried them to the far corner of the yard and plopped down, munching happily.

First we stretched, at Alan's insistence, and then he suggested we start exactly where we'd left off a few days ago, when he whooped me. Feeling equal parts silly and uncomfortable, I assumed the position with him on the living room rug. He lay on his back, and I dropped to my knees between his. He locked his ankles around my back. Even knowing this was as normal as grappling exercises came, I already hated it.

"This is called closed guard," he started.

I couldn't stop myself retorting, "I know."

"Okay, smarty pants. What did you do wrong?"

"I gave you my arm."

"Exactly. You know everything, lesson over."

"Don't be a jerk."

We went through a few iterations of Alan repeating the choke hold he'd used on me, explaining each step until I could parrot it back to him. His words and movements were so clinical I felt my discomfort fading effortlessly away. After he was satisfied I understood the technique, we switched positions so he could show me how to get out of it.

Though I'd known this was coming and expected my discomfort to return, I wasn't quite prepared for the rush of anxiety I felt when he knelt down between my legs. Unfortunately, he noticed.

"Are you sure you're okay with this?" he asked.

"Yes. Please don't ask again."

He did stop bringing it up, but the awkwardness was only getting started. We went through five different submissions, all of which seemed so complicated that I couldn't help but be dubious about ever using them in real life. It was like playing twister, but with more ways to mess up, a lot less laughing, and a lot more tapping out. After about an hour, Alan excused himself to the bathroom and I understood the first lesson to be over. I let Dude inside and helped myself to some bacon, trying to go over it all in my head to help it sink in.

"Tired?" I taunted casually when Alan emerged.

He grabbed a piece of bacon and answered around it, "You wish."

"So you're ready for some deadly, deadly Krav?"

"I'll try to keep an open mind."

I grabbed a wooden spoon and beckoned him back to the carpet. He obeyed, but I didn't like the smirk on his face.

"You're gonna kill me with a spoon?" he laughed.

I twirled the 'weapon' menacingly. "It's a knife. Use your imagination."

I taught him a few disarms and was pleased to see his smirk fade as he concentrated on absorbing my lesson. He was finally starting to get it when Dude began barking, making us both freeze in place. At first I thought he was objecting to Alan putting me in a wrist lock. Then we heard the car pulling up in the driveway.

After the first surprise visit from Doreen, I'd decided to

keep the curtains drawn, so this new arrival didn't cause nearly as much scrambling as the last time. Alan simply grabbed a cup of coffee and retreated upstairs while I peeked through the curtains: Doreen was back.

I realized as she climbed out of her little Subaru that I hadn't seen it here the first time she showed up. She must have walked all the way from her own cabin. Impressed, I grabbed Dude's collar and opened the door, dragging him away from the door so she could come inside. Sometimes he forgot he was so well behaved.

"Sorry. He's excited," I explained as Doreen carefully side-stepped him. "He won't jump on you or anything. Okay if I let him go?"

"Oh, sure."

As soon as he was free, Dude bounded up to her and skidded to a stop right at her feet, sitting down and wagging his tail while he waited for pets. She happily consented, then looked around the room as though only just seeing it.

"Did I interrupt anything, dear?"

"This? No—I was doing some yoga. I'll put it all back."

"I wanted to talk to you about that man who came to the cabin yesterday."

"Oh?"

"He had a picture of you. I think he's looking for you."

"You're kidding."

"It really made me very upset, the way he pretended to want to buy this cabin, and told who knows how many other lies. Look, I have his picture, too."

She pulled out her phone and opened it to show me Philip's email avatar, unintentionally shared when he'd established contact with her. I was doubly impressed.

"Do you know him?" she asked.

"Yes," I admitted. Of all the things for which I'd been woefully unprepared so far, it felt pretty good to be ready for this one. "He's my ex-husband. I'm—uh—kind of hiding from him."

"Oh my goodness. Oh I'm so glad I didn't tell him your name. When he showed me the picture, I saw your hair was a different color and something told me to lie to him. I acted like I'd never seen you before."

"That's—that's incredible, thank you so much."

"Obviously, I'm not going to sell the cabin to him. Or anyone, as long as you need to stay here."

"Really? Thank you… I can't tell you how much that means to me, really. I feel awful for putting you in this position."

She waved away my apology, asking, "Dear… is he dangerous?"

"Honestly? Very."

"Do you think he might try to hurt you?"

"Oh yeah."

"Don't you think you better talk to the police? You can get a restraining order."

With herculean effort I kept myself from rolling my eyes and said, "I—yeah, I'll probably do that."

"Good. Well, I'll let you get back to your yoga. But if you need anything, you let me know. You and your sweet puppy here can come over to our house anytime. Ernest and I will keep you safe. We'll be praying for you, dear."

I watched her drive away, unsure what exactly I was feeling. My chest hurt, and the cabin felt stiflingly hot. I heard Alan come downstairs and assumed he'd heard everything.

"You okay?" he asked.

"What—yes—why?"

"You're as white as a ghost."

"I'm feeling… things. I don't know. Do you want to keep going or take a break?"

"You need a break. Drink some water."

Ignoring the bossiness, I wandered into the kitchen to do just that. I wanted to keep training, but a shadow of a more cunning instinct told me now was a time to talk, not to train. Pouring a glass of water for myself and one for Alan, I passed one into his hand.

I took a moment to marvel at the sheer size of his hand around the glass before asking, "Why are you staying?"

After a long drink, he said, "I told you yesterday. This is my spot. Screw that guy."

"That's not really an answer, though. When we first met, you acted like the sky was falling just because I knew you were here. What changed?"

He shrugged but didn't answer. A guarded look in his eyes told me to drop it, but I pressed on.

"Where will you go, when you do leave?"

"What about our association so far makes you think I'd answer that?"

It was my turn to shrug. "I don't know. Maybe I'm kinda worried you don't really have somewhere to go. Maybe I think this is your last stand, too. Why else would you stick around?"

"Well, don't worry. I know exactly where I'm gonna go, and you'll be relieved to know it's a heck of a lot more comfortable than this place." He took another swig, smiled at me, and added, "Boring, though."

"I guess that'll have to do for now. Back to it?"

"Back to it."

We chugged the last of our water and resumed training, and we kept at it for over an hour until we were both too tired to go on. I grabbed a quick shower while Alan made dinner. When the time inevitably came to pick a movie to watch, I took the opportunity to draw him back in to the Kevin Bacon game with *Anastasia*. For a few hours I was able to convince myself I was on vacation, that I was nobody doing nothing as I'd told Alan in the beginning; but then it was time for bed.

Dude curled up on the couch with Alan, leaving me alone upstairs with a persistent mental image of Philip rummaging through my underwear drawer.

I wasn't going to call Philip, and he knew it. He was already planning his next move, and I wasn't nearly smart enough to guess what that might be. I could wait for Alan to take another shower and fire up my laptop, sending the SOS to my boss and asking him what I should do, but *that* I could guess: I'd get pulled out, Alan would slip through our fingers, and we'd be back to square one.

I didn't know how much time Philip would give me, or how

much longer Alan would take to crack; but I thrived on deadlines, even arbitrary ones.

"One week," I whispered into the darkness, unheard by my companions snoring downstairs. "You can do this."

16

Tuesday, June 30, 2020

The next morning when Dude licked me awake again, he had the decency to slobber all over my hand instead of my face. I whipped my hand under the covers, groaning. Dude's bright eyes and wagging tail, the scent of bacon, it was all the same as yesterday. I was worried "I Got You Babe" would erupt from my alarm clock any second, completing the illusion that I was stuck in *Groundhog Day*.

I got dressed and ventured downstairs, where Alan had already amassed a pile of crispy, fried bacon and was busy scrambling what looked like a dozen eggs at once. An empty bag that used to contain shredded cheese was discarded on the counter next to the stove. At this rate, I was going to run out of groceries much sooner than anticipated.

He caught sight of me, dressed for training again, and nodded approvingly. "Eat up. You're gonna learn some basics today—muscle memory stuff. It'll wear you out quick."

I grabbed a couple pieces of bacon. "I guess I'll do the same to you. You're so eager to end up on the ground, should I assume you know how to fall?"

"In my experience, gravity takes care of the formalities when falling."

"Oh yeah? Can you do this?"

I waited until he looked up at me again, then backed onto the rug. In one smooth movement I fell backwards, hit the ground rolling, and sprang to my feet. I took a bite out of the bacon I'd held onto, and Alan shook his head in unwilling admiration.

"You really should stretch before you start showing off."

We ate breakfast, stretched, and got down to business. Though I had planned an attempt to extract basic, totally harmless information from him—where he was born, how old he was, et cetera—Alan wasn't kidding about wearing me out. I was unable to carry on any kind of conversation for the hour that we drilled, and we both needed a long break before moving on to my half of the instruction. While we stretched and hydrated, our breathing and heartrates slowly returning to normal, I tried to think of an innocuous way to ask my questions.

I settled on, "How'd you learn all this? Are you a black belt, or what?"

"Yeah, I guess I'm unofficially a black belt. The guy who taught me was a third-degree, won a couple championships when he was younger, but he wasn't exactly qualified to hand out belts himself. Once he tried to kill me and ended up taking a nap, he figured I was at a black-belt level."

I leaned forward over my extended legs to stretch my hamstrings and hide my astonishment. That was the longest answer he'd given me in a while. Three whole sentences! Maybe jujitsu was my way in, in more ways than one.

"He tried to kill you?" I asked.

"He was drunk," Alan answered. "Which you'd think would make him less lethal, but no."

"You've had a much more interesting life than I have."

He made a wordless, non-committal noise, and I understood the question-and-answer window to be closed again. We worked on falls and rolls for another hour, then geared up for a long hike. Alan had agreed to show me the cave near the summit, and he estimated we could get there and back before dark if we maintained a good pace.

"Sure you're up for this?" he asked as we were headed out the door.

Considering my full hiking regalia and backpack laden with food, water, and emergency supplies in case we had to spend the night up there, I couldn't help but be confused by his question.

"Well, yeah. Why wouldn't I be?"

"It's a tough hike. If we get stuck up there, it's gonna be a cold night, too."

I grinned at him. "I've survived worse. Lead the way."

Though he turned and started guiding Dude and me up the incline behind the cabin, I didn't like the look he'd given me. Annoyed or suspicious, I couldn't decide. I was lost in thought immediately, wondering what about my answer could have caused that reaction. Alan was kind enough not to interrupt my thoughts with a single word, and Dude must have sensed the tension. He stayed between Alan and me, never straying from the path or trying to run ahead.

By the time we stopped for a break two hours later, I had a pretty good guess where I'd screwed up. Everything he thought he knew about me simply didn't make sense in the aggregate. I had money, perhaps enough that he'd consider me rich or spoiled, and I was hiding out in fear of my ex-husband; but by Alan's own estimation, I was already more than equal to laying Philip low—at least physically. I'd let my ego lead me around by the nose for the past two days, "showing off" as Alan said. And I hadn't been lying when I told him I'd survived worse than a tough hike and one chilly, uncomfortable night on a mountain. He'd no doubt heard the ring of truth in my words.

So was I a tough girl, or a battered spouse? Could I be both? I *was* both, and that was a fact I had no reason to hide from Alan. I just had to make it make sense.

I passed him an unsolicited bag of beef jerky from my backpack, asking, "Want some?"

While Dude looked on with keen interest, Alan took the bag, tore it open, and devoured half of it before speaking. He must have been lost in the same thoughts that had occupied me.

Saving me the trouble of bringing it up, he said, "I need you to help me understand something."

"Oh… kay."

"That little guy—that squishy pencil pusher I saw at the cabin, your ex—How are you afraid of him? You're not even afraid of me."

I shrugged. "The worst you can do is kill me. Philip could

burn down my entire life."

"So why hasn't he?"

"We aren't technically divorced yet. He's dragging his feet. He needs a wife. It's part of the wholesome, super normal image he needs to maintain. He still thinks he can get me to come home."

He frowned. "So you're not afraid he'll hurt you, you're afraid he'll… convince you?"

I shook my head. "I'm afraid when he realizes he can't convince me, things will get real ugly real fast. I know they will."

"You two have any kids?"

The perfectly reasonable question shocked me into several seconds of tense silence. I occupied the time by adding a packet of electrolyte powder to my water bottle and shaking it up. Once the powder was dissolved, I mumbled, "No."

Through a sigh, he asked, "So you're just gonna hide from him for the rest of your life?"

"No. Eventually someone else will catch his eye, someone who can give him—who can be the picture perfect wife for him, and I'll be off the hook. All I have to do is wait somewhere safe."

"Give him what?"

I stood up, re-zipping my backpack before slinging it too-roughly over my shoulders. "You said we didn't have time for lollygagging, right? Let's go."

Not counting our few, brief rests, the hike from the cabin to the cave took just under five hours. Alan led us on a course that diverged early from the path I'd forged to the summit. We were directly south of it when I scrambled over a house-sized boulder, close on Dude's heels, and caught my first sight of Alan's home-away-from-home-away-from-home.

"Cave" was a bit generous. The tunnel behind the presumed still was more of a cave than this. An overhang of rock formed a barely sufficient barrier between the sky and a twin mattress-sized, sandy stretch of ground. Alan had made a half-hearted attempt to disguise the remains of his most recent encampment. I could see footprints, the impression of a sleeping bag, and even a bright orange corner of what I suspected was a candy wrapper. Dude made a beeline for it, sniffing and scratching at the spot, hoping to uncover something tasty. Alan seemed to be looking at the area through my eyes.

"Yeah, I got a little lazy last time I left. I was in too big a hurry to leave."

Seeing no evidence of a campfire or a woodpile, I asked, "You don't have fires?"

"Absolutely not. Someone spots one little bit of smoke, and I'd have volunteer firefighters raining down on me in minutes. Way too risky."

"This is… depressing," I said. "So why were you at the shack?"

"I'd seen you nosing around. I needed to hide my stuff."

I forced a laugh. "If only you'd come a day earlier."

"Yeah… Want to see something cool?"

"Nah."

"Oh, come on. It's like ten feet away."

I followed Alan around the southwest corner of the rocky

outcropping, to the western slope of the mountain. This side was significantly steeper, but we didn't have far to go. He picked his way along a rather treacherous path to a larger overhang, this one almost deep enough to be called a cave. It was better hidden too, a massive deadfall shielding it from sight to the north.

"This is way better," I said. "Why don't you hide here?"

"I thought it would be disrespectful," he answered, pointing into the cave.

Though the light was fading, the wall of rock to which he pointed was bathed in an orange glow from the sinking sun. For several moments I couldn't decide what I was looking at. Were the pale shapes emerging from the rock wall merely bands of different stone, or the result of weathering? The longer I looked, the more shapes I saw, and the more sense they made. Dude stepped forward, trying to get into the cave, but I called him back.

I spotted a group of stick-figures surrounding a fat, cow-like creature; a cartoonish sun over three wavy lines that might have represented waves; a primitive, edged weapon for which I had no name; and even something loaf-shaped that sure looked like a swaddled baby.

"Oh, my God," I breathed. "These are petroglyphs. These are... God, they're incredible."

Alan echoed, "Petroglyphs? Never heard that word before."

"Rock art. These are..." I thought hard, trying to remember what I'd learned about the area. "Ute, maybe? Navajo? I wonder if anyone else knows they're here."

"I doubt it. How do you know so much about this stuff?"

"I studied art history in college," I whispered. The thought of the people who'd created these drawings, and how long ago they'd done it, was overwhelming my senses. I desperately wanted to touch one of them, but I knew better.

Dude, who was obediently heeling at my side, gave a low whimper. Something cold struck my right cheek, and I held out a hand, palm up.

"It's raining," I announced. "Figures."

I hadn't noticed the clouds rolling across the sky, but when I looked up, there was no doubt we were in for a respectable rain shower. It wouldn't be a full-blown storm, at least.

"Want to wait it out?" Alan asked.

I checked my watch. "Let's give it an hour. I'm hungry."

We adjourned to the smaller cave and took shelter from the rain, with Dude stretched out at our feet. He was making no effort to keep out of the rain and seemed perfectly happy where he was once I poured him some water and gave him a rawhide to chew on. Alan and I broke out the human food and went to work, chewing in companionable silence for several minutes while the rain picked up just beyond the toes of our boots. I thought of my unintentional nap under the cedar a couple days ago, when Alan (I assumed) had scared the crap out of me and several turkeys.

I wanted to ask if he'd seen me sleeping there, but instead I asked, "You're still a little bit suspicious of me, aren't you?"

He breathed a laugh. "Oh, yeah."

"So why are you still sticking around? Really?"

"I've become very attached to Dude."

"Uh huh…"

"And as you keep saying, where else can I go?" Alan asked.

"You told me you have a place to go."

"Not one with free martial arts lessons."

"Ah, there it is."

He snatched a bag of trail mix from my hands and helped himself. "You ask a lot of questions. Is it just that you can't help yourself, or…?"

"I'm not trying to help myself," I argued. Turning to him, I waited for him to meet my eyes before adding, "I'm trying to get to know you. It's what humans do."

He held my gaze for so long, I was starting to wonder if he'd initiated a staring contest when he said, "Stop. I mean it."

Dude, who'd been lounging on his side letting the rain pelt his thick fur, rolled over and fixed a steady gaze on Alan. I should have taken my cue from him, but I shook my head.

"I'll ask whatever I want to ask. Answer, don't answer— that's up to you."

He turned away, scowling. Though the rain hadn't let up and scarcely half an hour had passed, he said, "Let's go down."

The descent was even quieter than the climb, and much faster. We didn't stop for a single break. The rain held out for a while, soaking us both through and turning an otherwise pleasant return journey into a soggy chore. No sooner had it stopped than twilight fell, and with it the temperature. Nightfall was close at hand when we got back to the cabin. As I sat down to peel off my boots and socks, Alan disappeared into the bathroom. I heard the shower come on and laughed in disbelief.

"So much for ladies first," I grumbled.

All I could do was change into dry clothes and wrap a towel around my wet hair. I laid another towel on a chair so Dude could curl up in it. Soon Eau de Wet Dog had filled the small cabin, overpowering the more pleasing aroma of olive oil, garlic, and onions in the spaghetti sauce I was making. Alan took a long shower, finally emerging when dinner was almost ready.

Forcing a light tone, I said, "Hope you're hungry."

"It's all yours. I'm out of here."

Struck by his flat tone, I looked up from the bubbling pan of sauce and saw that he'd gotten dressed in a clean set of hiking clothes. He'd even put his boots back on, which had to be profoundly uncomfortable. I turned off the burner.

"Why?"

Already strapping on his wet backpack, Alan said coldly, "You know why. Don't do anything stupid. I might be outside the range of your incessant questions, but I'll be keeping an eye on you."

I couldn't think of a way to respond to that, and in seconds it was too late. Alan had stalked to the door, paused to give Dude a parting scratch behind the ears, and left.

17

Wednesday, July 1 to
Friday, July 3, 2020

Plagued by Alan's abrupt departure and wretched, pessimistic thoughts of Philip, I hadn't fallen asleep Tuesday night until it wasn't Tuesday night anymore. Whatever Philip knew or thought he knew about who was renting Doreen's cabin, by now he would have uncovered a name and looked up Abigail Breckenridge, matching my face to the alias and confirming what he'd somehow already guessed when he put his business card in my bra. I tossed and turned, imagining Philip sitting in a hotel room in Durango, waiting for me to call.

How much longer would he wait before he resorted to something more direct? My backwards progress with Alan made the question screech through my head like an alarm clock, rendering my "sleep" no more than a fruitless battle to quiet my own mind.

Nevertheless, when the sun rose, so did I. Exhausted, I

practically crawled into the shower to try to jar myself awake with cold water. When that didn't work, I made a pot of strong coffee and turned the last of my eggs and bacon into a meager breakfast.

I let Dude outside, and when he didn't come back after a few minutes as usual, I figured he was searching for Alan. That chore could keep him busy for hours; I didn't know whether Alan had retreated to the shack or the cave, or a third place he hadn't seen fit to tell me about. Dude and his big nose would have no trouble tracking him down.

I was sore from my neck to my toes, but at least my head didn't hurt. The lingering effects of yesterday's physical exertion felt good now, a healthy reminder of a whole body workout I certainly needed. The entire day would be a good memory, were it not for the way it had ended. What kind of idiot was I, pushing and prodding at Alan like that? Of course he was going to shut down.

The one bright spot I could see was that Alan had chosen retreat, not attack. If he posed any danger to me, it wasn't apparent from where I was sitting.

After breakfast was eaten and cleaned up, I sat on the couch and reviewed my options again. I still didn't want to resort to asking my boss for help. That amounted to giving up, which I wasn't ready to do. If he knew about Philip's trip to Hesperus and hadn't already pulled me out, that meant he still had faith in me. If he didn't know, I wasn't going to be the one to tell him.

I could probably get Dude to lead me to Alan, then apologize to him and promise to stop asking so many questions. Except that I couldn't stop asking questions, so that would backfire on me even if it did work. If I went for a hike just to pass the time, and ran into Alan, what would I even say?

Resigning myself to a day inside, I popped a movie into the VHS player and embarked on another deep clean of the cabin. It wasn't necessary, but it was something to do.

As each successive hour passed, and Dude still hadn't scratched at the door, I found it harder and harder not to worry. I couldn't articulate these worries to myself, but that didn't stop them from making me glance at the clock every five minutes.

When dinner time was fast approaching, I stepped outside to call for him. Rather than seeing Dude galloping toward me as I wanted, I saw dust rising from the driveway as a car worked its way up to the cabin. Panic gripped me, vanishing in an instant when I recognized the green Subaru. It was just Doreen.

I waited on the front step for her to park, climb out, and walk toward me with a white envelope in her hand.

"Afternoon," I greeted, smiling. It was actually nice to see another person.

"Hello. I need to put a phone line in, don't I? I do hate to show up unannounced." She reached me and held out the envelope, face down. "This was in your mailbox."

"I have a mailbox?" I asked, taking the envelope and flipping it over. There was no return address, but there was also no postmark. That told me all I needed to know.

"Well sure, right down there next to ours at the end of the drive. I don't normally check, but the postman left the door open so I'd see it."

"Right. The postman," I muttered, distracted. "Thanks for bringing it. Do you want some coffee? Maybe a glass of wine?"

Call me selfish, but even Doreen's diminutive presence made me feel safer. To my dismay, she shook her head.

"Ernest and I are headed to church soon. You're welcome to join us, of course. But you probably don't want to be seen around town, do you?"

"Yeah, I better stay here. Thanks, though."

We said our goodbyes, and I waited for her car and its attendant dust cloud to fade away before I tried calling for Dude again. The utter silence that responded made me so lonely, I felt a perverse eagerness to open the envelope and see whether its contents were as bad as I guessed they'd be.

I went inside, sat down at the table with a glass of wine, and tore open the envelope. Expecting a letter, I was surprised to see a 4x6-inch photograph slide out, landing face down on the table. On the back, in Philip's handwriting, were the same two words: "CALL ME."

I flipped the photograph over. Whatever I'd been subconsciously expecting, it certainly wasn't a crisp photograph of my neighbor, Dominique, entering the front door of our apartment building on Dupont Circle. It was a surveillance or stalker-style photo, taken with a telephoto lens. It was night, and Dominique was alone, unaware of the camera, her attention fixed on the keypad on the door. The only other person in the photo was a distant, blurry pedestrian walking away from her.

The implication was clear. I flipped the photo back over and scanned those two words again and again, my mind oddly blank.

I nearly jumped out of my skin when something scratched at the front door. I did spill my wine all over the photograph, but fortunately I caught the glass before it rolled off the table. Leaving the mess, I dashed to the door to let Dude inside. He was filthy, but his tail was wagging and he seemed quite pleased with himself. I watched him trot to the water bowl, smiling as slobbery water rained down on the freshly-mopped floor.

▼

Thursday plodded by, a dismal repeat of Wednesday without even the excitement of more threatening letters from Philip. After a halfway decent night's sleep, I woke up Friday morning with newly-minted determination. I would not stay cooped up for a third day. I couldn't keep cleaning. There was nothing left to clean.

If I bumped into Alan, so be it. He couldn't avoid me forever. He still had my Glock.

So far I'd explored exclusively to the north of my cabin, so when Dude and I struck out at mid-morning for a destination-less hike, we headed southwest. Soon we were behind and above Doreen's cabin, and I found a trail that looked as though it benefitted from regular maintenance. Though I never saw any barbed wire or No Trespassing signs, the path I was following passed between two rotting, wooden fenceposts that could have marked a property line in the past. Since the trail was so well groomed compared to the falling-down posts, I thought little of them.

As the sun climbed and so did we, I began to wish for another rain shower. The cobalt-blue sky wasn't marred by even a speck of cloud, so this wish was in vain.

Around noon, my southwesterly course veered straight west, and soon my footpath converged with a rough, unpaved road. I set up a cairn where the path ended, then set off down the road. In another few minutes, I'd reached a gully three times the size of the one Alan and I had crossed, but this one was spanned by a bridge of thick, weathered wooden slats.

I checked again for signs or fences or something to give me a clue whether I was trespassing, but, seeing nothing, I struck out across the bridge. Dude rocketed ahead of me, reaching the other side and disappearing into a tangle of bushes.

"Get back here, dork!" I called.

Dude's selective hearing kicked in, and he stayed in the bushes. I could hear him rustling around, yelping his exuberance and having a grand time. When I got closer, I saw tiny white flowers and green, unripe blackberries dotting the emerald leaves. Here and there a darker berry peeked out, and without a second thought I found myself hunting for a blackberry that was ripe enough to eat.

When I realized several minutes had passed without a peep from Dude, I called, "Dude? Where you at, buddy?"

I paused, listening. A gentle swish of leaves off to my left drew my attention, and I turned to see a snout protruding from the bushes. Between him and me, I spotted a fat, ripe blackberry just begging to be eaten. As I stepped toward it, the animal attached to the snout stepped out of the bushes.

It was not Dude but rather a chunky, sleepy-looking black bear. I froze in place, my arm still stretched toward the blackberry. Slowly the bear turned, gave me a disinterested look, and saw the same berry I was reaching for. I watched its beady black eyes, looking for some sign of aggression. It occurred to me that, in the absence of bear spray or my Glock, I probably should have done some research about what to do when you surprise a bear in the middle of the wilderness.

Step one turned out to be: Don't stare at it. Between my unintentionally aggressive gaze and outstretched hand, the bear seemed to conclude I needed to be dealt with. It took two quick steps toward me, rearing up on its hind legs, and swiped a warning paw through the air between us. I held my ground, but not out of courage; my feet seemed to be sewn to the ground.

I didn't appreciate how quiet the whole encounter was until an explosion of sound behind me caused both the bear and me to twitch in alarm. Beneath Dude's deafening, enraged barks, I heard Alan shouting, "You better have that magazine on you!"

The bear reacted by falling back to all fours and lumbering closer, putting me within easy reach of his claws. I fell backward and landed hard on my backside, but my hand was already diving into my pocket. I yanked out the magazine, tossed it behind me, and squeezed my eyes shut as the bear leaned over me, snuffling.

18

Friday, July 3 to
Saturday, July 4, 2020

One shot rang out, the bear gave an indignant grunt, and suddenly sunlight was shining directly onto my face, turning black to red. I peeked one eye open and saw the bear's round backside shrinking into the distance. Dude barreled past me, still barking. He stopped a few yards away, motionless as he tracked the bear's retreat.

I felt myself hauled to my feet by a giant hand around my arm.

"What the heck is wrong with you?" Alan demanded. "You don't play dead with a black bear! They'll literally eat you alive! You play dead for a *grizzly*, Abigail!"

Wrenching my arm away, I cried, "Nothing I just did was a conscious decision! *Stop yelling at me!*" Though he was clearly angry and still wielding my loaded Glock, I threw my arms around his neck, sobbing, "Ohmygod you just saved my life."

He returned my embrace one-handed, then peeled me away. "Good thing you kept that magazine on you, huh?"

"Oh… yeah. Just habit, I think."

"Dude is hurt," he said, causing my heart to painfully skip a beat. He hurried to add, "It's not bad. I think he sprained his back leg when he took off after the bear. Weird angle."

I turned to watch Dude, who deemed the bear defeated and started loping back to us. Sure enough, he was favoring his back left leg so much it barely brushed the ground.

"Oh, no," I moaned.

"He'll be fine." Alan turned me back around and surprised me by pressing a hand to my cheek. "What about you? You okay?"

"I'm… yeah, I… Wait a second, were you *following* me?"

His hand dropped to his side. "I was about to ask you that," he replied. "*I* was here to pick berries. Carefully. And by the way, next time you surprise a black bear, you raise you arms over your head, wave them around like crazy, and make as much noise as you can. Got it?"

"… Sure."

"Don't do that with a grizzly. They'll kill you just to make a point."

"Enough with the bear trivia! You're stressing me out." I felt Dude walk up next to me and press himself against my thigh. He was breathing hard, now holding his leg completely off the ground. "I have to take him to the vet. How the heck are we going to get back to the cabin?"

"I'll stay here with him while you get your truck."

"I don't know how to get here from there," I argued. Despite the receding wave of adrenaline making me sleepy, panic was creeping back in. I couldn't carry Dude. Even Alan couldn't carry him, not for any significant distance.

"Take a breath," he ordered, pressing the gun into my hand. "I'll get your truck, and you wait here with Dude. Where are the keys?"

"On a hook by the back door."

"Okay, I'll be back soon." He started to go, then turned back to me, asking sharply, "What do you do when you see a black bear?"

"Put my head between my knees and kiss my butt goodbye."

"Uh… okay. Hang tight, I'll be right back. See if you can get him across the bridge at least."

I watched Alan jog away, not across the bridge but straight north along the row of blackberry bushes. Dude lurched forward as though to follow, and I grabbed a hold of his collar. With one hand on the gun and one on Dude, I slowly guided him toward the bridge. We got halfway across, but there Dude sat down and then eased over onto his right side to lick his injured leg. I knelt down next to him and looked for any open wounds, but I didn't see any. I just hoped his leg wasn't broken.

"I guess this is as far as we're getting," I sighed. I sat down with Dude at my back, facing the blackberry bushes with my gun at the ready, and waited.

The sun beat down on me, turning a latent sleepiness into full-blown fatigue. I didn't count the minutes that Alan was gone, but after I'd nearly nodded off about a million times, I felt like I'd been sitting on the rough wooden surface of the bridge for hours. The water I'd brought was long gone and I was getting dangerously thirsty when Dude jerked behind me, attempting to stand up. I twisted around to hold him down and saw a dust cloud in the distance.

A minute later Alan was there, and I struggled to my feet to help him load Dude into the back seat of the pickup. I traded Alan the gun for the pickup's keys, thanked him, and that was that. I followed his directions back to the county road and then turned north toward Durango.

▼

Alone, tired, hungry, and sick with worry, I returned to the cabin that evening. Dude's leg was neither sprained nor broken. He'd been bitten. The vet found the bite on his leg, started talking about rattlesnakes and antivenin and overnight observation, and I nearly lost it. A bear *and* a rattlesnake? Fat chance I'd ever get near a blackberry bush again, let alone allow Dude near one. I let myself into the cabin, ready to throw myself down on the couch and have a good cry, but the sight of Alan sitting at my kitchen table changed my plans.

He stood up. "I thought you were never coming back."

"Why are you here?"

"I wanted to make sure Dude was okay. Where is he?"

I sank down onto the couch, closed my eyes, and recited, "He must have been bitten by something before he took off after the bear. The vet's treating him for a rattlesnake bite. He said I could pick Dude up when he's pulled through, but he'll have to spend the weekend there."

Alan swore under his breath. I heard him sit back down.

I said, "It doesn't sound like you're leaving, but just in case you were considering it, I have a request."

"What's that?"

"Don't. I'm on the verge of starvation, but after I get something to eat, I'd really like to get in some training. I need the distraction. If I have to sit here alone thinking about… I know you don't want to be here, but… I promise I won't ask you any questions."

"I'll hold you to it." He stood up again, walked around the couch, and sat down next to me. I opened my eyes in time to see his hand move toward mine, then change course and flop awkwardly down between us. He said, "He'll be okay. He's a big guy, and you got him to the vet in time."

"That's what the vet said."

"There you go. We can't both be wrong. What do you want for dinner?"

Alan somehow turned my dwindling supplies into a feast, one of which he partook with gusto. Stuffed to the gills, we agreed to wait a half hour before we started rolling, which turned into two hours of watching an entire movie. By then I was nodding off again, but I knew sleep would taunt and evade me all night if I turned in that early.

Alan taught me some submissions, claiming they were the simplest ones he knew. They didn't seem all that simple to me, but I didn't complain. The harder I thought about which arm to put where and what angle to form against my opponent's leg and all the rest, the less brainpower I had to wonder if Dude was going to survive his rattlesnake encounter.

We kept at it until I fell asleep mid-arm bar. Alan woke me up and asked, for the third time, if we could be done for the evening.

"It's past midnight," he said, practically begging. "I'm bushed."

"Giver upper."

I allowed him to help me to my feet, then trudged toward the stairs. It was a slow climb. When I got to the top, I glanced over the banister to see Alan standing by the couch, staring at the door. Something about his body language conveyed uncertainty.

Impulse told me I should ask him to stay, but discretion won out. I crawled into bed, turned out the bedside lamp, and listened. After a few minutes, the downstairs lights went out and I heard Alan stretching out on the couch.

▼

I was paralyzed, splayed out on the ground under the shadow of a hundred-foot high wall of blackberry bushes. I tried to scream for help as the black bear locked his jaws around my left foot and started dragging me away, but not even a whisper would come out of my throat. My chest was seconds from bursting open with the force of my desperation to make some sound, any sound.

The bear stopped, let go of my foot, and asked, "Abigail? Hello?"

I jerked awake, saw Alan standing at the foot of the bed, and screamed.

"Hey, whoa!" he stammered, backing up so quickly he nearly tripped. "Jeez, you wake up violent."

I had already clapped a hand over my mouth, embarrassed. In the tense silence that followed, I heard a rapid series of knocks at the door and Doreen calling, "Abigail? Are you all right?"

"You have a visitor," Alan said. I could tell he was trying not to laugh, which made me want to laugh. "Bad dream?" he asked.

"Bear dream. Did she see you?"

"Nope. But I think she heard you scream, so you better get down there."

His words proved prescient. No sooner had I rolled out of bed than I heard the front door open.

Doreen called, "Abigail?"

Alan backed soundlessly away from the banister, and I hurried downstairs. Doreen was standing on the front step with the door halfway open. She sighed with relief when she saw me.

"I heard a scream. Are you okay?"

"Got a splinter in my foot," I lied with uncharacteristic ease. "What's up?"

"Doctor Fugere in Durango called and said Dude made it through the night. Dear, what happened?"

Mentally kicking myself, I rushed through the story of Dude's rattlesnake bite and trip to the vet, ending with, "I'm sorry, I meant to tell you. I don't have a phone, so I told the vet I was staying on your property and he said he'd call you with an update. So Dude's okay?"

"Yes, he said the danger has passed, but Dude needs to remain under observation for a couple more days."

"Thank God," I breathed.

Unfortunately, my version of the story had made it sound as though the bite happened right behind the cabin. Doreen asked, "Were you able to kill it? If not, that's okay. Ernest can come take care of it, if you'll just point me toward the spot. He's probably still nearby."

"I—yeah, I got it. No worries." The additional lie wasn't so easy. I knew there was a reason I usually tried to stick to the truth.

"Okay, well, I'll get out of your hair. But I brought you this." She handed me a two-way radio, similar to the ones Alan and I had used to record her conversation with Philip. "They claim to have a range of five miles, so I may be able to radio you from home if anything else comes up."

"Great idea. Thank you."

She left, and Alan waited a minute before coming downstairs. I eyed him warily, wondering if he'd leave again, but he walked right into the kitchen and poured himself a cup of coffee from a pot he must have made while I was asleep. He poured me a cup, too.

"You owe me a lot of Krav after last night," he said.

Trying not to smile, I asked, "Um… Do you want to learn some disarms?"

"Not before I've had some pancakes."

19

Saturday, July 4, 2020

"So here's the thing," I started in, apropos of nothing, after Alan and I had finished with Krav for the morning. "When I got here, I bought enough food and supplies to last at least a month."

"Smart," Alan said.

"And then you showed up, and you eat significantly more than I do, and you can see where I'm going with this."

"Time to hit the grocery store?"

"Yes," I said, relieved not to have met any resistance so far. "Are you… going to let me do that?"

"You've already gone to the vet, might as well hit the grocery store," he said carelessly. I didn't quite buy the nonchalance, but I appreciated the effort.

"Okay, great, that was easier than I thought. Will you make a list of what you want?"

"I don't have any money."

"I don't have any tattoos," I shot back.

"… What?"

"Oh, I thought we were saying random things that have no bearing on the conversation. Just write down what you want."

I dashed upstairs to get dressed, slipping Philip's business card into my wallet for good measure. When I came back downstairs, Alan presented me with his list. I scanned it quickly.

"Fireworks?" I asked.

"Sure. It's Independence Day, isn't it? I like fireworks."

"So do I," I said, too ardently. I *loved* fireworks. I smiled at him, seriously considering it, but I had to push back. "We can't set off fireworks. We'll burn down half the state. I guess I could get some of those snake things." I kept reading through the list and sputtered, "Weed, seriously?"

"Can't hurt to ask."

"I'm not buying weed."

"Hm," he mused, looking smug, as though I'd unwittingly revealed something.

I crossed my arms defensively. "What?"

"In my experience, there are only two kinds of people that don't like weed: cops, and religious nuts."

"I'll pray for your soul," I said sweetly, adding, "If I'm not allowed to figure you out, you can't try to figure me out. It's not fair."

Alan added a few more items to the list, none of them objectionable, and I set off. The moment I hit the county road, windows down to let in the breeze, radio blaring, a heady sense of freedom came over me. I drove too fast, then forced myself to stick to the speed limit once I hit the state highway.

When I reached Durango, the feeling of freedom abruptly faded away, replaced by caution. If Philip were still hanging around, and I was certain he was, Durango was where he'd try to catch me. Still, errands had to be run, and the quicker the better.

Dude was first on my list. He was resting in the back of the vet's office where customers rarely tread, lying on his side within a massive dog crate. At the sight of me, his tail began to wag, but he only managed a few halfhearted pumps before going still again.

Seeing my distress, the receptionist who'd escorted me back said kindly, "He's just tired. All the meds. He's happy to see you."

I sat on the floor next to the crate and stroked Dude's massive paw. His tail thumped twice more. "So he'll be okay?" I asked.

"Doctor Fugere thinks so. He's such a funny guy. Dude, I mean," she added, laughing to herself. "So smart. Everyone's head over heels for him, of course."

Slightly cheered, though not nearly enough, I said goodbye to Dude and promised him he'd be coming home soon.

My next stop was a beauty supply store to pick up a couple of wigs. I pretended not to know how to put on a wig, so the woman manning the store was nice enough to help me out. I exited the store wearing a blonde bob, having stuffed my jacket into my bag with the other wig, and headed to the liquor store hopefully looking like a different person.

Fortunately for me, everything I needed was in the same, crowded shopping center; but this also meant it was childishly easy for Philip to decide where to camp out and wait for me to appear. If he'd seen me go into the beauty supply store, all was lost. If not, I liked my chances. I hadn't spotted his New Mexico Ford anywhere in the parking lot, but there was also a car rental place right next to the beauty store. My luck could swing either way, but I wasn't leaving Durango without a substantial amount of food and a new burner phone.

My luck went a little sour in Walmart. I didn't see Philip, but the store was so crowded it took me an hour to get everything I needed, another half hour to check out. Hating shopping carts, wigs, and most of all, other people, I finally got back on the road. Ignoring the last gas station out of town (and the low gas warning light), I wanted nothing more than to get back to the cabin. I ripped the wig off my head as soon as I got out of town, cursing its insanity-inducing itchiness.

When I turned onto the county road, I immediately pulled over into an ancient, overgrown cemetery next to it. The spot was invisible from the highway and offered an excellent vantage point from which to see who, if anyone, had followed me. Ten minutes passed, but the only other car that turned down the county road was driven by an elderly Native American woman. If she were Philip, it was an impressive disguise indeed.

I unboxed my burner phone, powered it up, and texted my new number to my boss. He didn't respond, and I deleted the message before silencing the phone and tucking it into my bra. I'd decide later whether to tell Alan about it.

The closer I got to the cabin, the harder it became to ignore a building anticipation, an undeniable eagerness to get back.

I walked inside, saw Alan reading on the couch, and before I could give it a second thought I said, "I bought a new phone."

He lowered the book slowly. "Mazel tov?"

"I—sorry, I just… for some reason I felt guilty, and that just sort of popped out of me."

He half smiled, eyes returning to the pages of the book. "Thanks for the heads up."

"Um. You're welcome." I fled outside to start bringing in the groceries.

Given the late start, our usual hike was a lot shorter that day. We decided to go to the shack to get Alan's cooler, since the fridge was so packed with food now that it would barely close. On the way, as I'd feared he would, Alan asked, "Why did you get a new phone? Someone waiting to hear from you?"

"No, it just felt weird not to have one. What if there's an emergency?"

"Fair enough. As a reward for your honesty, I'm going to make you the best chicken enchiladas you've ever tasted."

We got to the shack and retrieved the cooler, plus a few other items Alan wanted. Setting a challenging pace, we got the cooler back to the cabin in time for dinner, which Alan got started on while I hopped in the shower. When I emerged sometime later, the cabin smelled of chicken, peppers, and spices, presumably the enchiladas Alan had been bragging about all the way back from his shack. He asked me to watch the oven while he took a shower, so I blow-dried my hair in the kitchen, one eye on the timer.

Alan hadn't alluded to leaving again, and I sensed I was back on reasonably thick ice with him. Now that I had two demands for contact from Philip, the pressure was doubled to get something, anything out of Alan before Philip escalated things again. Knowing that escalation could hurt Dominique instead of me was almost too stressful to contemplate.

As the last drops of moisture disappeared from my hair, the oven timer went off and a novel thought popped into my head. Why not go for broke? I was running out of time. I had nothing to lose by running Alan off again, because in a matter of days—probably less than a week—I'd be back in Washington, licking my wounds.

Whatever Philip did next was certain to drive Alan or me away from Hesperus, and when that happened, I'd either know something or I wouldn't. The former was preferable, obviously, but I couldn't possibly know unless I asked.

I took the enchiladas out of the oven. The shower turned off, and I figured I had less than a minute to finish this mental exercise.

What if I told Alan everything? Who I was, who Philip was, and what I wanted from Alan? He might be angry. He'd *definitely* be angry. But would he tell me what I wanted to know?

I had to get my boss' permission to play it that way. That was the sticking point. He'd never agree to it. I knew he wouldn't, because before I'd even left Washington I'd proposed the same thing. According to him, my idea was "suicidally idiotic." But my boss wasn't here, I was, and desperate times called for suicidally idiotic measures. My mind made up, I had only to decide when to start the conversation. On that point, my stomach was loud and clear: after dinner.

Dinner was served, *Twister* was screening, and I was losing my nerve. I ate quickly, then nursed a cup of hot tea while Alan took his time eating. When he finally finished, I took his plate to the kitchen, refilled it, and brought back to him.

"Thanks," he said, accepting the massive helping of seconds without question.

I carried on upstairs, calling, "Be right back, don't pause it."

"'Kay."

I sat down on the bed and took a few deep breaths. My heart was racing. A few more breaths did nothing to slow it, so I did a series of stretches and changed into pajamas. Examining myself in the mirror calmed me down a bit. This wasn't going to be that dramatic. Alan had a belly full of good food, I looked like a nosy babysitter, and somehow I'd earned enough trust that he hadn't taken my new phone away. I thew my hair in a ponytail and headed back downstairs.

When I returned to the couch and sat down, I was pleased to see Alan smiling, though he was still staring at the TV.

"What?" I asked.

"You look like a Furby."

"I was cold," I defended. "And I…" I trailed off, twisting the ends of my fingers together. As badly as I wanted to go on, I found that I couldn't.

"And you what?" He turned toward me, but he didn't pause the movie.

Looking at my hands, I said, "Well I was thinking, since you've been so cool—not counting the first few hours of our acquaintance—but still, I probably owe you an apology."

"I've never seen someone use fuzzy PJs as an apology before, but okay."

"Cut it out."

I started to reach for the remote to pause the movie, but I withdrew my hand. Plying him with a full stomach and un-challenged custody of the TV remote could only work to my advantage. Helpfully, Alan caught my movement and paused the movie himself.

Silence ringing in my ears, I let myself feel every bit of the disquiet raging inside me. I hadn't been all that honest with Alan so far, and I was about to tell him something not only true, but classified.

I forced out, "I'm sorry I've been pestering you. It's hard not to be curious."

"Seems like you've gotten over it," he said, a verbal shrug that subtly invited me to move on.

He was so not into this. I weighed my options, disliking all of them. Philip's notes flashed before my eyes again, and I steeled myself. The words almost popped out of me, fully formed and blunt as a baby spoon, but I stopped myself. I couldn't say it.

Though Alan's eyes had strayed back to the TV screen, my prolonged silence regained his attention and he said gently, "It's okay. I understand."

"I'm trying to tell you something," I said through a sigh.

"Why?"

Meeting his eyes, I said simply, "I don't know."

"Have you been drinking wine again?"

"No." I shook my head and turned to face the TV, mumbling, "Just forget it."

"Okay…" After he hit play and let the movie run for a few seconds, he added, "We're still stuck here together, like it or not. Whatever it is… Maybe you don't need to tell me."

I was distracted from my anxiety long enough to wonder what in the world he thought I was trying to tell him. Before I could ask him about it, he started talking again.

"When I caught you snooping around, the only thing that made sense was to kill you. I don't know why I didn't. It's not like I've never—whatever. I can't do it now. I still should, and I can't."

Wide-eyed, I waited for him to go on. I couldn't believe what I was hearing, let alone what I was feeling. For all this casual talk of killing me, I didn't feel a whisper of fear.

He glanced sidelong at me, but his eyes snapped back to the TV screen. "When I saw that bear coming at you, thought about what it was about to do to you… Nah. I can't let anything bad happen to you. And this is working. Pretty soon I'll be gone, you'll have the place to yourself, and there'll be no harm done. Right?"

"Right."

"Doreen is covering for you, so that lousy little worm won't find you here. Right?"

He'd lost me. I stood up, thinking a small glass of wine might not be a bad idea. Maybe it would open my mind a bit, help me see this situation from Alan's perspective. I found the cluster of bottles from today's supply run and sorted through them, not sure what I wanted. Alan walked into the kitchen and stood behind me, his nearness goading me into turning around.

"What do you want me to say?" I asked.

"That you'll be okay. Just that."

"Why do you care?"

He took my face in his hands and kissed me.

20

Saturday, July 4 to
Sunday, July 5, 2020

With Alan's lips pressed against mine, I couldn't help but think of my boss again. When my hands found his chest and slid up toward his neck, savoring the feel of muscles rippling under his t-shirt, I could almost hear my boss saying in his most condescending tone, "Told you so, kiddo."

I found the willpower to push him away, but only a few inches. I asked, "What is this? What is happening right now?"

"You don't know what it's like. You—I don't know, maybe you do. I haven't spent this much time with one person in years. Always moving around, hiding, trying not to leave any trace. It's hell, and you're—Having you here with me feels too good." He kissed me again, lightly, and said, "You get it. I can tell you do."

He was right, in a way. I got it. But if he knew *what* I got, why I'd felt a connection to him since before we met, why I caught myself feeling grateful to him in my darkest moments, then his hands around my face might not be so gentle. He might even change his mind about killing me.

His lips found mine again, and I let myself enjoy the simple pleasure of it for just a few moments longer before pushing him away.

"I'm going to go to bed," I said levelly. "And I think you should, too."

"I have a better idea," he breathed.

"I know. I'm sorry."

I sidestepped out of his embrace and headed for the loft. My fear that he'd follow, that he wouldn't take no for an answer, was groundless. He remained in the kitchen right where I'd left him, watching me climb the stairs.

▼

Rather than the deep, dreamless sleep of exhaustion, I snapped awake in the early morning hours while it was still dark. My too-short sleep had been one nightmare after another, now a series of nonsensical half-memories that were already fading: chasing tornadoes with Philip; a hunting accident when I was ten; trying to get into a warehouse in Houston and the gut-wrenching, unbearably real sensation of failure; the hotel room with Tommy, one side a cutaway so the entire world could be our audience; and finally, just before waking, that horrible, winding tunnel into the mountain.

That was the clearest part. I'd stood there, staring into the tunnel, waiting for something to come out. I didn't know what it was, but I knew it would try to kill me.

That naked, nameless fear, coupled with the darkness and disorientation of waking up so suddenly, made me feel like a little kid again, afraid of the dark and too scared to move, even to turn on a light. I knew the solution, though.

"Dude?" I called softly, fearing to stretch my hand out until I heard his paw steps carrying him upstairs. For a moment, I thought his huge, fluffy silhouette was framed against the relative brightness of the living room, and then I remembered he couldn't be there. He was miles away, sleeping off a rattlesnake hangover at the vet's office.

How many times had I called his name in the middle of the night, asking him to come over to the bed and push his nose into my outstretched hand? It was a little ritual we shared. In that one word, he'd could always hear how anxious and scared I was and knew exactly what I needed. I'd rub his face and ears, feeling silly after he'd brought me down to reality, and then he'd curl up next to the bed and I'd fall back into an untroubled sleep.

The best I could do now was imagine the comfort of Dude's presence, pray he was okay, and look forward to getting him back.

No time seemed to have passed when I woke up again, but the scene couldn't have been more different. The cabin was sunny, already warming up, and I was so rested, content, and comfortable, that if I stayed very still I couldn't feel my arms and legs. I closed my eyes and waited for the smell of breakfast to hit me as it usually did. Instead, after a few minutes of silence,

I heard Alan coming upstairs. I feigned sleep as he sat down on the bed next to me, but somehow he saw through my act.

"Are you awake?" he whispered.

"No."

"Okay, good. Sorry about last night. That was stupid."

I stopped faking slumber and sat up on my elbow, asking, "It was?"

"Look, we've barely known each other a week, and in less than two months we'll go right back to not knowing each other. Right?" I nodded, and he went on, "I'm not trying to catch feelings for you, not with a firm expiration date like that."

"You think I am? I don't want you getting upset when I can't come with you when you leave."

He was blindsided by this, stammering, "Hold on—When I—Who said anything about you coming with me?"

"No one. I just wanted to get it out there, so there's no misunderstanding."

"There's no misunderstanding. We're crystal clear," he said coolly, abruptly standing up and heading for the stairs. "I'm ready to train when you are."

I came downstairs minutes later to find him stretching on the rug. I ducked into the bathroom to pee and brush my teeth, then joined him. While I stretched, he launched into a monologue about what we'd be training today and how it incorporated techniques I'd already learned. His tone was all business; but as I leaned forward over my legs, stretching my hamstrings, I felt his hand slide around my left ankle, grasping it firmly enough to make me wonder if he was angry.

I looked up, still stretching, and asked, "What?"

"Why did you have to put that idea in my head?" he demanded, accusing.

I leaned back on my arms. "What idea?"

"You know what idea. Don't give me that innocent act."

"I just wanted to be clear. You kissed me, remember?" I pulled my legs away, breaking his grip. "Now are we gonna talk or roll?"

His only response was to rise to his knees in front of me, ordering, "On your back. Open guard."

I complied with poor grace, making no attempt to hide my annoyance. In short order, however, my foul mood dissipated. Alan had resumed the role of dispassionate instructor, and I needed to concentrate on what he was saying. We practiced for about forty-five minutes, and except for a few submissions that were executed perhaps a little more roughly than was strictly necessary, he gave no indication our argument might continue. To end the lesson, as we had the last couple times, we dispensed with the instruction and really sparred.

I was quickly disabused of the notion that I was starting to get good at jujitsu, and instead I realized he'd been going easy on me. About five seconds after we started rolling, I was tapping out, my right arm trapped in an Americana—but at least I remembered what the technique was called.

"I'd say you've learned approximately nothing," he snapped, releasing my arm but not, as was courtesy, getting off of me. "Why'd you put your hands on the ground?"

"I'm sorry, I panicked," I shot back. "I didn't know you

were gonna come at me like that."

"In real life, it's always one hundred percent."

"In real life, I would've bitten you in the eyeball," I retorted. "Since there wouldn't be any stupid rules. Get off me anytime, by the way."

"Make me."

"We going straight to Krav, no break?"

"Sure."

Needing no further invitation, I initiated an all-out, thoroughly inelegant brawl that I might actually have won, had I been willing to play dirty; but I wasn't, and Alan knew it. The fight ended with me on my back again, winded and dizzy from tumbling over and over no fewer than ten times in quick succession. My wrists were trapped in his hands, and nothing I knew how to do managed to break his grip. I squirmed and struggled for a couple of seconds before accepting defeat.

"For someone who hates losing, you sure lose a lot," he taunted.

"For someone twice my size and stupidly strong, you sure take a while to win."

"Why cut the fun short?"

I glared at him until he released my wrists, then rolled up into a sitting position to inspect my right elbow where I'd scraped it against the carpet. The rug burn was mild, but still annoying. I felt a stab of pleasure at the thought of how Dude would have come to my defense, had he been there.

"I'm starting to think it's best to surrender to anyone who knows jujitsu," I grumbled. "Or stab them."

"Don't be so hard on yourself," he chided. He took my arm and inspected the rug burn, nodding approvingly. "You're no quitter, that's for sure."

"Well, how long did it take you to get good?" I asked, pressing my lips together as an irritated frown appeared on his face. "Never mind, I withdraw the question. Sorry."

Though he still seemed annoyed, I also sensed he was about to kiss me again. I used his shoulder as a support to climb to my feet and retreat upstairs to grab my phone. Calling the vet was a convenient distraction, but it also needed to be done.

Alan watched me thumbing around on the phone and asked, "What are you doing?"

"Looking for the vet's number. I want to let him know he doesn't have to call Doreen anymore."

"Doubt he'll answer on a Sunday," Alan commented.

I waved him off, but he was right. The call went to an after-hours voicemail after several rings, and I didn't leave a message. I turned the phone over in my hands several times, thinking, then asked, "Want to go for a hike?

"Aren't you hungry?"

"No. I want to get out of here."

We hiked until about four o'clock, Alan showing me the more direct route to the blackberry bushes that he'd discovered. The bushes, which were not a hundred feet high as they were in my dream, yielded up about a pint of ripe blackberries, and no snakes. We kept an eye out for the black bear, but if he was still around he was staying out of sight. As pleasant as a day of picking berries could have been, worry for Dude weighed me down during the trek home. I sank down on the couch when we got back to the cabin, staring at the blank TV screen. Alan brought me a glass of water.

"You're worried about Dude," he said. "Try calling again. Maybe they open late on Sundays."

"Yeah… okay."

I called again and was preparing to leave a voicemail when a chipper, androgynous voice answered, "Fugere Veterinary Clinic, how may I help you?"

"Oh! You're open. I was calling to check on my dog, Dude? The German Shep—"

"Oh, Dude," he or she said, a smile in their voice. "What a charmer! We all miss him already."

I heard papers flipping in the background and asked sharply, "Miss him? What do you mean?"

"I'm looking now—ah, here it is. He was picked up yesterday right before we closed. Doctor Fugere wasn't happy about letting him go, but they insisted. How is Dude doing, by the way?"

I paused to breathe through a surge of anger. "Who picked him up? Was it Doreen?"

"No, the file just says 'he,' no name. Could have been Ernest. We don't see him as much, and some of the newer front desk staff don't know his name."

I met Alan's eyes as I summarized, "So, someone who was *not* me came into your office yesterday evening and took my dog *before* he was ready to be discharged, and y'all didn't even write down his *name?*"

My tone finally sank through the receptionist's skull, and

they said, "I… yes, that's what the file says. He didn't bring Dude home?"

"He did not."

"It must have been Ernest. Who else could've taken him?"

"Literally anyone, I guess. Thank you."

I hung up, already angry at myself for giving the receptionist a hard time. Obviously they hadn't personally handed Dude over to a stranger. Alan had listened to the conversation and was already on the move, searching the cluttered kitchen counter for something. He found the two-way radio Doreen had brought over and pressed it into my free hand.

"Right. Good idea," I mumbled. I pressed the talk button and said, "Doreen? Ernest? Can you hear me? Uh… over?"

Twenty seconds passed like half an eternity. Finally, a sound issued from the little radio, but I didn't catch a voice. It sounded like someone had pressed the talk button, then released it without saying anything. Anger stomped through my veins again.

"Jeez, do they even know how to use a walkie-talkie?"

"Go over to Doreen's and see if she's seen him."

"Yeah." I stood up, halfway revived. "You don't mind me going alone?"

He stared at me, looking almost offended. Was I imagining things? He dismissed me with a wave of his hand. "I think we're past that, Abigail."

I decided to walk the three and a half miles to the Perkinses' cabin, knowing I needed to give myself time to cool down. I took my time, arriving at Doreen and Ernest's cabin just before 5:30.

I had only seen their home from a bird's eye view on satellite images and once from the summit, which didn't tell me much other than the size and location of the cabin. Having imagined a larger, somewhat nicer version of my own cabin, I was surprised to find a gracefully aged work of 1960s architecture a la Frank Lloyd Wright. The east-facing front of the cabin was mostly glass, through which I could see a brightly-lit, empty living room and open kitchen. I followed the flagstone path around the south side to what I assumed was the front door. There was no doorbell, so I knocked, only to find the door unlatched. Not a single bark heralded my arrival.

My intuition tingled uncomfortably at the unlatched door. Even if the Perkinses left their door unlocked like I did, they wouldn't deliberately leave it ajar. The wildlife would have a field day. There were no cars in the driveway, which meant either they parked in the garage, which was closed, or they simply weren't home.

Steeling myself, I gently pushed the door open and stepped inside.

"Doreen?" I called. "Mister Perkins? Are you home? Your door is open."

The interior was silent, no doors opening and closing, no water running, no television or radio playing. My gut told me they weren't home, and a tiny voice in the back of my head wondered if they'd failed to close the door all the way when they left. A cursory glance into the first room I found, which seemed to be an office, revealed a massive gun safe and a collection of ammo and other accessories. No way would they leave without making sure their door was locked.

Realizing how I would react to someone letting herself into my house and scaring the crap out of me, I called again, "Ernest? Doreen? It's Abigail. Is anybody home?"

Most of the house was dark except for the living room, but down one hallway I could see a glow of light. I crept toward it, falling silent as my heart began to race. If they were in there, but they couldn't or wouldn't answer me… I shook my head, dismissing this for now. No reason to get worked up… yet. As I passed the kitchen island, I saw a piece of paper tucked under a two-way radio.

In a tidy cursive hand, the paper read, "Abigail has the other one, if you need to reach her."

I turned a corner and saw a door cracked at the end of the hallway. From what I could see through the crack, it looked like the master bedroom. I opened my mouth to call again but thought better of it, opting for silence.

I nudged the door open, revealing a half-lit bedroom. It was luxuriously large, immaculately neat, and, to my relief, empty. To my left, another door opened onto an ensuite bathroom, which was much brighter. I headed toward it automatically, freezing when I heard the bedroom door snap shut behind me.

Turning, I was more resigned than surprised to see Philip standing in front of the door, his expression unfathomable in the dimly lit room.

21

Sunday, July 5, 2020

I stared at Philip, and he stared right back, waiting for me to speak.

"You heard me on the walkie-talkie?" I asked him. When he didn't answer, I pressed, "Why are you here?"

"I wanted to talk to Doreen. She's been screening my calls."

His voice now bore little resemblance to the silky tones on the recordings Alan and I had made. That Philip was trying to be charming and likeable; this was the real Philip.

"Did you hurt them?" I asked.

"Who, the Perkinses? Why would I do that?"

"Did you?" I tried to keep my voice level while my insides seethed and twisted, anger and disgust fighting for prominence with fear.

He let me squirm for a while before answering, "They're not home. For God's sake, I'm not a monster."

"You took Dude."

"I got your attention, didn't I?"

My heart stopped, and I could practically feel the blood draining from my face. I hoped the poor lighting would hide any other outward signs of panic. I hissed, "Where is he?"

He took a few meaningful strides toward me, saying, "He's safe. I'm surprised Jackson let you out of his sight."

"Jackson?" I asked, a beat too late.

"Can we skip this part? It's not that I'm in a hurry, I just hate being lied to. Luke Jackson, the man we both came here to find. Is he waiting at the other cabin, or is he outside?"

I said nothing; and though I should have retreated when Philip came toward me, I stood my ground, bringing my hands together in front of my chest to pick nervously at my fingernails. Being within arms' reach worked more in my favor than his, as he was undoubtedly armed with at least one handgun. He hadn't been a fan of knives last time I checked, which I hoped hadn't changed. He was a mere three feet away, close enough that his one-inch height and reach advantage was just noticeable.

As though he'd read my thoughts, he took half a step back and warned, "Don't start a fight. I don't want to fight you."

"I wouldn't, either. Why don't you tell me where my dog is, and I'll decide whether or not I want to get physical."

"I told you, he's fine."

"Where. Is he?"

"Albuquerque."

He managed to surprise me with that one, and I didn't bother trying to hide it. "Why?"

"How else could I get your attention? You ignored my notes,

that Perkins woman won't return my calls, I'm losing patience. All I want to do is talk some sense into you, and the harder I try the farther you run. So, you get to go to Albuquerque to get your dog. Then you can go back to Washington where you belong, and I can have some alone time with Jackson."

"Dude wasn't ready to leave the vet! Who's watching him now? Do they know he was bit by—"

"I told you, he's fine. I've got an ICE K9 handler babysitting him for the moment, and he knows Dude is recovering from a snake bite."

"ICE?"

"Friend of a friend. He thinks Dude's a working dog. I'm sure they're getting along beautifully."

I was, recent developments notwithstanding, overcome with relief at the thought of Dude hanging out with an experienced dog handler who probably had no reason to hurt him. That was all assuming Philip was telling the truth, of course, which was no more than fifty percent likely.

"How did you find me?" I asked.

"I didn't. Not on purpose, anyway."

He sat down at the foot of the bed, forcing me to turn to keep him in front of me. I glanced over my shoulder toward the bedroom door, wondering if he was turning me away from an accomplice, but no one else was visible in the shadows.

Philip said, "I told you, I came here to find Luke Jackson."

I wondered how he'd managed it, but instead I asked, "Why?"

"Same reason you did. Jackson is the only one left alive from that night in Houston. Except for you, of course. He has to know what really happened. How you made it out alive, why Tommy didn't. He could have pulled the trigger himself, for all I know. You've been no help, so I'm looking for the next best thing. Guilty conscience, maybe? Why don't you want me to talk to him?"

"I'm working on him. I can figure it out. Why can't you just leave me alone?"

"I don't have to explain myself to you, Bowman. Or should I say Abigail Breckenridge? What are you posing as, a kindergarten teacher? I'm not surprised you beat me here, but I was a little surprised to see Jackson alive and kicking today. I saw you two going at it. What are you doing, teaching him your Krav Maga nonsense? I can't imagine why you'd let him live, knowing what he knows."

"You can't imagine a lot of things," I hissed.

"Ouch, that hurt my feelings."

"If you're so hot and bothered to get to the bottom of the Houston fiasco, let me work. He trusts me. He likes me. He'll kill you on sight."

"No way. As soon as you get what you need, he'll be toast. I need you out of the way."

"What—you—You think I'm gonna *kill* him?" I asked, aghast.

"Why not? If anyone alive knows what you did, it's him."

"You really think I sold Tommy out? My own partner? And, what, I'm working for the cartel, now?"

"Please, again, I would prefer to skip the poorly delivered lies."

"You're such a stupid, narcissistic psycho," I snapped, barely overcoming a sudden urge to strike him. "You think you know everything, don't you?"

"Obviously not, or I wouldn't have come all the way to No-where, Colorado to get information from Jackson. What did you tell him about me, by the way? Vengeful mob boss? Abusive ex-husband? Loan shark?"

"The second one."

"Smart. So you get a bodyguard, and he gets—what—a roll in the hay every now and then?"

I inhaled a slow breath, letting it out even slower. "I can't go back to Washington, not yet. I need more time. I know I can get to the bottom of this—"

"Spare me." He stood suddenly, forcing me back a few steps. "*You* are at the bottom of this. The best thing you can do for yourself is go back to work and start telling the truth to the people who matter. It's time to do right by Tommy."

"Philip, *please*—"

"Save it."

I was seriously weighing my chances of an imperfect self-defense plea when the front door slammed, forcing his attention and mine away from the conversation for a split second.

Alan's voice cut the silence, calling, "Abigail?"

I met Philip's eyes as Alan called my name twice more, his voice closer each time. Utterly relaxed, Philip watched the door and waited for him to find us. I felt like running, but my feet were stuck to the floor. I heard a knock at the bedroom door, and Alan's voice again.

"Abigail? Are you in there?"

"We're here," Philip called before I could answer.

Several seconds passed before the door opened. I refused to turn toward it, instead easing ever so slightly closer to Philip while his gaze was focused on the bedroom door. Whether he noticed or simply decided he was too close to the light from the bathroom, Philip sidestepped away from me as Alan entered Glock-first. An involuntary groan escaped me.

"Get away from her," Alan snarled.

"We're just having a conversation, no need to get territorial," Philip said, reverting to smarmy charmer.

"Abigail, are you okay?" Alan asked, not taking his eyes off Philip's hands.

"Yeah, I'm okay."

"Come here."

I started toward him, but in the blink of an eye Philip's own weapon was drawn, pointed at my chest. He said, "Stay right there, *Abigail.* Why does he have your gun?"

"He took it from me," I said at once. Even Philip couldn't deny the ring of truth in my answer, but he shook his head as though dismissing it.

"I don't buy it."

"Hey, I'm as mad about it as you are."

Alan cut across Philip's retort with, "Point that thing somewhere else, or I start shooting."

"Oh, I'm not really going to shoot her," Philip wheedled, the effect of his words somewhat undermined by the fact that his gun was still pointed at me. "How could I kill my own, precious, loving wife?"

I stared at Philip, uncomprehending. Why was he playing along, when a few words from him would turn Alan against me in the blink of an eye?

"Yeah I'm not really interested in the dynamic here," Alan shot back. "Just put the gun down."

"You first."

Hoping to prevent a shoot out, I squared my shoulders and walked to Philip's side, explaining to an openly perplexed Alan, "He's got Dude. I have to go with him to Albuquerque to get him back."

Alan shook his head, looking like he'd love nothing more than to squash Philip like a bug. "What kind of piece of—"

"All's fair in love and war," Philip said with a smile, redirecting his weapon at Alan.

Unimpressed, Alan breathed, "You know you can't go with him, right? Please tell me you know that."

"I can't let anything happen to Dude."

"He's just a dog. I know you love him, but you can't throw your life away for a dog."

"Throw her life away?" Philip demanded. His imitation of indignance was so good it almost fooled me. "You think I'm going to hurt her?" I flinched as Philip's hand slid around my back, grasping me by the waist. He kissed my temple. "I'd rather die than hurt her."

"Deal," Alan growled.

"Put the gun down, please," I begged.

"I am not letting you leave with him."

"Doesn't look like she needs your permission, buddy."

Finally, though he still looked angry enough to explode, Alan lowered my gun. Philip followed suit, and I took the chance I'd been waiting for as Philip's finger slipped out of the trigger guard.

22

Sunday, July 5, 2020

I lunged for Philip's gun, tearing the weapon out of his hand before he could get a shot off. Alan sprang into action, snatching up Philip's gun as he tackled me to the floor. Though I landed on bottom again, this time I was ready and even eager for it. Alan stood back while I went to work. Within a minute, Philip was losing consciousness in the grip of a sloppily executed but nonetheless effective triangle choke.

"Well done," Alan concluded as I stood up, struggling to catch my breath.

"Good thing he… didn't expect that…" I gasped. I was pleased with myself, but already I could feel an ache in my right shoulder where I'd hit the ground. I'd be feeling it from head to toe by tomorrow morning. "How'd you know… he was here? You must've left… right after me."

He withdrew something from his pocket and held it up so I could see. Philip's business card.

"I'm not proud of it," Alan preempted, by which I assumed he meant going through my wallet. "But at least it got me here. You failed to mention he works for the FBI."

I took a deep breath, pulse slowing to normal. "I still don't see the connection."

"I thought you were calling him. I ran the whole way here to try to stop you."

My gaze fell to the ground, settling on Philip's inert form. He was already starting to stir as the buildup of blood in his brain dissipated. Why hadn't Philip blown my cover and told Alan the truth about why we were here and how all three of us were connected? Did some small part of him believe, despite his insistence otherwise, that I was telling the truth about Houston?

I looked back to Alan, who had apparently sprinted a 5K to try to stop me from calling my purported ex-husband. He had said we were past this sort of mistrust. Was that a lie, or was there a different reason he wanted to stop me? I forced my eyes shut, overwhelmed by the chaos of a dozen trains of thought all converging.

Alan derailed every train at once by saying, "I can't let this guy live. You know that, right? I don't need an FBI Agent on me, Abigail."

"You can't kill him," I whispered.

We both stared at the man in question, who was almost fully conscious. Philip had a lot of questions to answer, and I wasn't about to let that information die with him. But we had to beat him to Albuquerque, to the ICE Agent who was unwittingly holding Dude hostage.

I offered no protest as Alan hogtied Philip with a phone cord and stuffed a washcloth in his mouth as a gag. From this humiliating position on the bedroom floor, Philip locked eyes with me; not pleading, not worried, just a deadpan stare that made it nearly impossible to think.

Alan said, "He can't cause either of us any problems if he's dead."

I briefly considered and then recoiled at the idea, shaking my head fiercely. "We can't kill a federal agent."

"I'm fine with it."

I almost said, "I know," catching myself in the nick of time. "I—need to think. Find his phone, will you? And hurry. We need to get out of here before they come back."

While Alan dug around in Philip's pockets, I fought with myself. If Philip were dead, he couldn't beat us to Albuquerque, but he also couldn't tell me why he hadn't blown my cover. He couldn't answer for his crimes if he were dead. How could I express any of that to Alan, whose sincere intention to kill Philip was as plain as daylight?

Alan found Philip's phone, pressed Philip's thumb against it to unlock it, and buried his nose in it while I watched. At length he said, "I can't turn off the fingerprint lock without the passcode. There aren't any texts, but he's called the same five-oh-five number a few times today. That's probably Albuquerque," he added in response to my blank look.

"Dude," I breathed.

"I know, he might have been telling the truth about that."

Alan said the number out loud and I echoed it back twice,

trying to memorize it. The simple exercise sparked an idea, and I said, "We've got to get the heck out of here. Can you carry him?"

Alan looked down at Philip. The two men contemplated one another in strained silence, and then Alan said, "Fine. Let's get going, it'll take a while with this sack of crap."

"Right behind you, I need to grab something."

Dashing back to Ernest's office, I rifled through desk drawers and cabinets until I found an old expand-o-file. Inside, under 'B' for Breckenridge, I found Abigail Breckenridge's rental agreement. It was a gold mine of my personal (if almost entirely fictional) information. I took it, then replaced the expand-o-file and returned to the kitchen to add the note with Abigail's name on it to my stolen file. Seeing a row of keys hanging on hooks by one door, I opened it to reveal a long, three-car garage. It was empty but for a massive, old Ford F-250 in the farthest space. Its tires looked brand new. Since one set of keys bore a decorative Ford keychain, I had to assume the thing ran.

I met Alan on his way out of the back bedroom. He'd thrown the smaller man over his shoulder in a fireman's lift and seemed unbothered by the weight, but I could tell by Philip's expression that the arrangement was anything but comfortable for him.

I couldn't help but ask, "Did threatening my dog seem like a good plan, Philip? Does it now?"

"What's that?" Alan asked, nodding at the file in my hand.

"My rental agreement." In response to his questioning look, I said, "Look, if we're going to murder my husband, I'm not leaving a paper trail the cops can see from space. We have to remove any trace I was ever here."

"What about Ernest and Doreen?" Alan challenged.

"Their word against mine?" I suggested. "Don't even go there. I mean it."

"Fine. Let's get out of here."

The three-plus mile trek back to my cabin took nearly an hour, at the end of which Alan was clearly fatigued by his 200-pound burden; but the complaints, arguments, and questions I expected didn't come. He tossed Philip into the back seat of my Ram, checked his restraints, and then turned to me.

"It's probably better if you let me handle this," he said in a low voice. "Where are the keys?"

"I left them in the front seat," I said. Telling him this made me remember where my laptop was: under the other front seat. I needed it to find Dude, and my boss would skin me alive if I lost it. Scrambling, I said, "Look, can you give me a second with him? Alone? This is… I'm not sure about this, Alan."

"What do you have to talk about?" he demanded.

"Please. Two minutes, that's all I ask. You can get started packing. I've got stuff all over that cabin, and you're better at bugging out than I am."

He snorted. "Fine. Two minutes." He pressed my gun into my hands, presumably keeping Philip's gun for himself. "Promise me you'll shoot him if he tries anything."

"Gladly."

The moment my cabin's door closed behind Alan, I darted around to the passenger side and pulled a messenger bag from under the seat. While I tried to decide where to hide it, I glanced at Philip. He was facing away from me, motionless; but I was certain I'd seen his hands moving out of the corner of my eye. His restraints did look a bit loose now.

His death at Alan's hands was imminent, and I couldn't let that happen. With another glance, I confirmed my pickup's keys were in the driver's seat where I'd tossed them. My gas-guzzler was running on fumes. The gas in the tank wasn't enough to get Philip to a filling station, but it would get him far enough away to save his life. My mind made up, I tossed the laptop bag into the scrub oak by the driveway and returned to the driver's side.

"This isn't over, not by a long shot," I told him.

I grabbed the phone cord binding his hands and twisted off one loop, constricting the rest so much that he cried out in pain. When I let go, the bindings fell so loosely around his wrists that he'd have to be an idiot not to get out of them. I backed away, aimed the gun, and fired one round into the woods. Philip flinched, then froze.

"Unless you want Jackson to kill you too, wait five minutes."

I slammed the door closed in his disbelieving face, hoping I'd broken his stupid nose, and ran into the cabin. Alan was gathering all my possessions on the kitchen table, but he was missing something rather essential to the packing process. He didn't know my luggage was hidden behind the bed upstairs.

"What was that? Did you shoot him?" he asked.

Dazedly, I answered, "He got free and tried to take the gun. I had to. I… just wanted to stop him, but I think I killed him…"

He took the development in stride, saying, "I'm sorry you

had to do that, but it's for the best. I'll take care of the… Where the heck is your luggage?"

"Let me do this. You need to get your things from the shack, right?"

He swore. "Yeah, I do. I'll be back in an hour."

I followed Alan to the door and closed it behind him, silently begging him not to open the pickup to verify Philip's supposed death. With a sigh of relief, I saw Alan disappear into the woods without a second glance at the pickup. I kept my nose pressed to the glass, counting out the minutes as I knew Philip would be. At five minutes on the dot, the pickup roared to life and peeled away.

"Be a little louder about it, you ungrateful puke," I complained.

I dashed outside to retrieve my laptop bag, then got busy packing everything up. If Alan had heard Philip's noisy departure, he didn't rush back to talk about it. Within fifteen minutes, I'd packed everything and dumped it in a pile outside the door. After scrawling a hurried note to Alan, I sprinted back down the road toward the other cabin.

All the recent cardio paid off, and I made it to the Perkinses' cabin in under half an hour. They were still gone, probably yakking it up at evening church services the way my parents did. The return trip to my cabin in my liberated Ford F-250 was much faster, and Alan still wasn't back yet.

Once I'd loaded all my luggage into the old pickup, I had nothing left to do but wait for Alan. He'd told me to give him an hour, and that hour was almost up. If he didn't show, would that mean it was time to go our separate ways? I decided it didn't matter; what I needed now was to get to Albuquerque and find Dude.

Left to my thoughts, I began to worry in earnest about Dude. Would some missed check-in with Philip incite the unknown ICE agent to act? I didn't think he'd hurt Dude, but would he leave Albuquerque? Would he pass Dude off to someone else? Would Dude escape and try to get back to me, only to be lost in the two hundred, mostly empty miles between Hesperus and Albuquerque?

The surge of emotion brought on by this thought was nearly enough to make me cry. I pulled out my phone and considered calling the 505 number I'd memorized, but I thought better of it. Once I got to Albuquerque, I could find Dude without tipping off the agent holding him. Instead I dialed my parents' home number.

The machine answered, unsurprisingly. My parents would be at church, and even being an hour ahead they'd likely be out longer than Ernest and Doreen. They liked to socialize.

"Hi Mom, hi Dad," I muttered, as though Alan would somehow hear me. "I just wanted to check in, let you know I'm okay. I had to leave DC kind of suddenly, and I'm not sure when I'll be back. So, you know, if my landlord tries to evict me, be sure to grab your dining table before it gets auctioned off. Just kidding. Kind of. Um… I'm okay. Love y'all. Okay bye."

Why I'd done it, I couldn't have said, but as soon as I hung up, I heard Alan returning. He came inside fuming.

"Where's your truck, Abigail?"

"He must not have been dead. I was packing everything up when I heard him drive away."

Alan let out a string of so many swear words that I wanted slap him. I rose to my feet and said, "The tank was nearly empty. He won't get far. I took the other truck from Ernest's garage. Do you want to cuss, or do you want to get on the road?"

"Once we find him, the guy's toast. I don't give a—I don't care what you say. After that, you take one truck, I take the other, and that's that. Got it?"

I nodded, swallowing a lump in my throat.

"Fine. Got everything?"

"Yeah, I'm ready to go."

Alan tossed his stuff into the open bed of the pickup and didn't argue when I climbed into the driver's seat. He slammed himself into the passenger seat, anger radiating from him in wave after wave. We hit the road, four hours of uninterrupted question-and-answer time facing us both.

23

Sunday, July 5, 2020

From my driveway to the state highway, Alan didn't utter a single word. I was too frightened to speak, knowing that we'd be overtaking Philip at any moment. I'd turned south, away from Durango and toward the New Mexico border.

Finally, when I was about to scream from the pressure, he growled, "I'm sorry. I should have made sure he was dead. That's on me."

I went on the offense, asking, "Why did you go through my wallet?"

To my surprise, he gave an unwilling chuckle and said, "I wanted to see your driver's license."

"Why?"

"To see if it was fake." He glanced at me, and I made no attempt to hide my irritation. Unabashed, he added, "Abigail Breckenridge doesn't suit you at all."

"Abby does," I corrected. "That's what my friends call me."

"Okay, Abby. Are you an FBI agent, too?"

I laughed. "No. I'm just an accountant."

"For?"

"Huh?"

"Who do you work for?"

"Oh—OPM."

"What is OPM?"

I explained in brief, describing not my job but a Krav Maga classmate's job. It wasn't quite time to tell him the truth. If that time was ever going to come, it would be when I blew past Philip instead of stopping so Alan could murder him. I could wait. He seemed to accept my answer.

"That sounds like the most boring job the world."

"You're not wrong. So… what exactly do you do?"

He laughed again. "Uh… pass."

"Fine. I'm not sure I want to know, anyway."

"Uh huh. Speaking of not wanting to know…"

"What?" I asked.

"Are you sure you don't have a kid?"

I gasped, "Excuse me?"

"I saw your C-section scar last time we rolled."

Furious at the ambush, I accused, "You're so mad at me for Philip getting away that you're gonna call me a liar? Real classy, Alan. It *wasn't* a C-section."

"Sure looked like one. My mom had one, I know what it looks like."

"Are you seriously asking? Because you're gonna wish I hadn't told you this."

"I can handle it."

I took a deep breath. "My high school boyfriend knocked me up. When I told him about it, he told me to get an abortion. I didn't want to, so naturally he had no other option but to stab me. I lost the baby and the horse it rode in on."

"How old were you?"

"Seventeen," I snapped.

"You're right. I wish you hadn't told me that."

"At least now you don't think I'm the world's worst mom or something." I tore my eyes away from the road for half a second to look at him. "Still think I'm a liar?"

He chose not to answer, and we lapsed into silence, more questions queuing up. Night was falling, and the deserted country highway was devoid of homes and headlights alike. We still hadn't overtaken Philip, and I was beginning to wonder whether he'd gone south at all. Alan thought of another question before I could.

"Where exactly in Albuquerque are we going?"

"Ugh. I don't know. We can't track down—find Dude tonight. We just need to pick out a place to stay the night, somewhere we can think for five minutes."

"You can't think now?" he asked.

"Ernest has probably already reported this truck stolen. There are only a handful of highways we could take, and plenty of state troopers and sheriff's deputies to stake them out. It'll be a miracle if we make it to Albuquerque."

"So what you're saying is, we need to ditch this ride."

"At the earliest…" I trailed off, following Alan's gaze.

Something on the right shoulder had caught his attention, and I thought I knew what it was.

Sure enough, there sat my pickup, dark and evidently abandoned. As we zipped by, Alan and I both tried to see inside. I didn't see anyone. I turned back to the road and gave it my full attention, refusing to acknowledge his eyes boring into me.

Alan's next words weren't quite what I expected. "What about phone calls? Emails? Documents on their computer? I know you're smart enough to know taking a paper file wouldn't slow down even the dumbest investigator."

"So?"

"So if you weren't trying to cover your tracks, what *were* you trying to do?"

I left the question unanswered, for all of seven minutes. Looming out of the darkness and coming into focus by the old pickup's feeble headlights, Philip was unmistakable. He was walking along the shoulder, thumb out, and turned as we got closer. He was clearly uninjured. I didn't slow down. As we passed him, despite the dramatic difference in our speeds, I had no trouble locking eyes with him for the briefest of moments.

Alan turned to me. "You let him escape."

"I didn't want you to kill him," I whispered.

"Why?"

His calm tone sent a shiver through me, and I gripped the steering wheel as hard as I could. "I'm not like you. I couldn't let you kill him."

"You're gonna get *me* killed," he muttered.

That was it. The eruption I'd expected, his demand that I

turn around and go back so he could kill Philip, threats to my life, none of it came. Not even yelling. I swallowed another lump in my throat.

"We can find another car somewhere else. Okay?"

"Okay."

Unfortunately, opportunities for stealing a new car were few and far between. We stopped halfway at a little gas station casino in New Mexico, but the only car in the parking lot old enough not to have an alarm was also occupied by a snoozing, elderly man. We didn't see so much as an outhouse until we reached Cuba, New Mexico. By then it was so late only gas stations were open, and they were all too crowded. We gave up and decided to find Alan a ride in Albuquerque, the lights of which we finally spotted around midnight.

I headed south on the main interstate, looking for a likely place either to stay or to steal. I pointed out another casino, a huge, grandiose hotel surrounded by acres of landscaping, parking lots, and a golf course. Alan was not impressed.

"Are you crazy? Half of northern New Mexico is in there."

"Right, we should stay at a seedy, cash-only motel where we're sure to be the only non-crackheads for a mile. Do you want to blend in, or get stabbed?"

"All right, all right. Point taken."

Though it was past midnight, the Sandia Resort and Casino was as bright and crowded as though time were meaningless. The hotel lobby merged seamlessly with the casino, and even to someone who was less than enthused about gambling, it looked pretty inviting; but after paying for a room with Abigail Breckenridge's credit card, we abjured the flashing lights and cigarette smoke and headed straight for the elevators.

I had condensed my basic necessities into the same backpack I used for hiking, and Alan had everything he needed in a duffel slung across his shoulder. Even in our grungy hiking clothes, we didn't attract much interest from the staff and other guests. Once isolated in the elevator, Alan let out a long breath of air.

"Okay, you're probably right," he admitted.

"Plus, this is more fun. Bet you wish you'd been hiding here all along." He didn't answer, but I thought I saw the ghost of a smile on his lips. I said, "I noticed you're coming up with me instead of taking your leave."

"Yes, you're very good at noticing things."

Our room was near the top of the hotel, facing the mountains to the east. Even though I'd asked for the cheapest room available, it was still a far cry more luxurious than I'd hoped. I longed more than anything to pass out on the fluffy, white duvet, but I sat down at the desk instead. There was no time like the present to reveal the laptop I'd shoved into my backpack. Alan, who was happily starfished on the king-sized bed, sat up when he saw it.

"Where were you hiding that?"

"In my pickup."

"Okay… why were you hiding that?"

"I didn't want you to take it and do something stupid that would help Philip find me," I answered easily. It was mostly true. "But that ship has sailed. I need to figure out where Dude is."

Though I hadn't been planning for quite this scenario when I first had Dude microchipped, I'd had no doubt I'd eventually have to resort to modern technology to find him. Not only was he an escape artist, but several people in my apartment building had warned me—half-jokingly—that I better watch out or someone might steal him. So, he got the Cadillac of microchips: Not only would any vet, pound, or animal shelter be able to scan it and pull up my contact information, but the chip itself came equipped with GPS. I logged into the hotel Wi-Fi, then the website that translated the signal from his chip and transposed it onto a map. Alan got out of bed to watch over my shoulder.

"This seems like a bad idea," he groaned.

"Philip doesn't know about the microchip. And how else are we gonna find Dude?"

"He probably took Dude's collar off anyway."

"It's not on his collar."

"Want to tell me why you didn't use this secret weapon sooner?" he asked shrewdly.

"I told you, I was hiding the laptop from you."

Alan huffed his annoyance but let it slide. I clicked the Find button and watched while the circle from which Dude's tracker was transmitting gradually shrank, zeroing in somewhere in southeast Albuquerque. I zoomed in.

"He's at the airport?" I asked, dismayed.

"Did Philip tell you who he's with?"

"An ICE agent," I intoned, sitting back. "He said it was a friend of a friend."

"Are you *kidding* me?"

I glanced up, jerked out of my brief reverie by his sharp tone. "No?"

"FBI, OPM, now ICE… That's my limit, Abby. That's a third of the alphabet."

"What are you talking about?"

He grabbed his duffel bag off the floor, avoiding my gaze. "I was hoping to grab a shower at least, but that's my cue. I can't be involved in your crap anymore."

"You're not going to help me get Dude?" I asked sadly.

"I never said I would." He stared at me, then let out a gusty sigh. "Just find the guy, look at him like that, and he'll give you Dude and whatever else you want."

"Where are you gonna go?" I asked. When he of course didn't answer, I whispered, "Alan, I need you. Please…"

"Stop it." He dropped his bag and knelt in front of me, almost supplicating. "Every minute I spend with you now puts me at risk. If our places were reversed, you'd do the same thing."

My mind raced, searching for the right question, the last one I'd ask. I knew he'd cut and run eventually, but *where?* Hamming it up a little, I whispered, "You said being with me felt good."

"No, I said it felt *too* good." His jaw was set, his mind clearly made up. He stood up and I sat there, dazed. Struggling through the wave of panic and defeat he'd unleashed, I sat up a little straighter and tried to adopt a disinterested tone.

"Are you taking Ernest's pickup?"

"No, Philip saw it. I'll find something else."

"Where you're going… Will you be safe there?"

"You know I can't tell you that."

"Okay," I said firmly, standing up. I groped around in my backpack for the manilla envelope which had, until very recently, been in the front pocket of my laptop bag. I pulled out five hundred-dollar bills and handed them to him. "At least take this."

"Are you serious?"

"You said you have no money. Money tends to help."

"You can't give this to me. This is—"

"Just take it," I snapped, forcing the bills into his hand. "We're even now."

I turned away from him and sat down at the desk again, opening my laptop and hiding behind it while he stood motionless, saying nothing. Eventually I heard the crisp sound of bills being folded and stuffed into a pocket. He came around the desk and turned my chair toward him, taking my face in his hands. His next words took me off guard, but I managed not to react too joyously.

"By Christmas, I'll either be dead or in London. You can come find me there, if you want."

"London?"

"Don't make me regret telling you that."

He kissed me, grabbed his duffel bag, and left.

24

Monday, July 6, 2020

The next morning, I was wrenched from a mercifully deep sleep by the hotel phone ringing. Some psycho had set the ringer to full volume. It cut through my sleep like a hot knife and I struggled upright, disoriented and panicking. I picked it up, prepared to give some crank caller an earful.

"Who is this?" I demanded. My voice was a painful rasp and I coughed, almost missing the light chuckle coming through the receiver.

"Good to hear your voice, Anna."

A full five seconds passed in complete silence while I processed what I'd heard. I cleared my throat.

"Jim?"

"So you do remember me. I was beginning to wonder."

"How the—Why are you calling me? *How* are you calling me?"

"Circumstances have changed. I've got someone here who

really wants to see you. Meet me at the dog park on Louisiana and Corona."

He hung up, leaving me reeling as reality settled over me. I lay back and covered my eyes with my arm, intoning, "Anna Bowman. My name isn't Abigail Breckenridge. It's Anna Bowman. I live in Washington, DC and work for the FBI. Agent Jim Camposanto is the jerk who ruined my life and made me go to Colorado to find Luke Jackson, to find out what happened to Tommy in Houston."

I'd been dubious at the time, when Jim made me write down that very spiel and memorize it before I left for Colorado. He hadn't been amused by the "jerk who ruined my life" part, but he also couldn't argue with it. How could someone forget who she was? But he was right. I was so deep into being Abigail Breckenridge that I had to repeat the mantra twice before it sank in.

The fictional Abigail and I had one or two things in common, though. Chief among them was Dude. Knowing Jim had him, somehow, brought relief washing over me. I got out of bed and groaned as my shoulder gave a twinge of protest. It was sore from the fight with Philip, but not injured. I did a few perfunctory stretches and took a long shower. Now that I knew Dude was safe, my boss and his questions and his patronizing attitude could wait.

I found my way to the appointed place around ten in the morning. I hadn't bothered to find a replacement for Ernest's stolen pickup; as Jim had said, circumstances had changed. I picked out Dude's booming voice as soon as I stepped out of the pickup, and I followed it toward the off-leash area on the north side of the park. At midmorning on a workday, the park was sparsely occupied by three other people and about half a dozen other large dogs.

Dude bowled me over at the gate, licking my face and behaving as though we'd been apart for seventeen years. Far from being hurt or abused, he seemed to be thoroughly enjoying life; and if he was still feeling any ill effects from his snake encounter, I couldn't see it. Once I'd been greeted, Dude leapt up and started chasing a pair of huskies around the park. I stood up, brushed dirt and wood chips off my clothes, and headed toward the bench where a tall, lanky, dark-haired man in his early forties was looking painfully out of place in a three-piece suit. He stood up when I got close.

"Anna."

"Jim."

"Have a seat."

I complied, torn between annoyance and worry. "How did you get Dude?"

"You finally used your laptop. I saw you track him to the Sunport, so I went there and explained to the agent holding him that Philip Levin asked me to pick him up."

He finished this terse tale and looked expectantly at me, as though he'd explained everything. I was bursting with questions—How did he know Philip was the one who'd delivered Dude to the agent? How did he know I was at the casino hotel last night? How in the ever loving *heck* did he know "circumstances had changed"?

I held all my questions back and merely said, "Thank you. I was so worried about him…"

"I've been worried about you, too. No contact since you left Washington, phone and laptop totally dark, not so much as a 'Happy Fourth of July' email. You can see why I'd be concerned."

"Luke wasn't too keen on me reporting my progress to the FBI."

Jim sat up a little straighter, eagerly asking, "You found Jackson?"

"Sure, I told you I would. He's calling himself Alan now. He'd shaved off the beard. He knew someone was looking for him."

"And?"

"And nothing. Philip caught up with me a few days ago, and I didn't get a chance to find anything out before Luke ran for it."

"Levin knows Jackson was there?"

"They met. Briefly."

He swore. "So Jackson knows who you are."

"No." I squirmed under his penetrating gaze, struggling to explain, "Philip played along. I don't know why. He just… We didn't get a chance to talk about it."

"Where's Levin now?"

I scoffed. "You're asking me? I thought that was your job."

"Don't get smart with me, kiddo."

Frowning at the nickname, I admitted, "I let him escape. Jackson was going to kill him. He's probably on a plane by now."

"Do you have any idea where Jackson is going?" Jim probed.

"Yes, sir, I'm happy to report that I know where he'll be and when, and I have no reason not to tell you," was what I should have said. What came out instead was, "He didn't leave a forwarding address. He didn't trust me."

Jim grabbed my right hand, pressing his index and middle fingers to the underside of my wrist. "Are you sure he didn't tell you where he was going?" he repeated.

Fuming, I met his gaze and said, "I don't know. He was at the casino with me last night, and he freaked out. He said he couldn't be involved with my crap, and then he left."

He released my hand, satisfied.

"You should work with someone you trust," I snarled. "I don't want to do this anymore."

Completely ignoring this, he pressed a set of car keys into my hand and said, "You're tired. We can debrief later. I need to focus on Levin. Go to your parents' house, get some rest. I'll contact you when we figure out where Jackson is."

"And Philip?"

"If he shows up, you call me immediately. Got it?"

"Got it."

I stood up to leave, but he grabbed my hand again. Rather than repeating the improvised polygraph nonsense, he squeezed my hand and asked, "Tell me you're okay, Anna."

Though I would've loved nothing more than to yank my hand away and explain in detail how very *not* okay I was, I nodded and waited for him to let me go. Looking down my nose at him, I said, "I'm okay enough for your purposes. See to it that Ernest Perkins gets his pickup back."

I called to Dude, and we left the off-leash area to find the car that went with the keys Jim had given me. I found it a few spaces down from the pickup: an unremarkable Mazda sedan, barely large enough for all my luggage and Dude. We squeezed inside, and I entered my parents' address into the navigation system. The soothing female voice cheerfully informed me that an eleven-hour, forty-one minute trip lay before me. I glanced over at Dude, who had taken up his place in the passenger seat.

"Time to meet your grandparents."

25

Monday, July 6, 2020

My parents' house was the last place in the world Philip Levin, or anyone, expected me to go. In all his weeks of hounding me, Philip hadn't, to my knowledge, even called my parents to see if I was there. This was why Jim sent me to Texas, why that had been the plan all along, but the strategic wisdom of it didn't make showing up unannounced at my parents' house in rural northeast Texas late Monday night any easier.

My little sedan had eaten up the highways from northern New Mexico to my home town, Manchester, near the Oklahoma and Arkansas borders. I'd stopped for gas and a bathroom only as often as Dude needed the latter, otherwise refusing to prolong the journey any further for such trifles as hot meals, stretching my legs, or simply resting.

I'd used the hours to game out various scenarios, everything from my mom running across the yard to welcome me (unlikely) to my dad greeting me at the door with a loaded shotgun (less unlikely). If Dude, in the passenger seat, thought my silence a strange departure from the chatterbox I'd been on the drive from Washington to Hesperus only a few weeks ago, he made no comment.

My parents and I weren't close anymore, but we'd settled into a reasonably civil, almost halfway normal relationship until about a year and a half ago, when my older sister Emily had decided to unseat me as the black sheep of the family. At the end of that debacle, my sister was in jail, my parents were raising her two daughters as their own, and I was on their blacklist for siding with Emily.

Given the circumstances, I decided not to give them any more warning than my awkward voicemail from Colorado letting them know I was alive.

Even though I wasn't expecting a warm welcome, it was fortifying to arrive at the home of my youth and see that very little had changed in the two years since I'd last visited, just as very little had changed in the previous three decades. It was past nine o'clock when I stopped at their front gate, and the little town through which I'd driven looked like it had been asleep for hours.

The lower story was illuminated, and as soon as I entered the gate code, I could see movement inside. I had no hope of surprising them. As resistant as my parents were to most trappings of twenty-first century life, they had bitten the bullet many years ago and shelled out a substantial amount of money for an electric gate. I still knew the code to get in, but my opening it so late had set off an alarm inside the house.

Though I couldn't see much more than shadows rippling across curtained windows, I knew what was happening: They were throwing on robes, my dad was arming himself, my mom was peeking through the curtains to see who it was, and my seven- and five-year-old nieces were most likely oblivious to it all, having once slept through an EF-3 tornado.

I drove up the long, gravel drive, parked, and turned to Dude, who was wriggling with quiet enthusiasm in the passenger seat. He had never been here before, in fact had never been within a hundred feet of a child in his life. I hoped my nieces were made of sterner stuff than their mother, who would've been terrified of any dog his size.

"Well," I said, breaking my eleven-hour silence. "You better wait here. This is going to be…" I trailed off, unable to think of the right word, shrugged, and stepped out of the car.

I picked my way across the dark front yard and up the porch stairs, and I was almost to the front door when it was jerked open from the inside. I ground to a halt in the middle of the porch.

"Annie?"

I winced at the nickname but let it slide. "Hi, Mom."

One look at her told me I had seriously misinterpreted the situation. She was not dressed for bed and seemed wide awake. My oldest niece, Emma, hovered behind her, looking curious. My dad and younger niece, Ellie, were nowhere to be seen.

"I didn't think—We were just getting ready for bedtime—Goodness, come in, come in."

She dragged me inside and then disappeared into the kitchen, saying something about coffee. Emma and I stared at each other for a moment, unsure how to proceed.

"You remember me, right?" I finally asked.

"Uh huh."

"Oh good. Okay."

She smiled at me, which I knew from experience was all the greeting I could expect. She was like me—not a hugger. Instead she walked boldly toward me and addressed the holstered Glock on my right hip.

"Papa let me shoot his gun before he left. Can I shoot yours?"

"Uh… mine would knock you over, Ems. Where did he go?"

"Sucklahoma."

"Emma Marie Bowman," my mom snapped, re-appearing in the entry way. "We don't say that."

"Papa does."

"*We* don't. It's not nice. Come sit down, Annie, you look exhausted."

"I will, but, um… I left my dog in the car. Can I let him run around? He's been stuffed in there for a while."

"Of course…" she said uncertainly, asking, "Is he… he's a big dog, isn't he?"

"Some would say."

"Is he safe to be around the girls?"

"He may scare the crap out of them at first, but he's not dangerous." My mom clucked disapprovingly, Emma giggled, and I added, "Sorry."

"Hm. He can stay outside for now, okay?"

Dude was only too happy to have the entire two-acre yard to himself. He disappeared into the darkness as soon as I opened the door, and I returned inside to find my mom and Emma at the kitchen table in the midst of a heated exchange.

Mom was saying, "Bedtime is bedtime, no matter who's here. You know that."

"But I want to play with the dog! And Anta said I could shoot her gun!"

"I did not, don't drag me into this," I defended, joining them. My mom slid a cup of coffee my way.

"Emma, you promised Grandpa you'd behave while he was gone. Didn't you?"

"Yes…"

The way Emma forced out the word without even moving her lips nearly made me laugh. My mom shot me a warning look, and I held it in.

"Okay. Go brush your teeth."

Emma stomped away toward the stairs.

"And don't wake up your sister!"

Mom's eyes followed Emma's progress up the stairs and remained fixed on the ceiling for several seconds, as though she could see through it. Finally she sighed and looked down at her own coffee. "She's going to be just like you."

"Sorry."

"Anta, she called you." She laughed. "I thought she'd forgotten about that."

"Aunt Anna is a mouthful, even for an adult."

She laughed again, still staring at her coffee. I took a few sips of mine, and gradually the silence became strained and uncomfortable. I could tell she was about to think of another innocuous topic, so I cut her off.

"Mom, my boss sent me here. I didn't have a choice. Did you get my voicemail?"

"Yes, it was very distressing."

"I said I was okay like nine times."

"You didn't sound okay. How can your boss send you home to your parents' house, that doesn't make any sense."

"He needs me to lay low for a while. He figured you wouldn't be able to turn me away."

"He sounds very controlling."

"Well… yeah."

"Are you in trouble?"

"… Yeah." Her gaze shifted to me, finally, and I could see her question before she asked it. "Y'all won't be in any kind of danger because I'm here. I promise. I would never do anything to put those girls at risk."

"How long do you need to stay?"

"Uh—I don't know."

"This is… I don't know. Your father isn't going to be happy about this."

That hurt more than I would've guessed. I took a sip of coffee to hide my expression, but I couldn't hope to fool my own mother.

"I don't mean that you're here. He'll be happy to see you. I just mean… the circumstances…"

"I'm sure if I tell Jim I can't stay here, he'll figure something else out."

"Jim is your boss?"

I nodded.

"You tell him you can stay here as long as you need to."

"Thanks, Mom."

We sipped at our coffee in silence for a minute, but it wasn't the tense non-conversation it might have devolved into. Eventually I could hide my curiosity no longer.

"Why is Dad in Oklahoma?"

"He's doing some training. They hired a lot of new engineers in May and he needs to get them up to speed. He'll be back on Friday."

"Did he… hear the voicemail?"

"He was already gone when you called. I was at church."

I knew it. "Have you told him, though?"

"There wasn't much to tell, Annie."

It struck me that I'd sent the voicemail in question less than twenty-four hours ago. It felt like a week had passed. I sank a little under a wave of exhaustion as the energy drinks, coffee, and caffeine pills that had kept me going in the interim all gave up at once. My stomach growled angrily, but it was easy to ignore; a few more hours, all of them asleep, wouldn't kill me.

"You need to sleep," my mom said firmly, taking my coffee cup and carrying it to the sink. "We can talk about this in the morning."

Those last few sips of coffee got me through feeding Dude and setting up a pile of old blankets on the porch for him, up the stairs to my dad's vacant man-cave-office-guest-room, and through the rigamarole of brushing my teeth, going to the bathroom, and struggling into borrowed pajamas. My brain's last act that day was a reminder that there were two children in the house. I unloaded my gun, hid it on the top shelf of the closet, and stuffed the magazines in my backpack.

26

Tuesday, July 7, 2020

My first night at my parents' house was surprisingly comfortable, all things considered. The air conditioner was blasting arctic breezes well into the early morning hours, and under three blankets I was as snug as a bug in a rug. Their little corner of Texas was as peaceful and nearly as remote as the cabin in Colorado, and I was so far beyond tired that I would've slept until noon if my nieces had let me. Since they'd probably been awake since dawn, I was impressed they didn't disturb me until half-past nine.

I was jolted awake by two giddy little voices preceding their owners up the stairs to the guest room. Emma was filling her little sister, Ellie, in on the previous night's events. I feigned sleep, and at the top of the stairs their voices dropped to conspiratorial whispers. Thankfully, the darkness of the room hid my body shaking with laughter at their breathy conversation.

"—and that really big dog outside is hers, and he knows lots of swear words and can see in the dark, and Anta has brown hair now like yours, but a lot longer."

"I want to play with the dog—"

Emma clucked just like my mom and said, "You can't, he'll eat you."

"Can I ride him?"

"Probably, if you ask real nice. Hey Anta… Anta?"

I flinched as a tiny finger poked me in the cheek.

"Can you wake up now? Meemaw made breakfast and Ellie wants to play with your dog."

That she was still whispering, even while trying wake me up, was too much. I opened my eyes, laughing, and peered at them in the semi-darkness. "Who are you two? Where am I?"

That got me a nervous giggle from Emma, though Ellie was trapped in some kind of awed silence.

"You know who we are!" Emma insisted.

"Hm… it might be coming back to me… but I need some coffee to be sure."

I earned myself a few minutes of peace as both girls dashed downstairs to secure the requested beverage. By the time they'd convinced my mother to let them carry a full cup of hot coffee up the stairs, I was on the way down. I rescued the cup from Emma in time to prevent a tragedy of spilled coffee and ceramic shards on the stairs.

"Thanks, you two. Man, you've gotten big. What are you, like sixteen and eighteen now?"

Ellie started to correct me, but Emma retorted, "Yep, Ellie's taking her driving test tomorrow. Everyone in town is terrified."

I stared at her, bewildered by her quick wit. I could see what my mom meant. A mere seven years on this earth were enough to make it clear Emma was going to be a handful and a half. I loved her, but I did not envy my parents.

My mom had breakfast ready and waiting when we all arrived in the kitchen. She dismissed my offer of help and ordered me to the table, where I was presented with a huge portion of her famous breakfast casserole. I was several bites in before I realized something.

"Doesn't this have to sit overnight?" I asked her as she sat down to enjoy the fruits of her labor.

"Always has," she breezed.

"When did you make it?"

"After you went to bed."

"Since when are you such a night owl?"

She shrugged. "I couldn't sleep after I put Emma to bed. The coffee, I guess. Sorry they woke you. I couldn't keep them at bay any longer."

"I was already awake," I lied. "They—uh—they really want to see Dude."

She glanced over her shoulder at the back door, where both girls were standing at attention and waiting for the all-clear to go outside. They were almost vibrating with excitement.

"You're sure he won't hurt them?" Mom asked.

"Positive."

She seemed convinced but insisted they eat breakfast first. I watched in unwilling admiration as she wrangled them to the table, coaxed them both through a bowl of cereal apiece, and managed to foist a second helping of breakfast casserole on me. She hardly broke a sweat.

Half an hour later, while they were dutifully washing their hands, I said, "Dang you're good at this."

"Annie, don't cuss."

"'Dang' is not a cuss word, Mom."

"It is in this house."

"All right, your house, your rules. You wouldn't happen to have a swear jar, would you?"

"I'll make one," she offered, and she wasn't kidding.

I went outside to calm Dude down and show my mom, who was watching through the window with the girls, how well behaved he was. After a few tricks that had the girls laughing so loudly I could hear them from outside, she allowed them to dash outside.

My mom and I were sitting on the front porch, nursing our second cups of coffee each and watching Dude play with the girls, when the phone in the kitchen rang. My mom went to get it and came back a few seconds later, announcing in a low voice to the exclusion of Emma and Ellie, "It's for you."

"Sorry—what?"

"An Agent James Camposanto of the FBI. I'm assuming that's your boss, Jim?"

"Yes. Crap."

"Annie."

"Sorry."

I went inside to answer the phone, making sure my mother wasn't listening at the door before I picked up the receiver.

"What."

"When did you get to Manchester?" The voice on the other end was tight, cluing me in that I might have messed up somehow.

"Last night," I said.

"And you didn't think to maybe let me know?"

"I mean, obviously I didn't. You didn't tell me to."

I bit back a smile as a long, slow sigh preceded Jim's answer.

"I would think, given the circumstances of your departure, you could easily infer I would want to know you arrived safely."

"… I arrived safely."

"And your parents?"

"Mom's cool with it, Dad's not here."

"How much do they know?"

"Jim, you already know how much they know. Why are you wasting my time?"

He paused for several seconds, most likely composing himself. Jim had a confoundingly even temper, and I was rarely able to resist the impulse to test it. In my defense, I'd never wanted to work for him in the first place. His voice was a study in serenity when he finally answered.

"I have to ask these things. You know that."

"I know."

"We need to talk about Colorado, and I need to give you an update on you-know-who. It has to be in person. Meet me at the Choctaw Casino in two hours. I'm in room fifteen twelve."

Before I could assemble a response, he hung up.

▼

The casino was less than an hour away across the border, which allowed me plenty of time to argue with my mom about why I was leaving again so suddenly, convince her that Dude wouldn't snap and turn into a killing machine the moment I drove away, and finally take a shower and make myself more or less presentable.

Had I bothered to guess how crowded a casino would be on a Tuesday morning in Oklahoma, I would have been wrong. Apparently this was the place to be for anyone within a hundred miles who wasn't at work, and I had trouble finding a parking space. This casino was only about half the size of the casino in Albuquerque, lacking that establishment's ineffable touch of vitality, and a painful reminder of one Alan-slash-Luke Jackson's abrupt and troubling exit from my life in the wee hours of Monday morning. Again I struggled to accept how little time had passed since then. I was already in a totally different world here.

I found Jim's room number and hesitated at the door, checking my watch. Three more minutes would make it exactly two hours from when he'd hung up the phone. I waited, watching the second hand on my watch. Quiet footsteps on the carpet behind me broke my concentration.

"Can I help you?"

I turned to see Jim, his expression shifting from wariness to recognition to irritation. He was wearing swim trucks, flip flops, and a towel draped over his neck.

He said, "Oh, it's you. What's with the wig?"

Having donned my previously unused, electric blue wig for the occasion, I grinned. "Like it? I bought it in Durango. Didn't get a chance to deploy it."

"Are you actually in disguise, or are you just messing around?" he demanded, letting us both into the room.

"Can it be both?"

"With you, that's almost a guarantee."

I waited by the door while he extracted a t-shirt from his suitcase and thew it on.

"Why the casino?" I asked, just to make sounds.

"Closest hotel to your parents' house."

"No it isn't."

He shot back, "Closest one with a pool where I can get a drink at ten in the morning."

"Wow, a few hours in Oklahoma and you're already descending into unapologetic hedonism. What's meth like, by the way?"

He laughed appreciatively, looking me up and down. "That wig… I thought you were a prostitute or something."

"Gross."

Since I was planted against the wall by the door, he came back to me, standing too close. I looked up at him, glaring a warning. "Don't you start with me," I snarled.

He tugged at the wig experimentally, felt how loose it was, and pulled it off. The wig cap came next, allowing my hair to tumble free, while I stared at the wall behind him and wondered what life would be like if I had a boss with an ounce of professionalism. Jim's hand twisted into my hair.

"Jim, for God's sake. You *have* been drinking, haven't you?"

"You smell so good."

"You said you needed to talk to me about Philip."

"I do."

"You said it had to be in person," I reminded him.

"It does."

"So…?"

"Give me a second to catch my breath, kiddo."

"Please don't call me that. It's so demeaning."

"Sorry." He ran his thumb across my lips. "I've been so worried about you."

I finally met his eyes. "Can we please not do this? Just pretend you're sober, and a professional."

He took a deep breath, nodding. "Right. Okay. Fine."

As he retreated, I unstuck myself from the wall and followed him into the room, muscling past a vague sense of disappointment that he'd given up so easily. It was for the best, I told myself. This partnership was already strained and dysfunctional enough.

"What's going on with Philip?" I asked.

"He took a personal day yesterday, and now he's back at work. He's re-focused the search for Jackson on the Four Corners area, but he's back to overseeing everything from Washington."

"Has he told anyone I was there?"

"Doesn't look like it." He sat down on the bed and said, "Why don't you start from the beginning."

"Like… nineteen eighty-seven?"

"Anna, I swear…"

"All right, all right."

I launched into a detailed description of everything that happened in Colorado, beginning with finding Luke's cabin and ending with his departure from the casino. Of primary interest to Jim were Philip's surprise arrival at the cabin and our brief conversation a few days later when he showed up at Ernest and Doreen's cabin.

"He told you he tracked Jackson there?" Jim asked eagerly.

"Uh huh."

"Did he say how?"

"No."

"So he could still get to Jackson before we do."

"Easily."

"Did you get anything out of Jackson at all?"

Disliking the subtle dig at the job I'd done—or tried to do—I argued, "I'd barely gotten him to start thinking about considering the possibility of trusting me before Philip screwed everything up."

"How did you do that?"

"Take a wild guess."

"No."

I shrugged my shoulders defensively, then forced myself to relax them. It wasn't as though I'd done anything wrong. Luke's last words flitted through my head, unbidden: "By Christmas, I'll either be dead or in London." I asked myself for perhaps the thousandth time why I wasn't telling Jim. For the thousandth time, I had no answer.

I sighed, "Apparently, he felt some… feelings."

Except for a brief narrowing of the eyes, Jim hardly reacted to this, asking, "You said he didn't trust you. Why?"

"He said I asked too many questions."

"And he never told you what's supposed to happen on August thirty-first?"

"Nope."

"I've got to say, Anna… not your best work."

I flared up at once, spitting, "Will you give me a break? You were supposed to keep Philip off my back, and that lasted, what, a week?"

He grinned, unimpressed by my fury. "You're devolving before my eyes."

"The heck is that supposed to mean?"

"Can you not hear yourself? Your accent is thick enough to slice with a knife."

I crossed my arms, fuming, robotically articulating my next words. "Well excuse the crap out of me. It gets worse when I'm stressed."

"It didn't use to. You used to have ice in your veins."

"Yeah, well… it's hot in Houston."

For a moment he almost looked abashed, but he recovered quickly and said, "We'll know when Philip starts zeroing in on Jackson again. I won't be able to give you much notice, so keep the essentials packed and be ready to go when you hear from me. How soon can you get to DFW Airport from your parents' house?"

"Depends on the traffic. Two and a half, three hours maybe. Why?"

"He could leave the country, and if we know where, you'll be right behind him. I'm working on getting Abigail Breckenridge a passport and some more cash. How much do you have left?"

I hesitated, provoking his suspicion immediately.

"How much?" he repeated.

"About a thousand."

"How the…?"

"Stuff's expensive in Colorado."

Plus I gave five hundred dollars to Luke, but Jim didn't need to know that yet. Misappropriation of government funds would be the least of my worries.

"Whatever, fine. I'll try to get you five thousand, but you better learn to live on ramen and hot dogs just in case."

"I can live on less than that."

He eyeballed me in a way I definitely didn't like. "You are taking care of yourself, right?"

"What do you call learning jujitsu?"

"That's not what I mean."

"Ugh. Don't go all mother hen on me, Jim. I already have a mom."

"Is she as hot as you?"

I clenched my fists, turning away from him. "You're trying to provoke me. It's not gonna work."

"So you can dish it out, but you can't take it, huh?" When I offered no response other than to glower at him, he left off to fish something out of his suitcase. He tossed me a new phone. "Try not to break that one, please."

27

July to September 2020

My passport arrived by courier three weeks after my meeting with Jim. The courier, who buzzed the gate at 8:30 at night, refused to allow my mom or dad to sign for it and demanded I come to the gate personally, which my mom waspishly informed me of while I was taking a bath. I threw on a bathrobe and signed for the package, then returned to my room to inspect its contents.

Ellie had been moved into Emma's room so I could occupy the space that had once been mine, and so my dad could have his office back when he got home from Oklahoma. I found myself anachronistically surrounded by the trappings of a carefree, cripplingly naïve, and hilariously gawky teenage me: Cheap prints of Renaissance paintings were still meticulously pasted over forbidden posters of Good Charlotte, Weezer, Buffy the Vampire Slayer, and the like. Volleyball trophies crowded out older artefacts from art class and Bible school on my bookshelf.

The only items that appeared to have been touched were my small VHS library, where I found a VHS box that concealed a toy cell phone instead of a Sailor Moon movie, and my little jewelry collection, which now belonged to Queen Emma and Princess Ellie and was routinely disgorged onto the carpet for dress up.

Ellie didn't seem to mind being displaced, though she did occasionally "forget" she'd been moved and sneak into my room in the middle of the night to snuggle up next to me. Just in case she decided to go for it while I was reviewing the contents of my Eyes Only GSA Approved container, I locked the bedroom door behind me.

Inside was a U.S. passport issued to Abigail Breckenridge, whose picture bore one striking difference from my current appearance that goaded me into calling Jim.

"Hello?" he answered, his guarded tone catching me by surprise.

"Did you not save this number in your phone?" I asked.

"Oh—Anna. I have the number of the phone I gave you. What phone is this?"

Hadn't I texted him from this number after I'd bought the burner phone to replace the one I broke? While I was trying to decide how or whether to ask about that, Jim moved on.

He asked, "Did you get the passport and the cash?"

"I did, yes, thanks, but… quick question. Why is Abigail blonde?"

"Because redheads stand out."

"So do blondes. That's why we dyed my hair brown."

"Which Philip has already seen."

"You could have given me some advance notice, you know. It takes time to go blonde, especially after dying your hair."

"Wow, am I glad I didn't know that."

"I'm not taking crap for not being this blonde in time to leave the country, if that even happens."

Wearily, he asked, "When have you taken any crap ever?"

"I'm serious."

"It's not that big a deal. Besides, think how sexy you'll look as a blonde. I know I am."

"You're just loving having this much control over my life, aren't you?"

"I don't hate it," he agreed.

"… Any news?" I asked.

"Nada."

"Are you back in DC?"

"Yep. How's Texas?"

"Hot. I'm starting to hope he turns up in Siberia."

"Well, keep your fingers crossed. I'll call you if anything comes up. Just enjoy the break."

That was easy for him to say. Every other conversation with my parents was either a wild bid for information about my job, which I couldn't give, or a rapid-fire barrage of questions about my plans for the future, which I didn't have.

Having mostly gotten over my sudden appearance at his house demanding room and board, my dad was descending back into disgruntlement with each conversation that ended in, "I can't tell you." Occasionally I required him to save me from one of the spiders that came out of the woodwork to scare me, which always gave him a laugh, so at least his mood wasn't entirely sour.

My parents required me to attend church with them three times per week. The actual church part was fine with me. It was the people I couldn't stand, a two-dimensional cast of unlikeable characters who had known me my entire life. I thought I'd escaped them, yet thanks to Jim I was in their clutches once more.

The nasty ones were easy to deal with through simple avoidance; it was the nice ones I had to watch out for. They wanted information, and they were more assiduous than any interrogator. When they failed to get information out of me, they went for my parents. When my parents clammed up, they went for the girls.

Fortunately, Emma and Ellie knew nothing about me and were happy to make up whatever tale gained them the most interest from adults. Two weeks in, the busy bodies figured out my nieces were unreliable sources. Some started on me again, and others joined the nasty camp. Had I not been mired in the middle of it, it would've been hilarious.

I hadn't seen Jim since we met at the casino, and my thoughts swung back and forth between him and Luke—or Alan, as I'd known him—until one night when my real ex-husband, Aaron, popped up along with a wayward thought that he probably still lived in our house, two miles down the highway. Within seconds of this horrifying thought, I was in full flight mode. I needed to get out of town, and there weren't many places to go.

That was August 30, and as I slipped through the gate to

kill some time at the same casino where I'd met Jim, I wondered what was happening tomorrow on August 31. Had Philip not made an appearance in Hesperus, I would've spent this entire time carefully probing Luke for information. I hadn't thought about the date in a while, let alone made any effort to figure out its significance.

I put the riddle out of my mind and resolved to have a good time, even if I was having it all by myself in a sea of strangers. I gambled, drank free beer, and chatted with locals for a couple hours, then retired to a room at the hotel. Since that hadn't been the plan, I called my parents and let them know I wasn't going to make it back to Manchester that night.

▼

I woke up stressed, my efforts last night to ignore the August 31 enigma making it all the more vexing this morning. Next to my phone charging on the nightstand, I saw the note I'd written myself before falling asleep last night: "What is happening on August 31?" I threw the note away and got in the shower.

To kill more time, I visited the hotel's business center to use the computer. Searching "what's happening on August 31" generated no results for the current year. Princess Diana died, Malaysia gained its independence, a plane crashed in Argentina, and Richard Gere was born; but nothing important appeared to be slated for today.

I had given up and was checking out of the hotel when my phone rang. I didn't recognize the number and ignored the call, only to get a second call in my car a few minutes later. Assuming it was a telemarketer or wrong number, I answered warily.

"Hello?"

"Hello, Anna."

I had been backing out but changed my mind, returning to the parking space and earning a blaring horn and middle finger from the person who was waiting for my spot. I had to put the car in park and catch my breath before I was able to answer.

"Philip."

"Sorry I didn't say goodbye in Colorado."

"You're welcome for letting you live. How did you get this number?"

"It's good to hear your voice. You and I still need to talk, don't we?"

"We're talking," I snarled.

"I want you to come see me. It's that, or I come see you at your parents' house. You decide."

I had to take another moment to compose myself, finally saying through clenched teeth, "Threaten my family and something bad is gonna happen to you."

"I'm not threatening anyone. Just giving you options."

"I'll take door number three: Leave me alone until you find Jackson, and then give me first crack at him."

"I'm not looking for Jackson anymore."

"Yeah, right."

"You misunderstand me: I already found him. He was even easier to track down than you were, once again."

"Tell me where he is."

"So you can pump him for information again? That got you so far last time."

"It would've gotten me farther if you'd left me alone and let me work. He's sure not going to tell *you* anything."

"You really think I'd let you near him? How stupid do you think I am?"

"I don't think you're stupid, I think you're evil. And you don't want me talking to Luke because he knows something about you, doesn't he?"

During the tense seconds of silence following my question, I realized my mistake and shut my eyes, willing the words back into my mouth. Philip's voice was different when he spoke again, a gloating smile evident through the phone.

"So you and Camposanto are after my dirty laundry, is that it?"

"My relationship with him is none of your business."

"Not gonna work, Anna."

Words failed me completely and I hung up the phone, blocking the number before calling Jim.

"I messed up," I said when he answered, skipping any sort of greeting. "Philip knows what we're doing."

Jim said, "Slow down. Tell me what happened."

I walked him through the whole conversation, ending with, "I'm sorry, Jim. He came at me from the side, I never saw it coming."

"It's… it's fine," he forced, clipped tones betraying the fact that it was absolutely not fine. "He was going to figure it out eventually. Why else would you want to talk to Jackson?"

"In Colorado he was still acting like he suspected me. Then he parroted my cover story to Luke, and I thought maybe he was starting to believe me… that it was neither of us, and he wanted me to get it out of Luke somehow."

As though any of that made sense to Jim, he fired back, "It was just a mind game. He knows exactly who's responsible."

"But what if it wasn't him? What if he's in bed with them but didn't make Tommy, what if they both were?"

"I'm not following you at all."

"No, listen: If Philip had told the cartel Tommy was a fed, the only logical thing to do when he found Luke and me in Colorado was to kill us both. Make it look like Luke killed me and then toss Luke's body where no one would ever find it. But he didn't, he tried to separate us by making me go to Albuquerque after Dude."

"Why?" Jim prompted.

"I don't know. To get me out of the way? Maybe he wanted Luke all to himself. And he still does. He's still looking for Luke. Maybe he thinks… What if Philip thinks Luke can prove he's dirty? He can't really be trying to pin the whole thing on me anymore, not after finding me there trying to get information out of Luke."

"It would still make more sense for him to kill you both."

"Not if he wants to find out what Luke knows first."

"Okay…" he said, clearly wanting more.

"I—I can't prove any of this. Not without Luke."

"So you need to meet with Philip and find out where he is."

"But… now he knows I—we—suspect him. If I were him,

I'd kill me."

"So would I," he agreed, evidently not picking up on the fear and panic in my voice. "We just need to give him multiple reasons not to. He's already got one."

"What's that?"

"It's illegal."

"Jim! This is serious."

"Two, you already have an in with Jackson that he can't hope to replicate. Three, you're working for me, which means killing you would be tantamount to a confession, and three, you—"

"You already said three, you're on four."

"—And D, he still might think you know something about that night. If not something that implicates you, then something that implicates him."

"And we're back to him killing me," I sighed.

"Not necessarily. If he thinks you can help him, he'll take that risk. It's like he told you in Colorado: You and Jackson are the only ones left alive from that night. He had a chance to get rid of you both and didn't take it. He wants to know what you know."

He had me mostly convinced, but the fear of coming face-to-face with Philip again was visceral. I was silent long enough that Jim shifted to a more sympathetic tone.

"It's normal to be scared. I'll be watching over you the whole time."

"He'll definitely want me to come alone, et cetera."

"And he'll assume I'm there anyway, so I will be."

"Jim…"

"Call him, find out where and when he wants to meet, and then call me back."

I did as I was bidden and then drove home. My dad was already at work in his office-slash-man-cave, and my mom was busy homeschooling the girls. I vaguely answered her inquiries about my night out, then grabbed a sleeve of crackers and a cup of coffee and plopped down in front of the TV.

I was slightly hungover from the excessive fun the previous night, so spending the whole day on the couch wasn't exactly unpleasant. I endured a twenty-four hour news cycle, flipping among every local, national, and even international news source available until the sun came up on September 1.

Nothing at all happened on August 31.

28

Friday, September 4, 2020

Friday morning found me clutching my new passport and boarding pass to my chest, shuffling forward in line at a TSA checkpoint at the Dallas-Fort Worth International Airport. With a refundable ticket to Washington, DC and a carry-on backpack filled with enough clothes and other necessities for two nights away from home, I blended in easily with the other weekday travelers.

I'd used my fake Abigail Breckenridge driver's license many times, the accompanying credit card more times than that, but the passport was next level. I'd been combat breathing since my dad dropped me off at the terminal, and it was barely keeping my pulse in check.

I reached the front of the line and passed the passport book and boarding pass to the TSA agent, silently cursing Jim's name for making me do this. I wasn't even getting on the plane. If I actually used my boarding pass and flew to Washington just for kicks and giggles, I wouldn't be leaving the United States. Even if I *were* to leave the United States, I wouldn't need my U.S. passport to get through the first TSA checkpoint. Nevertheless, Jim insisted I use the passport. In his infinite wisdom, he'd convinced me I needed practice using a fake passport before I actually had to travel internationally.

I still owed him a kick to the shins for making me bleach my hair blonde to match the passport photo, but he was probably right about the need for a change of appearance. He was usually right about everything, but I'd shave my head before I told him that.

My passport was good enough for the first agent, boosting my confidence for the rest of the checkpoint. I was still so visibly nervous that I got pulled aside for secondary screening, but once that was over I was free to move about the secure area of the airport.

This had been one of Philip's requirements, explicitly to ensure I wasn't armed when I met him. The ticket to Washington was Jim's idea, so I could bug out if needed and avoid returning to my parents' house. It wasn't a direct flight, though. Jim had booked the flight with the most legs, affording me the option of stopping in Denver or Atlanta or going all the way to Washington.

Aside from having to leave Dude behind with my parents, the possibility of escaping to pretty much any other town was undeniably inviting.

I found the gate from which my flight would be leaving without me in two hours and sat down facing the main thoroughfare through the terminal. Five minutes later, I saw Jim duck into the family restroom across from the gate, and I got up and followed him in.

"Lift up your shirt," he said by way of greeting, already unplugging a cordless microphone from its charger.

"At least buy me dinner first," I grumbled.

"We can flirt later, hurry up."

Reflecting his businesslike mood, I stood compliant and still while he clipped the microphone to the middle of my bra. I put my shirt back on, tested to make sure the microphone was transmitting, and exited the bathroom less than three minutes later. Stopping outside the door to adjust my shirt, I accidentally made eye contact with the woman who'd been sitting next to me at the gate. She pressed her lips together and looked away. Suppressing a fit of nervous laughter, I dashed away to find the coffee shop where Philip had said he'd be waiting.

He had chosen a seat by the window, basking in the warm midmorning sun that slanted through the wall of windows through which the curious could watch planes taxiing around the gates. He stood up when he saw me, and I slowed my pace to a cautious two miles per hour, stopping behind the empty seat across the small, round table from him.

"Philip."

"Anna. Nice hair."

"Let's get this over with, okay?"

"Have a seat."

I removed my backpack and set it down under the table, and as I reached for the chair I saw his left hand start to move toward his hip. Denial robbed me of half a second's reaction time. How could he have gotten a gun through security? As I cut to my left, Philip's weapon followed me, sending a round down the terminal before I could get my hands on the gun. He missed my right lung by no more than a couple of inches, the shot passing between my torso and outstretched arm. As screams erupted all around us, I barreled into him, knocking him backward. He kept his feet but lost his gun, which was mine for about two seconds before some instinct told me to drop it. I let it fall behind me and kicked Philip in the chest as he lunged toward me. He staggered backward but didn't fall, rushing me again as an alphabet soup of federal agents surrounded us and began screaming commands. I forced him back again with a shove, nearly knocking myself over.

"Get on the ground, now!"

Unsure if the officers around us knew who the aggressor was, I hesitated. I didn't want to be on the ground if Philip came at me again, but I also wasn't a fan of getting shot by the TSA. Fortunately, Philip moved first, rushing me again and collapsing with a groan as a bullet ripped through his right thigh.

I backed up two steps and lowered myself to the ground, trying to keep Philip in sight as we were both swarmed by bodies. I lost sight of him as I was marched back toward the security checkpoint and through a secure door, into the bowels of the TSA. Though I craned my neck as far as my meaty escorts would allow, I couldn't see Jim anywhere.

They found me a private room and locked me inside, alone, removing the handcuffs that had been slapped on me in the terminal. For fifteen minutes I watched the tiny window in the door with bated breath, praying for a familiar face; but when the door opened it was only to admit two strangers: a female TSA supervisor, and a Black man in a black suit. The latter sat down across from me and fixed me with an X-ray glare.

"Want to tell me what that was all about?" he invited.

Cowed, I whispered, "I don't know."

"What is your relationship to the man we took into custody with you?"

"I didn't know him."

"Why were you meeting him there?"

"I wasn't. I just needed a place to sit."

"Why would he try to shoot you?"

"Beats me. Shouldn't have let him skip the TSA checkpoint, huh?" I spat, unable to quell my anger at the near-death experience.

"Sandra, can you pat her down?" he asked, and to me, "Would you like some privacy?"

"I don't care."

I stood up, unbidden, and allowed the woman to pat me down. This wasn't her first rodeo; she felt the microphone through my shirt on her first pass and asked, "What's this?"

"Jewelry."

"Show me."

I glanced at the man, who stood and headed for the door, saying, "Knock when you're done, Sandra."

I watched him leave, begging my brain to think of a way out of revealing the microphone, but I was too amped up from the fight with Philip and couldn't seem to string two thoughts together. Just before the door snapped shut behind the man, Jim pushed through it into the room. The TSA woman turned, momentarily distracted from the pat down.

"Who are you?" she asked.

"James Camposanto, FBI," he intoned, flashing his badge. "This woman has been remanded into my custody."

"She's got to answer some questions."

"You can coordinate with my office," he said dismissively, handing her a business card and turning to me. He did not look happy. "Let's go, come on."

I threw an apologetic look at the steamrolled woman, who looked ready to fight Jim as he took me by the elbow and escorted me out of the interview room. We passed the other man on the way out, and he gave Jim a resigned nod. At the door that led to the unsecure area of the airport, I ground to a halt, looking around the office.

"Wait, my backpack—"

"They wouldn't release that, not yet. We'll get it back later. What's in it?"

"Just clothes and toiletries, and my cell phone, driver's license, cash, passport, house keys, and favorite book, you know, nothing much…"

"We'll discuss it later," he gritted, forcing me through the door. Though I tried to pry his hand off my arm as we headed for the parking garage, he held on doggedly.

"Where are we even going?" I asked.

"I don't know."

Our destination ended up being a remote corner of the parking structure's ground level, shielded from view by a massive SUV with tinted windows.

Jim finally let go of my arm, only to round on me, demanding, "Want to tell me what just happened?"

I knew he had heard the audio through my microphone and had probably also talked his way into viewing the security camera footage while I was waiting in the interview room, so I assumed his was a rhetorical question. He probably knew what happened better than I did, considering the tunnel vision and rush of adrenaline.

"Just the thing you spent so much time trying to convince me wouldn't happen!" I cried.

"What aren't you telling me? What else has Levin said to you? Did you get something out of Jackson that you're keeping to yourself? Because now would be the time to spill it."

That last question hit a bit too close to home. I didn't trust myself to answer, so I crossed my arms and stared at him, hoping I looked stony and indignant. He closed the distance between us and grabbed me by the shoulders.

"This is what happens when you lie to me," he said. "You could've been killed. And if it interests you, the bullet Philip sent into the terminal full of innocent people behind you hit a concrete pillar instead of the ten-year-old kid standing right next to it. He could just as easily have been killed, too."

I shrank at this, avoiding his eyes. The thought of a child getting shot was too much. I could feel my face turning red as my eyes began to sting with tears.

He let me stew in it for a few more seconds, then asked again, "What aren't you telling me, Anna?"

"It doesn't have anything to do with Philip or Tommy," I insisted somewhat weakly. His eyes narrowed, and I took a deep breath, telling myself it made absolutely no sense to withhold this. "Luke said… When he left the casino in Albuquerque… He said he'd be in London by Christmas and I could come find him there, if I wanted."

My admission seemed to have sucked all the air out of the parking structure. Jim stared at me, his face frozen, for an unbearably long time while his hands tightened around my shoulders.

"Jim?"

"Why are you just now telling me this?"

I moved my lips, but no sound came out: "I don't know."

"I do. You're protecting Jackson."

"No."

"Name one other possible explanation. Go ahead, I'll wait."

"I forgot."

"You were screwing him, and you got attached, didn't you?"

I shoved him away, snarling, "Screwing him? *That's* what you think of me?"

"Give me the mic, Anna."

I ripped the microphone off my bra and overhanded it at his head, but he caught it.

He ordered, "Go home and try not to do anything stupid. You'll be hearing from me."

29

Friday, September 4, 2020

Jim left me alone in the parking garage, shaken and angry. I refused to give a single thought to anything he'd said, instead focusing on figuring out a way to get home without so much as a nickel in my pocket.

It took me a while to work out what to do, which gave Jim plenty of time to depart. He was nowhere in sight when I emerged from the parking structure and slipped into the line waiting for a hotel shuttle. I shuffled onto the next shuttle with a dozen other passengers and was ferried to a hotel within the airport, where I used the hotel lobby phone to call my dad. I asked him to come pick me up, told him where I was, and started to explain what happened (albeit in a largely untruthful way), but he cut me off.

"We can talk about it when I get there."

I groaned as I returned the headset to the receiver, knowing what his tone forbode. He was sick and tired of getting jerked around. I was in for it, and my mom wouldn't be there to run interference.

He hadn't even made it out of the city before turning around, and I only had to wait in front of the hotel for about forty-five minutes before he pulled to a stop in front of me. I climbed up into his pickup, feeling at once perfectly safe and anxious to the point of nausea. He didn't look mad, but that didn't mean much in his case.

"Thanks, Dad," I forced.

"Where's your backpack?"

"It got stolen."

Sparing any extraneous details, I related the fictional account of my backpack being stolen before I could get through security, that my boarding pass and wallet were in it, and the ticket counter would not print me a new one, and I couldn't remember the confirmation number to print it myself, and I didn't have my cell phone to call anyone for help, and the airport wouldn't let me use a phone, and my only choice had been to sneak onto a hotel shuttle to find a phone, by which time my flight to Washington had departed DFW Airport. It was a bit of a jog around the truth, but I couldn't exactly tell him the TSA confiscated my backpack after a shoot out.

My dad listened expressionlessly and then asked, "Who hit you?"

"Huh?"

He pointed to my left cheek. I felt the spot gingerly and winced. It felt like a carpet burn, probably inflicted when the TSA was cuffing me.

"When he took my backpack, he pushed me against the wall."

"Why didn't anyone stop him?"

"It was in the parking garage. No one saw."

"What the heck were you doing in there? I dropped you off right in front of the airport, the door was ten feet away."

"I… I wanted a cigarette before the flight. To calm me down, you know I hate flying."

"Since when do you smoke?"

I lost my composure and snapped, "Will you quit trying to poke holes in my story? God, you're like the Spanish Inquisition."

To my astonishment he laughed, then asked, "Want to get a drink before we head home?"

I knew he meant coffee, not beer (it was barely noon), but the question still surprised me.

"I—uh—sure, that would be good."

On the way out of the airport, we spotted a Tex-Mex restaurant we both liked and decided to make it lunch. The hostess led us to a relatively private booth, perhaps sensing I was there to be interrogated. My dad ordered coffee, and I followed suit somewhat regretfully, thinking of how long it had been since I'd tasted a margarita. He waited until the coffee had arrived and we'd placed our orders to start back in.

"Annie, all I ask is that you don't lie to me and your mother. If you can't tell us, that's fine. Just say so."

"Sometimes I have to lie. I can't always tell you that I can't tell you."

He shook his head. "That's some convoluted nonsense."

"Brought to you by Uncle Sam."

That got me a grin. I could always score points with him by taking pot shots at the government. He wasn't a fan.

"And we call it a cover story, not a lie," I added. "Call it a parable, if that makes you more comfortable."

"It doesn't."

"Well… just know that if you think I'm lying, I'm probably doing it at my boss' direction, and I don't like it any more than you do."

"Were you really going to DC?"

"Yes."

"Was your backpack really stolen in the parking garage by a stranger who inexplicably got away?"

"No."

"But it was taken from you."

"I certainly didn't give it up willingly."

"Who hit you?"

"No one, Dad. I promise that's the truth." I decided not to add that Jim had definitely come close to hitting me. I'd never seen him that angry before. Again I pushed those thoughts away.

"Are you still going to Washington?"

"I don't know. Until I get my wallet back, I don't see how I can get on a plane."

"Do you really not know what happened at the airport today?"

I straightened up, asking sharply, "No, what happened?"

"Some kind of shooter, it happened right after I dropped

you off. I heard about it on the radio and tried to call you, but you didn't answer."

"You're kidding me."

"You expect me to believe you had nothing to do with that?"

"I didn't shoot anyone!"

"Were you involved?"

"I—" I swallowed the automatic denial that flew to my lips and said slowly, "Please don't ask me any more questions about that."

He sighed and leaned back, both palms resting on the table on either side of his coffee. My dad was a large man, six feet tall and built like a refrigerator. At sixty years old he was still an intimidating person, even to someone who knew he didn't have a violent bone in his body. The only people who weren't at least a little bit afraid of him were my nieces, who treated him like a giant, sentient teddy bear, and my mother, who wasn't afraid of anything. I could only imagine the terror he'd struck into the hearts of the green engineers he'd been instructing when I first arrived in Texas.

"I won't ask you any more questions, Annie, but I need to tell you something."

"What?"

"First I need you to promise not to be upset at your mother."

Oh, boy. "Of course, I promise."

"After you went up to Oklahoma to meet your boss, some-one else called the house claiming to be your boss. Your mother answered the phone, and she got a little upset. It wasn't the same person who'd called before, and she told him off."

"What did she tell him?"

"That she didn't believe him, and he'd better leave you alone. She told him your boss had already called and it was a different person, an Agent Camposanto."

I closed my eyes. "She told him Jim's name?"

"According to her, yes."

I opened my eyes again but couldn't look at him, staring into space instead as I counted backward from today. "This was on July seventh?"

"Right after you got to Manchester, yes."

"… Can I use your phone?"

"You have to tell me one thing first, and it better be the truth. Are my granddaughters in danger?"

"You really want the truth?"

"I always do."

No, you don't. "I think they were. They won't be anymore, because I'm not going back to your house."

He accepted that so quickly his next question seemed to come from left field. "What about Dude?"

"I can't take him with me."

Sighing again, he pulled out his phone and handed it to me, saying only, "Text your mother and ask her to pick up some dog food at the store."

I took my dad's cell phone to the relative seclusion of the women's bathroom and called Jim, who answered on the first ring. "Camposanto."

"Jim, it's me."

"What? What now?"

"I need your help. I can't go back to my parents' house. I can't put them in danger anymore. Please."

"Hold on."

I heard tapping on a keyboard, a few mouse clicks, and then more tapping. Several minutes passed without a word from either of us, during which another woman used the restroom, washed her hands, and departed.

"Are you in a bathroom?" he asked.

"Yes."

"Where?"

I told him the name of the restaurant, and he told me to hold on again. A minute later, "There's an Uber coming to pick you up. Red Jeep, driver's name is Rudy. He'll be there in eight minutes."

"Thank you."

"He's taking you to the Marriott on Grapevine Mills Circle. I'll meet you there." He hung up.

My dad was not the least bit surprised to be informed I was ditching him. He accepted my lack of explanation with a curt nod, standing up to give me a hug.

"You still into that kav magra stuff?" he asked.

"It's Krav Maga, Dad, and yes. I know a little jujitsu now, too."

He nodded his approval. "Don't you let anyone hurt you, Annie. You take care of yourself."

"I will."

Though my Uber was still five minutes away, I went outside to wait in front of the restaurant. I didn't think I could bear waiting with my dad, whose expression had seemed to indicate he was saying goodbye to me forever. Perhaps I was just being dramatic.

Once I'd been dropped off at the Marriott without incident, I planted myself in a chair in the lobby and waited for Jim to show up. He took longer than I expected, nearly half an hour, during which time the concierge came over three times to ask if I needed anything. The third time I dismissed her rather rudely, and I was pretty sure she was trying to figure out how to bounce me from the hotel when Jim finally appeared.

He spared me one quick glance before heading to the counter to check in, and then he simply beckoned to me to follow him to the elevators. If his intention was to impress me with his continued bad mood, it failed.

"Still mad at me for almost dying?" I asked tartly when the elevator doors closed on us.

"It couldn't be for withholding information in a federal investigation."

"Could be that. Maybe you're mad because you think I have feelings for Luke."

"Of course I am," he said, so quietly I wondered if I were meant to hear. I was surprised until he added, "You're obviously compromised, and I still have to use you because my other options are approximately nil."

"Use me?" I repeated.

Jim glared at me, then led the way out of the elevator without a response. I followed morosely, thoughts straying to my lost backpack and then to my nieces and Dude, who I thought I'd be seeing again in a couple of days at most. I trudged into the hotel room behind Jim, still lost in depressing thoughts, and was snapped back to reality by the feeling of his arms encircling me.

"I'm sorry," he said gruffly. "I'm glad you're okay." He held me at arms' length and asked, "You are okay, aren't you?"

I wasn't prepared for Jim to shift back into friend mode. He could have given me some kind of warning. I shook my head, imagining Dude roaming around my parents' house and yard looking for me. My face crumpled, and Jim wrapped me up again.

"I didn't sign up for this," I complained, voice muffled. "I was supposed to get information from Luke, pass it to you, and lay low until you sorted everything out. That was what you said."

"That was the original plan."

"How much longer do I have to do this?"

He let me go, only to slide his hand around the back of my neck, lightly gripping my hair. "You have to do this until it's done," he answered. "What happened? Why are you suddenly so sure your family's in danger?"

I explained how my mother had inadvertently spilled the beans—presumably to Philip—about Jim being my boss long before I had, which absolved me of that mistake but had given Philip a lot more time to mull over the implications. Now that I'd been marked for death, intuition told me my family could find themselves in the crosshairs at any moment. Jim didn't question my logic, or lack thereof, he simply nodded.

Defeated, I asked lifelessly, "So, what's next?"

"You're going to order yourself something to eat, and I'm going to the airport to get your stuff back. We'll go from there."

Enemy Cross // AK Waller

30

September to November 2020

I stayed in the hotel room for two nights while Jim found a semi-permanent residence for me to pass the time until I could go to London. This ended up being a modest, furnished apartment a couple miles south of the hotel, which whoever controlled his purse strings had allowed him to rent month-to-month under a name he pointedly refused to tell me.

Jim was making an effort to be nice to me, but I sensed a shift in our working relationship. My decision to withhold Luke's words about London was certainly the cause, but I wasn't as clear on the implications. Jim acted as though Philip's attempt on my life at the airport might have been foreseen, had I told him Luke was going to London. Since Jim didn't come right out and say that, I couldn't challenge him to make sense of it. It didn't matter, anyway. Jim had a nasty habit of not sharing information with me until he had no other choice.

Since all I had were the contents of my backpack, which Jim

had wrestled away from the TSA through what he wanted me to believe was pure finesse, the apartment was a dismal place. Jim insisted I behave as though I were in witness protection.

"Whoever Philip answers to decided they wanted you dead more than they wanted someone in his position in the FBI," he had explained, "and that should scare the daylights out of you. Never use Breckenridge again, and even though this goes without saying, I feel you need to hear it anyway: Don't use your real name, either, and don't call or visit your parents or anyone else you know. Don't even leave this apartment. If I see a single dog hair in here, your goose is cooked."

So, for three miserable weeks I hunkered down in the apartment, broken only by two massive grocery deliveries and one visit from Jim halfway through week two when I'd been washing and wearing the same three sets of clothes so much I wanted to rob a department store at gunpoint.

Jim had been on a miniature adventure, goading my parents and nieces away from the house with free tickets to Six Flags and sneaking in to collect all my things, including the Glock I'd left in my dad's safe. I had to admire Jim's fortitude, burglarizing a house guarded by a horse-sized German Shepherd who didn't know him from Adam. I may have come home with Jim's scent on me once or twice, but otherwise Dude had no reason to trust him.

Removing all my things from the house wasn't something Jim wanted to hide; the more people who saw, the better. Unfortunately for Jim, the opposite was true for delivering them to me. He had driven halfway to Alabama before meandering back to my temporary apartment. The whole ordeal had taken him two days, at the end of which he was so tired it took very little convincing for him to stay the night. He slept on the couch.

I was dealing with Agent Camposanto, not simply my Jim, and knew I would be until I caught a flight to Europe. Agent Camposanto had no interest in flirting with, sexually harassing, or even so much as touching me; he was so focused on the task at hand that he reminded me of a sand spider, which will wait in a hole for as long as it takes for prey to wander by, even at the risk of starving to death. I knew from experience that plain old Jim wouldn't resurface until all the planning, strategizing, preparing, and briefing had been completed to his satisfaction.

Spending the night, or even coming to my apartment again, was out of the question after he brought me my stuff. Like participants in an illicit affair, when we needed to meet, we did so in a random hotel and kept it brief. An exchange of information, a homework assignment, a reminder about the rules, and I'd be on my way back to the apartment alone. Luckily, the apartment complex had a gym and a pool, so I wasn't too murderously bored.

Now that the Abigail Breckenridge alias was burned to uselessness, Jim had supplied me with a new identity. Tegan Mercer, according to the Oklahoma driver's license, U.S. passport, and only-for-emergencies credit card, was to be my name for the foreseeable future. I had to memorize a few details about her but was otherwise left to my own devices as to her life story. That part took less than a day. The real meat and potatoes was preparing me to, in Agent Camposanto's words, "be set loose in

Europe with no one to watch your back or make sure you don't get yourself or someone else killed."

With the scant information from Luke that I'd finally passed on to Jim, that Luke would be in London by Christmas, Jim and his team were preparing me to go to London and operate completely alone, not to return to the States until directly ordered to. The target date for my departure was November 15, but that date came and went while Jim waited for confirmation that everything was ready. Finally, on November 23, I got the call: Get to the airport; your flight leaves in three hours.

▼

Ever since my first foray through college, which really was to study art history as I'd told Luke, I'd wanted to travel to London someday. The 2,000-year-old city was home to enough museums, monuments, architecture, and layer upon layer of raw history to keep an art historian busy for more than one lifetime. Jim knew my background, and he knew exactly how easily I'd be distracted by the city itself.

"You're not a tourist, and you're not studying abroad," he'd instructed. "You're just Tegan the Court Reporter from Hicklahoma, visiting family in the UK for Christmas. You don't care about statues, you're bored by museums, and as far as you care, London is just like any other city only much, much bigger."

Not one of my fantasy trips to London had been set in the winter, though. I doubted I'd be home any sooner than January, and the temperatures were only going to be dropping between now and then. Outside Heathrow, I shivered in line for a taxi in forty degree air that felt more like twenty, inadequately insulated by the light jacket in which I'd departed DFW. After a trip to the hotel to drop off my things, my next stop would be a store that sold the fluffiest, puffiest, downiest winter coats London had to offer.

Again Jim's careful guidance popped into my head: "You have to make this cash last as long as possible. If you lose it, get robbed, or blow it all on a fancy hotel room, you're going to be on your own until I can beg, borrow, or steal something else. Trust me, you don't want to be homeless in London in winter."

With this advice echoing around my head, I checked into my hotel and took a scalding hot shower to warm myself up. The eighty dollar per night room was hardly fancy, but it wasn't a long term solution. I was to sort that out on my own, without any assistance or input from Jim, the better to remain hidden for as long as possible. I wasn't to have any contact with him except for phone calls every two weeks at pre-appointed times.

"Don't forget to call. If you miss a check-in, the fastest I can get to London is a day, and I won't even know where exactly you are. By the time I find you, if I find you, I will be pissed. If you don't call, it better be because you're dead."

"Get out of my head," I snarled at the mirror.

I threw on two sweaters and my heaviest coat and left the hotel on foot to find something to eat. It was lunchtime in Texas, so it was dinner time in London, or supper if I wanted to be classy. Whatever I was going to call it, I needed food immediately.

Jim's disembodied voice refused to budge. Everywhere I looked, some piece of the advice he'd drilled into my head popped up to have its say. The hotel restaurant-slash-bar, the first and most obvious option for dinner, was ruled out.

"You don't want to be noticed anywhere you plan to return to. Don't hang around your hotel or go back to the same place more often than you need to."

So, I pulled my coat around me as tightly as possible and headed out into the darkening street. I had no idea which way to go, let alone how far I'd have to walk before I found something. I struck out to the west, simply because most of the people on the sidewalk were heading in that direction. I earned a lot of strange looks, shivering along in twice as many layers as everyone else.

"Even if you don't know where you're going, pretend to. You won't be able to avoid looking like a tourist, but you don't have to look helpless and lost. If you have to ask for directions, only ask for enough detail to get yourself oriented. You don't need to be telling random strangers on the street where you're going."

I had reached the level of hunger that provoked counterproductive behavior. Though I passed half a dozen cafes, restaurants, and food trucks, none of them appealed to me. For reasons unknown, I was fixated on finding a real British pub, and so I trudged on as the temperature fell and darkness settled in. I passed a department store selling exactly the sort of outwear I wanted, but fortunately I was hungry enough to resist the expensive impulse. Finally, I found a pub and ducked inside.

"Don't sit at a bar," Jim's advice butted in as soon as I glanced toward the restaurant's bar. "You'll get too much attention that way. Ask for a table near the back, and sit facing the door."

I settled into a booth that met with the invisible Jim's approval and ordered a Guinness and shepherd's pie from the pixie-like, too-young looking blonde woman who flitted over to wait on me. While I waited, I took in my surroundings, a much cozier and more enjoyable activity after the first few sips of beer.

The pub wasn't very busy, and I seemed to have stumbled across an establishment that wasn't known to tourists. Most of the patrons seemed to be locals, and the pub itself wasn't making any discernable attempt to attract more business. Still, I wasn't the only Yank in the place. At the center of the restaurant, being stereotypically loud and obnoxious, four college-aged men with New England accents were having an animated conversation about their adventures that day.

My waitress, whose name I remembered right when I saw her coming with my shepherd's pie, threw the college boys a sullen glance as she passed their table. They, in turn, exchanged crude comments about her that were decipherable only by their tone.

"Thanks, Alice," I said brightly when she placed the steaming plate in front of me. "Can you do me a favor?"

She seemed grateful for a reason to linger at my table rather than passing the college boys again. Smiling, she said, "Sure, name it."

"I want to buy all four of those kids a shot of Jack Daniels and tell them it's your finest single-malt Scotch, but I don't want them to know it's from me. Is that possible?"

She stifled a laugh. "Sure, I'll say it's from the bartender—Maybe the tip'll make up for them existing."

"That works."

"Any particular reason?"

"I'm bored and want to listen to them gas on about how much better it is than the cheap stuff."

"Now that I can get behind. Cheers."

I watched with childish glee as all four men loudly savored their cheap whiskey, nearly losing my composure when one of them pointed out how much better it was than Jack Daniels. Once they'd finished their aperitif and departed, plunging the pub into almost unnerving silence, Alice brought me an unsolicited third pint of Guinness.

"Sixty pound tip and three phone numbers," she announced as she set the beer in front of me. "Did you know those guys?"

"Nope, thankfully."

I drank my last pint in deep thought, little snippets of Jim's instruction still popping into my head at random. It hadn't been like this in Colorado. Granted, that situation was as different from my current one as possible.

In Colorado I was alone, free from distraction, and had every reason in the world to complete my mission, but Jim trusted me now even less than he had before. Why else would he go to such lengths to make sure I thought of him at every turn? He was like an overbearing parent hammering rules into his sheltered child before summer camp: Don't chew with your mouth open, don't forget to wash your hands, make good choices!

The more I thought about it the angrier I got, which tended to happen to me with a good stout stumbling through my bloodstream. So I'd withheld one tiny piece of information. That didn't make me a traitor, or even unreliable. It made me human. I didn't really want to find Luke again, because deep down I didn't believe he knew anything that could help us prove Philip was dirty; and I didn't want to put him in any more danger than he was already in because of me. And I had to admit, parting words or no, I was afraid he would not be at all pleased to see me.

I hadn't been on a short leash in Colorado so much as trapped in a tiny cage. Now, all of Europe was available to me. Thousands of dollars in cash, a U.S. passport, and fluency in the five most commonly spoken languages in the European Union would get me pretty darn far.

So far maybe Jim and the FBI would give me up for lost and leave me alone.

This insurrectionist thought bounced around in my head while I walked back to the hotel, distracting and causing me to miss the building entirely and have to double back to find it. I abjured the lift and took the stairs to warm up, and I was so tired when I finally stumbled into my room that I fell asleep face down on top of the covers.

Day one of my search was officially over. I hadn't found Luke, but at least I'd found a pub I liked.

31

November to December 2020

If you're wondering how a woman with very little investigative experience goes about canvassing a city of nine million people in search of one man who probably doesn't want to be found, you would've been asking Jim the same questions I was. Where do I start? What resources will be available? Can I partner with any British law enforcement agencies or hire a local investigator who knows the city?

Jim's answers, if they could so be called, had been maddening. No resources were available to me except those accessible to any person with an internet connection and basic reasoning skills. As for local help, that was a pipe dream. As had been the case with the Colorado search, no one outside Jim's purview could have any idea what I was doing; so, as far as Londoners were concerned, I wasn't looking for anyone, let alone a person of interest in a murder on U.S. soil.

To start, Jim had said, I needed to put myself in Luke's

shoes. Where would he go? What would he be doing with his time? What are his needs, his habits, his comfort zones? As though a couple weeks with the guy had given me such insights. I knew almost nothing that would help me find him. Thanks to Jim's research, I knew three of Luke's aliases and where he'd gone to high school. I knew he was a practitioner of jujitsu, but I doubted he'd be signing up for BJJ lessons at some London dojo. He liked to cook and was good at it, and he didn't like to talk about his past, present, or future. He knew the main character in *Jurassic Park* was named Alan. Not much to go on.

Jim knew a bit more, but for reasons unknown he was infuriatingly stingy with such information. Luke Jackson had never been issued a U.S. passport; neither had his primary alias, Blake Johnson. Neither one had an address in London or anywhere in the United Kingdom. If he was employed, such employment was not connected to any of his aliases or real or stolen social security numbers in any legal way; therefore, if he was drawing any kind of income, it was either illegal or so paltry as to be beneath the notice of at least two governments' robust and rapacious tax-collection apparatuses.

Jim's solution was simple, but not easy. I was going to have to resort to good, old-fashioned pavement pounding. As more than one lifetime would be required to accomplish a thorough-going foot tour of London, I would have to focus my energies and open-records surfing on narrowing down the places to look. For instance, I could cross off Westminster Abbey and the flight control towers of Heathrow Airport. See, we're already making progress.

The one piece of information that should have been encouraging, owing to its usefulness, was just the opposite. For nearly a year, I'd been unofficially part of Jim's chain of command. On paper, I worked under an agent named Christopher King in the Organized Crime Unit, where I'd been punted to take a breather after the Houston fiasco, but in practice I worked for Jim. Sure, I didn't know who our boss was, or what exactly we did, or even where in the FBI my empty office was located, but I was part of the team. I felt that entitled me to some information.

What I got instead was Jim tersely informing me that I needed to scrutinize any physical location associated with an import-export company that had offices in multiple countries. Presumably that describes all import-export companies, so this wasn't much in the way of a lead. Rather than telling me how he knew this, Jim ordered me not to repeat the "information" to anyone, not even to Google it, to simply forget he'd told me and go on about my business.

▼

Contrary to my orders, I returned to the same pub every night that first week after spending my days trying to find semi-permanent lodgings. By Friday evening I had a few options, but none was ideal. Since everything within walking distance of my hotel was too expensive, I'd spent Wednesday, Thursday, and Friday taking taxis to other parts of the city upon the recommendation of the hotel concierge, looking for apartments, and taxiing back to the hotel. Since I had no work visa, no job, and no references, options were further limited. Even so, I had six viable options, and I was determined to make a decision before I left the pub that evening.

Alice, the waitress, offered drive-by advice as she flitted back and forth, her hands more than full with the Friday night crowd. She nixed three places based on their location. A fourth was crossed off after I described my would-be landlord and she declared, sight unseen, that he was a serial killer.

She couldn't help choose between the last two, though, so I designated my empty plate of fish and chips the spare room in Clapham and my almost-empty pint glass the attic room in Shepherd's Bush and placed my dinner knife between them. I gave it a spin as Alice returned with my next pint.

"Now what's this?" she asked, coming to a full stop where before she'd only slowed down slightly on her way past.

"Flipping a coin, except without the coin. Or the flipping."

I glanced up while the knife was spinning, surprised she was still standing there. Only then did I notice how empty the pub was. I was one of three guests still hanging around. Checking my watch for the first time in hours, I realized the pub would be closing in seven minutes. I sighed expansively as the knife point stopped, directed at the pint glass.

"Shepherd's Bush," I announced. I pictured the chilly attic space and grimaced. "God, I wish I had a work visa."

"Haven't you?" she asked, surprised. "What're you doing in London, anyway?"

"Visiting family," I said with well-trained disinterest, adding on impulse, "or, I was. My uncle didn't pick me up at the airport, and I found out last week he's actually in the UAE, so… I don't know what I'm doing here. Waiting, I guess."

"How long are you here?"

"At least a month. But apparently I could stay as long as six months, if I wanted."

"Nothing waiting for you back home?"

I scoffed. "Nothing I couldn't live without." I offered a mental apology to Dude, without whom I definitely could not live, but Alice didn't need to know that.

"Hm." She gave me an appraising look, then wandered back to the bar, saying, "Hang about a moment, I need to check on something."

I assumed she meant I didn't have to leave, despite the fact that the second-to-last guest had just staggered out and the bartender had locked the door behind him. I nursed my Guinness and watched the door through which Alice had disappeared. Ten minutes later she emerged, looking pleased with herself. She sat down at the table across from me.

"I've solved it. I've got a room for you, and a job, so long as you're not too hung up on the legalities."

"At this point, the legalities can pound sand."

She grinned. "I just love your little American phrases. Pound sand? That doesn't even make sense. Anyway, you can buss tables here, and at five hundred pounds per month, you can stay in my spare room, walking distance from the pub."

I stared at her, uncomprehending. "You're joking."

"Not at all. You're a lucky lady: My flat mate moved out two months ago and left me in a crunch. I'd've mentioned it earlier, only I didn't realize you didn't have the proper visa."

To give myself time to think, I took a deep draught of beer. I'd gotten lucky before, but this seemed too easy. She sensed my indecision.

"I understand if you don't like the idea. You could get in a lot of trouble... but you probably won't."

I swallowed painfully. "You don't even know me."

She shrugged. "Don't need to. I'm not proposing to you, I just need a flat mate. And my spare room is leagues better than some cat lady's moldy old attic."

"I think..." I began to say I needed time to think about it, and ask if I could talk to her tomorrow night. Instead, I found myself saying, "... It's a deal."

"That's it! Come back to the office and meet Cat, the manager. Tell her you've got a degree in bussing tables."

"I do," I retorted, grabbing my backpack and coat and hurrying after her. "But in America we call it Art History."

A quick meeting with Cat, the enormous Scottish woman who only appeared outside of her office when a customer needed yelling at, convinced me this was going to be anything but too easy. She would be watching me like a hawk, and the pay was below minimum wage. I was to be paid entirely in cash under the table, and if I declared the income to anyone, she'd snap me in half (her words).

Once that was over with, I paid my tab with a generous tip for Alice and made plans to meet up with her in an hour at a nightclub; because, in her estimation, if we were going to live together for any length of time, she needed to see how I comported myself in a combat situation.

We met four of Alice's friends at a nightclub, and while they and Alice collectively consumed enough alcohol to kill a Russian sailor, I sipped unhurriedly at a couple of cocktails and babysat them.

One of Jim's most infuriating bits of advice was also the one I didn't need to be told: Don't get drunk. Ever. So, I minded my five new British friends and had a few laughs at their expense. This exercise culminated outside on the street in front of the club, where I was required to physically separate two of them. Alice was sober enough by that point to be impressed, and while she walked me back to my hotel she peppered me with questions about self-defense and jokingly wondered if Cat would pay me a bouncer's wages.

My first day on the job was Saturday, and I did not in fact have any days of the week off. That suited me, because once I'd moved my meager possessions into Alice's spare room, I had nothing to do during the day but search for Luke and occasionally venture into a salon to have my roots touched up. I had to myself one bedroom and one half-bath, more than enough privacy to crack open the new laptop Jim had supplied and use the accompanying mobile hotspot to access publicly available resources to conduct my search.

By then, with less than a month until Christmas, I knew intuitively that Luke had arrived in London. He'd said, "by Christmas," not on or after Christmas. For all I knew, he'd be gone again by Boxing Day. On the pretense of exploring the city, I left Alice's flat early each morning to reconnoiter, barely returning in time to change clothes and head to my shift at the pub.

My search was gradually heating up, but I had to be realistic. London was a big city, and I was only one woman. I could search for Luke for the rest of my life and never get any closer than I had that first night.

32

Thursday, December 24, 2020

By Christmas Eve, I'd worn the soles out of my warmest boots and tentatively crossed off dozens of locations from my mental list. With increasing desperation, I cut my arrival at work closer and closer, until on Christmas Eve I arrived fifteen minutes late. Cat was waiting for me by the locker where I exchanged my coat for my apron.

"You've got another job," was her opening accusation.

I was understandably taken aback. "I don't."

"Does your watch need winding, then?"

"It doesn't work that way. Look, I'm sorry I've been late. It won't happen again. Besides, it's nearer closing when you need me most," I said cheekily, referring to my frequently needed powers of not-so-gentle persuasion to eject unruly patrons.

She suppressed a smile and stomped away, muttering something that sounded awfully like, "too big for your boots." I threw on my apron and plunged into the chaos of the pub to start earning my keep.

Alice and I suspected word was getting around about the tall, blonde, American woman who sometimes played the part of bouncer at the pub. I hoped we were wrong, as everything about that scenario was the opposite of flying under the radar. Still, it was gratifying to see the pub more crowded than usual and halfway believe it was in some small part because of me. More likely the bigger crowd was due to the holidays.

My next scheduled check-in with Jim was tomorrow, Christmas Day, and I knew he'd be expecting me to have made some kind of progress even if we couldn't discuss it. I did not intend to tell him about my job or my accommodations, and we were obviously prohibited from discussing anything classified. He'd make sure I was still alive, I'd accept whatever increasingly hackneyed advice he'd thought up, and that would be that. I wouldn't have to admit I was no closer to finding Luke now than I'd been when I stepped off the plane in November, but even so it was not a conversation I looked forward to.

It was all too easy to push thoughts of the impending phone call away in favor of getting myself into the right headspace to be the best busboy-bouncer I could be. That started with taking stock of the customers in the pub.

For the past four days in a row, the same two men had been seated at the end of the bar when I arrived for work, so I automatically clocked them as I stepped into the dining room. On the rare occasions when I'd been able to catch snatches of their conversation, I'd heard a few words in French; but they spoke to one another so quietly that nothing was really discernable, and they paused any discussion when Alice or I got too close. They were so alike in appearance I decided they were brothers, and no one else who frequented the pub gave them any sign of recognition or friendship.

Needless to say, they made me a little nervous. I caught them eyeing me once or twice, but that didn't set them apart from any average patron. It was more a totality of the circumstances, and what Jim would have to say about them, that had me on edge. I kept the presumptive brothers in sight while I started clearing tables and chatting up whoever seemed in need of a friendly conversation.

My two mysterious Frenchmen usually only lingered long enough to drink a pint, but tonight they ordered a second round, then a third. Both were in their thirties, well-dressed and reasonably good-looking, so they garnered a respectable amount of attention; but all interested parties were dismissed kindly yet firmly. They seemed to want nothing more than to hold a muted discussion in a crowded pub on Christmas Eve.

During a lull in the activity, when for once I had no tables to clear and no messages to relay to Alice, the bartender, or the kitchen, I straightened my shoulders and marched right up to the bar, squeezing in between one of the Frenchmen and the German woman to his left.

I ordered a shot of Glenlivet from the bartender, who submitted to my request with only passing disapproval. Technically we weren't supposed to drink on the job, but everyone did, and I needed some liquid courage.

I drummed my palms on the bar while I waited, looking

around boredly. The German woman took a step backward, pushing me into the man on my right. She half-turned to apologize, and I reflexively answered in German before turning to pass the apology along in French like some sort of translating telephone game. The Frenchman frowned at me, more calculating than annoyed, and didn't offer a response.

My scotch arrived with their food, and I downed the former as quickly as I could, departing with a playful, "Bon appétit."

Since today marked the start of at least a three-day weekend, the atmosphere in the pub was especially merry. Before midnight I had ejected one pair of literal hooligans and one bafflingly strong older woman, all to general glee, and I was waiting for the high sign from the bartender to get to work on a deeply inebriated gentleman who was toeing the line between amusing and out of hand.

Sadly, midnight came and went, and the drunk gentleman showed himself out peaceably. People began filtering out as though his departure had been the signal that the fun was over. By 1:00 a.m., one hour to closing, the pub was downright peaceful. The Frenchmen were working on their fifth pint each, and it was clear they were in no hurry to leave. As soon as I got the chance, I dragged Alice into the kitchen for as private a conversation as we could hope to get.

"They're starting to freak me out," I said, as though continuing an earlier conversation. She understood immediately.

"You, too? Thought maybe it was just me."

"What should we do?"

"Is this really the first time this has happened to you? Obviously, we take the long way home and see if they follow."

"And if they do?"

"I imagine you'll have to rough 'em up," she grinned, painfully attempting an American accent.

I nodded, concluding distractedly, "They're creepy."

"They are at that."

I was so amped up for our little plan to get started that I was actually disappointed when the two French brothers left the pub about fifteen minutes before closing. Our Christmas Eve was fated to be as uneventful as usual. We closed up, fully intending to walk a circuitous route home, but the night was so cold we ended up taking a cab.

I fell asleep in the early morning hours, noting as I slipped away that I was about to spend my first Christmas abroad, surrounded by strangers, searching for a man who probably didn't even suspect I was looking for him.

33

Friday, December 25, 2020

The very last thing I expected to hear on Christmas morning was Bing Crosby crooning about silver bells while dishes clattered in the tiny kitchen next to my room. I lay awake with my eyes closed, taking it in, not sure exactly where I was. Finally I heard a metal pan crash to the floor, followed by a stream of imaginative profanity from Alice.

I concluded I really was in the spare room of a woman I'd met a month ago, flush with small bills from my lucrative busboy career, about to spend my thirty-fourth Christmas lurking around some of the least savory parts of London looking for Luke Jackson.

And, of course, I had to make a phone call.

I grabbed my watch off the nightstand and consulted its glowing face: nearly 8:00 in the morning. That meant it was nearly 3:00 a.m. in Washington. I had about six hours left before checking in with Jim, and I planned to make the most of them.

Even though I had nothing concrete to show for it, I had been anything but idle since arriving in London. I may not have found Luke yet, but I was zeroing in on him. There were only so many places he could be, and I was narrowing the search down the old fashioned way: looking. London was a big city, but I had used my time wisely.

My planned Christmas gift to myself was a trip to a place I had long ago placed at the top of my list of likely hideouts. It was a small office building in Dagenham owned by Frères Enterprises, a company whose name had cropped up several times in my research, usually when I went down the rabbit hole of public records.

A news article about prostitution, drug trafficking, or arms dealing would lead to an open record at the Met showing when and where arrests had occurred (names redacted to protect the guilty), and that would lead to property and business records, which would lead to a company's website, which would lead to another website, which eventually led back to the first website. I didn't always land on Frères Enterprises, but enough that I was convinced they were sketchy as all get out.

They had an international office in Atlanta that handled their North American business, and that piqued my interest. One of the few pieces of concrete information Jim had given me made Atlanta catch my eye: Of the twelve cars that had been stolen from outside the casino in Albuquerque the night Luke left, one had been clocked at a toll road heading out of Dallas. If that was Luke, he was headed east, which made Atlanta a possible destination.

I had identified over two dozen locations in the greater London area that were associated with Frères Enterprises, and I'd visited all of them at least once. I'd already passed by the office in Dagenham, just to get a feel for the place, but that had been early December when Luke might not yet be in London.

Today I was going to plant myself in the café across the street and hope for a miracle. Sure, there was a shocking amount of guesswork involved; but intuition had yet to fail me, at least when it came to Luke. And Jim had all but ordered me to focus on import-export companies, which just so happened to be the raison d'être of Frères Enterprises. I knew, as surely as I knew when I stood on top of the mountain in Colorado and looked down at a mystery structure that wasn't there two years ago, that I was on to something. In the interest of saving time and effort, I had refused to revisit the place any sooner than Christmas Day.

I climbed out of bed and, shivering at once in the cold air that attacked me, I dragged the blanket off and cocooned myself in it before finding Alice in the kitchen. She was already dressed, which was wildly out of character, and had somehow acquired a red and green elf hat with jingle bells. Even more bewilderingly, she appeared to be in the middle of cooking breakfast. Bells jingled as she turned to me.

"Happy Christmas, you!" she trilled. "And happy day off to us."

"We have the day off?"

"Sure, didn't Cat tell you? She's not opening the pub today at all."

"Uh… first I've heard of it."

"Well, better late than never. Wait, wait, stay right there," she said as I started toward the table to sit down. "You're just under it."

"Under what?" I asked, looking up.

A hand-drawn mistletoe had been taped to the ceiling, and with cheerful impunity Alice grabbed me by the face and kissed me right on the lips. She whisked away to continue wrestling with kitchen implements.

After a few seconds to recover from my surprise, I muttered, "Okay, tell me where all this Christmas spirit came from so I can get my own."

"I have no idea," she answered lightly, now consulting a recipe and extracting measuring cups from the cabinet over the stove. "Yuck, these are sticky. I don't think I've ever used them."

I sat down at the table to take in the spectacle in comfort. "It's usually madness to even attempt to wake you up before noon."

"I popped right out of bed at seven, bright eyed and bushy tailed, and thought I'd try my hand at Christmas pudding. What's the worst that can happen?"

"Fire?"

"O, ye of little faith…"

As much as I would've loved to stick around and watch, I had to dismiss myself. I reeled off my briefly-rehearsed lie. "Well, I'd love to help, but I've got to meet my uncle at nine for breakfast. He finally called last night."

"What?" she cried, abandoning the sticky measuring cups for the moment. "After all this time, what's the point?"

"Yeah, that's pretty much what I said. But he feels awful

and wants to take me Christmas shopping. So… submit your requests now. I bet I could snag just about anything if he feels guilty enough."

"Hm… I'll have to think about that one. When are you leaving? Where are you meeting him?"

"Kensal Green," I lied. "Guess I better leave in about thirty minutes."

"Too right, and you look a mess. Let me do your hair, will you?"

"Why, what's wrong with it?" I asked, self-consciously catching the tail end of my hair between my fingers.

I was afraid she'd spotted my week's worth of red roots peeking out, but she said, "It's unjustly imprisoned in a permanent ponytail."

"All right, fair enough. Let me get dressed."

I brushed my hair and allowed Alice to braid it, and her nimble fingers made it look ten times better than I ever had on my own. She insisted I throw on some makeup and allowed me to use hers, because I didn't have so much as a tube of mascara to my name.

"He's my uncle, not my boyfriend," I groaned as Alice appraised my work and started adding to it. "I don't need to get all gussied up."

"Gussied up?" she sputtered. "What on earth does that mean?"

"You know, looking hot."

"Looking hot is always an advantage, regardless of the circumstances."

I had to give her that. With forced patience I submitted to the application of several cosmetics, finally putting my foot down when she tried to slap a pair of false eyelashes on me.

"Okay, now you're just messing around," I protested.

"True, and you don't really need them. You clean up quite nicely, Tegan."

"Thanks," I said, and I meant it.

Alice sent me off with a request for the most expensive bottle of wine my uncle would shell out for, and as I emerged onto the street to hail a cab I felt a stab of grief. She'd turned out an excellent friend and roommate, and if things went south today I'd likely never see her again; but I couldn't say a proper goodbye, because that would only provoke her suspicion.

Feeling miserable, I looked up and down the street and realized there wasn't a cab in sight. It was Christmas Day, and hardly anyone was out. Annoyed, I set off to find a warm place to wait while I called an Uber.

I didn't arrive at the café across the street from the office building in Dagenham until well after nine, which was bothersome but not entirely disastrous. I didn't expect many people to be going in to work today, and even less for one of them to be Luke. I simply needed to 'suss out' (as Alice would say) how to get inside.

Setting up at a seat next to the window, I powered up my laptop and found a donut shop that was open for the holiday. I placed an order for delivery, sat back with my cappuccino, and watched.

About forty minutes later, a delivery van stopped outside

the office building, blocking my view of the entrance. Swearing under my breath, I grabbed my laptop, told the waiter I'd be right back, and stepped outside to get a better angle.

Gritting my teeth against the wind, I watched the donut delivery man walk straight into the building carrying a large, flat box and exit three minutes later, sans box. He seemed to be in a hurry but was otherwise unruffled. I was surprised and a bit disappointed, thinking maybe I had the wrong building. Nevertheless, I returned to the café to pay for my coffee and collect the rest of my things, thinking there was no time like the present to try to get inside myself. If nothing else, I could snag a donut.

Snow was starting to fall as I crossed the street. Inside the unlocked, double glass doors was a small, poorly-heated reception area which was vacant. No security cameras were visible, just as I'd noticed none on the building's exterior.

A pink coat and purse hanging from a peg on the wall hinted someone had been there today. I assumed the receptionist was walking around with a box of donuts, trying to figure out who had ordered them. Ready to bump into her but hoping not to, I let myself through the door next to her desk and found myself in a long, half-lit hallway lined by a dozen doors.

Next to each door was a nameplate holder, but most were empty. The last door on the right, the one door with a nameplate, was also the only one that was unlocked; but, as the name indicated, it was nothing more than a breakroom. I started to leave, seeing no reason to linger in a dead end with no escape routes, when one of the locked doors opened halfway down the hall.

I backed into the breakroom and listened to a muted conversation in French between a man and a woman. As expected, the woman was explaining about the mysterious donut delivery and complaining that she'd had to pay for it. I glanced at the counter behind me and saw the box in question, open and missing two of its original dozen.

The woman was directing the man to the breakroom to get one, since apparently the proper owner wasn't going to come forward. She excused herself to return to the front desk.

With nowhere to hide, I backed away from the doorway and prepared to explain myself to whomever entered. Whatever I'd been expecting, I forgot all about it the moment he stepped into the breakroom.

He stopped, freezing in the doorway and staring at me as though unsure his eyes were working correctly. Since he'd been speaking beautiful French moments before, I was equally shocked to find myself face-to-face with Alan, AKA Luke Jackson.

34

Friday, December 25, 2020

Luke recovered from his shock first, asking in a whisper, in English, "What are you doing here?"

I threw my hands wide and shrugged, momentarily robbed of the power of speech. He shut the breakroom door, locked it, and rounded on me. As I'd feared, he was the opposite of thrilled to see me.

"How the heck did you find me?" he demanded.

"You told me you'd be in London."

"Yeah, well, it's a big city, *Anna.*"

"I've been looking for a while."

"What—how—why?" he stammered.

"Which one do you want me to answer first?"

"You know what, never mind. I've got to get you out of here right now."

He grabbed me by the arm and started dragging me toward the door. I resisted as best I could, but he easily overbalanced me.

"What is your problem?" I hissed as he ducked his head outside, checking that the hallway was empty.

"Shut up."

He pulled me not toward the reception area but across the hall to an unlabeled door, which he unlocked. Behind the door were stairs, their foot lost in deep shadows. I recoiled automatically, but he dragged me through the door with very little effort. When it closed behind us with a delicate click, total darkness enveloped us both.

I whispered, "You're scaring me. What's going on?"

I heard an aggrieved sigh. "Stay here a sec."

Footsteps carried him down the stairs, where he found a light switch and flicked it on. I followed him down and saw that he'd pulled me into a storage basement. Before I could read the labels on the hundreds of boxes that nearly filled the tiny space, he grabbed me by the face just as Alice had done. It wasn't so he could kiss me.

"Don't look at anything. Do not come back here. You understand?"

His imperious tone finally cut through my fear, angering me. I snapped, "Yeah, I got it."

"That door leads to the street," he said, turning me to face said door. "Make sure it closes behind you." He pushed me toward it.

The push was too much. I spun around, demanding, "Why'd you tell me you'd be in London, then? You said I could come and find you, so I did. Why are you acting like this?"

I was pleased to see his stony expression waver a little. He glanced jerkily toward the door upstairs and then turned to me, forcing out, "Where are you staying?"

I spat out the address, and he repeated it back to me. As though against his better judgment, he said, "If I can, I'll come by tonight. That's the best I can do."

"If you're still a jerk tonight, don't bother," I retorted.

Without waiting for his answer, I threw myself through the outer door and up the metal staircase, onto the street.

Fuming, I began walking without any real idea where I was going. I was fairly certain I was headed in the general direction of Alice's flat. About the time I calmed down enough to take note of where I was, I found myself in front of a grocery store. At least Alice would get her Christmas wish.

I bought their most expensive bottle of wine, which wasn't really saying much, and started to call for another Uber when I saw a handful of people emerging from the Underground station across the street. I decided to take the Tube instead, if for nothing else than to give myself time to think before being peppered with Alice's questions.

At the station half a block from our apartment, I heard sirens before I gained the street level. My heart immediately began to race at the sound. I took the remaining stairs three at a time and ran toward my building, stopping at the street corner and peeking around the concrete fence post that stood there. Several police cars, a fire engine, and an ambulance blocked the street directly in front of my apartment building.

My blood froze, my head pounding with sudden, excruciating force. Realizing how suspicious I looked, I forced a few deep breaths in and out and rounded the corner.

A small crowd had bunched together at the caution tape stretching from the gate next to the building to the fender of the fire engine in the street. Forcing myself in among the onlookers, I asked no one in particular, "What happened?"

"Someone's been attacked in there," a man to my right said confidently. "They're not letting anyone in."

"Do... do they know who?"

"Sure, but they're not telling us, innit?"

"Right," I mumbled, already backing away, looking for an escape.

I couldn't fathom what was happening, couldn't shake the feeling that Alice—No, I had no reason to assume she was the person who'd been attacked. It might not be her. Even if it were her, maybe she was only hurt. Desperate to flee and with no idea where to go, I simply turned around and headed back to the station.

I rode the Tube for an hour, got off, and boarded the next train headed in the other direction. Then I did it again. After four hours on the Underground, I returned to my apartment to find the caution tape torn down, the emergency vehicles gone, and the crowd dispersed. Without giving myself time to think or dither, I walked directly into the building unchallenged.

Our apartment was on the tenth floor, and for once I rode the lift, not trusting my legs at the moment. The trip from the lift was short, ending when I spotted the uniformed constable posted at my door. I turned on my heel and rode the lift back down, numb and directionless.

What had happened? Was it safe to call her, or did the police have her phone? If they answered, I'd be hauled in for questioning by the end of the day. Certainly, they'd want to know who was living in the spare room, since Alice's name was the only one on the lease. It was only a matter of time before the police talked to Cat and the others at the pub and got my name, even if they didn't out me as her roommate. I needed every spare minute between now and then.

In the lobby, I stopped at the mailboxes and pulled a permanent marker out of my backpack. I hastily drew a chess piece, specifically a bishop, on Alice's mailbox. If that wasn't enough of a clue for Luke, he didn't deserve to find me. I set out on foot for Saint Paul's Cathedral, the seat of London's Bishop, hoping to find its doors open.

Halfway there I stopped dead in my tracks as though struck by lightning: I was nearly an hour late for my check-in with Jim! Hands shaking, I pulled out my cell phone and dialed his number, reaming myself under my breath. He answered on the first ring.

"Anna?" He packed a lot of anxiety into those two syllables.

"Sorry, sorry, I'm fine, I just got distracted."

"It better have been something big! I was about to call up the cavalry!"

"I think my roommate was attacked today in our apartment. Because of me."

The words tumbled out on their own, words I hadn't been able to articulate to myself yet. My eyes started to water, hands shaking so badly I was afraid I'd drop the phone.

After a tense, lengthy silence, Jim asked, "What happened?"

I explained as clinically as I could, starting with where I'd gone that morning and why I thought I'd find Luke at a building associated with Frères Enterprises. Jim didn't even bother reprimanding me for discussing classified information over the phone. I was on the brink of a total meltdown, and he had no trouble picking up on it.

"Take a breath," Jim instructed. "You sound manic."

"I am!"

"You don't know for sure she's… For all you know she injured an attacker and ran off."

"That's—yeah," I gasped, clinging to the idea like a drowning cat. "She could have. I bet she did."

"Where are you going now?"

"The cathedral… I'm freaking out, Jim."

"Just tell me you'll be okay."

"I'll be okay," I intoned dutifully, not even fooling myself.

"Check in again tomorrow, same time. Okay?"

"Yeah, right. I can do that."

"I don't have any new information for you, I'm sorry."

"That's okay. I didn't expect any."

"I'll look into Frères Enterprises though."

"Okay. Bye."

As I slipped the phone back into my pocket, my cold-numbed fingers betrayed me and it fell to the ground with an ominous crack. I picked it up, studying the spider web of fractures across its screen. I pressed the power button a few times, but it was dead. That did it. I sank to the ground, breathing hard, clutching my knees to my chest. Thankfully no one was around to see my episode except for a few passing cars, though I would've been grateful for the comfort of a kind-hearted, total stranger right about then.

It was Tommy all over again. Everything was different, but I still thought of Tommy. I couldn't process it, couldn't master the fury and grief and confusion. I sat there and had out with it until my butt was practically frozen to the sidewalk, then I picked myself up and forced myself not to stop again until I reached the cathedral.

I was so relieved to find the doors open that I nearly fainted. Shivering with a combination of cold and hunger, I paused inside the door and looked around in awe. Feeling tiny and safer than I had in months, I eased into a side aisle and leaned against the marble wall to catch my breath.

There were a lot of people inside, most of them listening to a choir singing Christmas songs in the apse; they were on "Silent Night" at the moment. Others were milling around, tourists taking it all in. A handful of men in cloth were gliding around, answering questions, directing some people to seats, and gently herding others away from roped off areas. One of them spotted me and came over, smiling serenely.

"Is there anything I can do for you?" he asked. He was a short, stocky, man with a steely grey hair helmet. His voice was soothing.

"I just needed to warm up," I whispered, vaguely surprised to find myself speaking Spanish. That wasn't a good sign. "Is that okay?"

He understood but answered in English, "Of course. Feel free to sit down, you don't have to stand."

"Thank you," I sighed, sinking obediently into the pew to which he gestured. He wandered away, but I knew he'd be back to check on me. I rubbed my fingers under my eyes, and they came away smudged with mascara and eyeliner. I probably looked like a wreck. I got up to find a bathroom.

Once I'd scrubbed away enough of the melted makeup on my face to not look like such a tragedy, I returned to the pew and rested my arms on the back of the one in front of me, listening to the choir. They were doing "Silent Night" again, but in German now. I was transfixed, soaking up the distraction for as long as it held out.

The priest returned and sat down next to me. "You seem very troubled, dear," he said in imperfect but confident Spanish. Beneath all the other emotions packed into me, I was touched by his effort.

"Something bad happened to my roommate today," I confessed, as though I'd done it. "I don't even know if she's okay."

"I'm so sorry. What a terrible thing to happen, and on Christmas." He paused uncertainly, then added, "Would you like to go and light a candle for her?"

"Can I?"

"Of course you can. You won't bother anyone. See, there's someone doing it now."

I looked up and followed his nod toward a bank of flickering candles just this side of the crossing. About twenty yards from where I sat, a man in a heavy black coat was lighting one of the candles. He crossed himself, turned around, and locked eyes with me.

It was the Frenchman from the pub, the one I'd bumped into on Christmas Eve.

35

Friday, December 25, 2020

For two full seconds, I was frozen in the grip of the French-man's gaze. I jumped to my feet as though pinched, causing the priest to lean backward in alarm and ask, "Are you all right?"

"I'm sorry, Merry Christmas," I gasped, already heading for the door. The bite of cold air outside was painful, but it woke me up enough to get the gears turning in my head, finally.

He had to have followed me from the apartment, which meant he'd waited there for me to show, which meant this *was* about me, not Alice. I looked left, then right, then across the square. I descended the stairs from the cathedral doors, stopped in front of the statue in the middle of the square, and waited.

The Frenchman emerged moments later, looking in all di-rections just as I had done. I waited until he looked right at me, then turned and walked resolutely toward the only other thing that was open, a sushi restaurant across the street. Without look-ing to see if he was still following me, I walked straight through the seating area toward the restrooms. A back door led to the street directly behind the restaurant, where I broke into a run toward the cross street that would lead me back to the cathedral.

It was an infantile plan, but that was probably why it worked. I stepped back inside the cathedral minutes later, out of breath and chilled to the bone again, resuming the exact same seat and watching the door while I tried to catch my breath again. The kindly priest with his good-enough Spanish did not come back to visit me.

I resolved to wait at least until 8:00, if allowed, before moving on. I wasn't about to vandalize the beautiful cathedral to leave Luke another clue with my marker. If he didn't go to my apartment, understand my first clue, and find me at the cathedral, I'd just have to start from scratch later, once I was safe again.

Though my eyes hardly left the doors for five hours, my pesky French shadow did not return through them. Luke didn't make an appearance, either. Back and eyes aching miserably from my vigil, I gave up at eight o'clock and headed for the doors.

I was ill prepared for the drop in temperature outside. Snow had fallen, and the square was slick with packed snow where hundreds of feet had crisscrossed it. Streetlights illuminated the scene, which was now devoid of any human presence but my own. I wrapped my scarf around my face and descended the stairs once more to go… I had no idea where.

Some tiny corner of my brain that was still functioning told me to walk toward my apartment. I didn't ask it why. I set my feet eastward and in seconds had left behind the halo of light around the cathedral's façade.

Hardly had I put a hundred feet between myself and the front of the cathedral before I heard footsteps. I looked over my shoulder and spotted a man mere yards behind me, unidentifiable in the darkness.

I broke into a run, flirting with breaking my neck on the icy sidewalk and literally sliding around the next corner into an open park behind the apse. I turned another corner, rounding the back of the cathedral, blind with panic when I saw that he was indeed chasing me. I'd really worked this out well, being out there alone at night pursued by, I assumed, the same person who may have attacked Alice in our apartment.

I lost traction and lurched to a stop, barely staying on my feet, and he crashed into me from behind, knocking us both to the ground. I managed to keep my head from striking the pavement by grabbing his jacket and leaning into him, but the impact still rocked me.

Before I could strike, scratch, or bite any part of him, I heard my name in Luke's voice. I peered through the darkness at his face, too winded to answer.

"You dork, why were you running from me?" he asked, and with a jolt of reality shifting into place I realized he was laughing.

I wriggled out from underneath him and sat up painfully, explaining, "I thought you were someone else."

He stood, offering me his hand. "How many people did you expect to come find you here?"

"Two to three," I answered with involuntary honesty, not

understanding he was mocking me.

"That's… pretty specific…"

I tried to explain further, gave up, and moaned, "Please take me somewhere safe and warm."

I could tell he was brimming with questions, but he held them in like a champ. He led me to a parked car about a block from the cathedral, and then we drove southwest for half an hour to a tiny row house across the Thames. Through what was rapidly deteriorating into delirium, I noted only that the house was blue before he ushered me inside and flipped on the lights.

I stood in the entryway, lifelessly compliant while Luke pulled off my backpack, coat, scarf, hat, and gloves. I shivered, and he wrapped his arms around me.

"I'm guessing a lot has happened since you found me this morning," he whispered.

Without raising my face from where it was pressed into his shoulder, I summarized, "I went home and my apartment was a crime scene. I left you the bishop. This guy who had been stalking us at the pub where I work followed me to the cathedral, but I waited for you until eight anyway. I thought you were him, or his brother."

"That's a lot to unpack."

"I think… I think he hurt my roommate."

"What?" He let go of me and bent down a little to look me in the eye. "Someone was stalking you and attacked your roommate?"

"Some French guy and his brother. They've been hanging around the pub where I work."

Even in my nearly catatonic state, I couldn't miss the color draining from his face. He said, "I think you need to back up a little."

"No," I groaned. "I haven't eaten all day. I'm cold and exhausted and confused. Please…"

He took pity on me, pathetic as I was, and showed me upstairs to the bathroom. One blistering shower later, temporarily clothed in a men's t-shirt and sweats, I followed my nose downstairs to find a grilled cheese sandwich and glass of wine waiting for me in the kitchen. I sat down at the kitchen table, not seeing Luke at the moment and not caring all that much. I was too focused on the food.

I had finished the sandwich and was working on the wine when I finally registered the taste of a decent merlot, which just so happened to be what I'd bought for Alice that morning. I had slipped it into my backpack before boarding the Tube.

I leapt up and dashed to the front door, but my backpack wasn't there. After a quick search through the downstairs rooms, I found it on the living room sofa, open. The only things missing were the bottle of wine and my passport. My laptop was still strapped in and apparently undisturbed.

Luke came downstairs to find me standing over my violated backpack, chewing on my fingernails. He tossed me the passport identifying me as Tegan Mercer.

"I'd love to meet your passport guy. That's about as convincing a forgery as I've ever seen."

"Thanks," I mumbled, stuffing the passport into my backpack and zipping everything back up. "Why were you going through my stuff?"

"We can talk about that later," he said firmly. When I started to argue, he silenced me with a kiss. My knee-jerk response was to push him away, and I was far too tired to fight it. He caught my wrists, wheedling, "Later, please. I didn't think I'd ever see you again…"

Too weak to twist out of his grip, I settled for glaring reproachfully up at him. "You think a grilled cheese is going to make up for how you treated me today?"

"It's a start."

"You've got some nerve—"

He cut me off again, pulling me into a kiss and then picking me up. Thinking resistance was probably futile in my current state, I allowed myself to be carried upstairs and deposited on a bed. Thankfully, Luke's intentions were benign. He helped me get comfortable, then sat down next to me on top of the covers. The warm, soft embrace of the well-worn mattress was dragging me down into a heavy sleep, but I tried to listen when he spoke to me.

"We've got a lot to talk about, Abby. When you wake up, we'll start with why you didn't object to me calling you Anna earlier."

"Mhm. Okay. Good night, Luke."

36

Saturday, December 26, 2020

Sunlight pierced the curtains, hitting me right in the face and breaking through my sleep. I tried to cover my eyes with my left hand and was unable to move it. Thinking I was waking up one body part at a time, I gave it a few minutes and tried again. A *thunk* of metal on wood brought my sleepy contentment to an abrupt end. I rolled over to confirm what the sound had alerted me to: I was handcuffed to the bedpost.

"Well, that's not good," I breathed.

I opened the drawer in the nightstand, searching for a pen or paper clip. I was too focused on this task to realize Luke had been sleeping next to me and was roused by me jostling the bed in my hurry to escape.

His hand closed around my right elbow and pulled it away from the nightstand, forcing me onto my back. I studied his face, decided he didn't look angry, and then decided I had no idea why I was handcuffed to the bedpost. I gave a nervous laugh.

"Good morning. Should I be worried?"

He nodded slowly. "Yes. We're talking now, and it's not optional."

"Oh." My smile faded. "What's with the handcuffs?"

"They're serving their intended purpose. Don't try to slip them or I'll cuff your right hand, too."

"Um… okay. You're kind of freaking me out now."

His first question came out of left field. "Aren't you curious about August thirty-first?"

It had been so long since I'd even thought about August 31 that for half a second I had no idea what he was talking about.

"No. Nothing happened," I finally answered. "I watched the news all day and nothing ever happened."

"You thought it would be on the news?"

"Well… if anywhere."

He stood up. From the desk by the door he extracted a red expanding folder, the sort I'd use to carry classified information around within the FBI. I was guessing that wasn't where he'd gotten it.

He pulled out a photo, addressing the image I couldn't see, "August thirty-first was when I got my next job."

He handed me a photo of myself. It looked like it had been snapped from a distance as I was leaving church in Manchester. My hair was still brown, which meant the picture had been taken sometime in July. I stared blankly at myself while he went on.

"I'm not supposed to exist between jobs. It's sort of a self-imposed rule. It makes everything easier. No one is supposed to know where I am, not even my boss, but thanks to you I had to come here. You can imagine my surprise when he gave me this." He pulled a sheet of paper from the folder and read, "Anna Claire Bowman, thirty-three, resident of Washington, DC, employed four years as an Intelligence Analyst at the Federal Bureau of Investigation. Last known location Manchester, Texas. Parents' house. Extremely rural, moderate security measures, including German Shepherd on the property. Armed, trained in defense tactics, speaks English, Spanish, German, French, and Italian. (I'm assuming that refers to you, not Dude.) Recently changed her appearance, blonde hair. Known contact with Agent James Camposanto, possibly a romantic relationship. Suspected involvement in an internal investigation of Agent Philip Levin." He lowered the file and asked, "Do I need to go on?"

While he'd been talking, I'd worked through my shock and arrived at the conclusion that the game was up. I shrugged. "That pretty much sums me up. Nothing about my shoe size, though?"

"You think this is funny?" he demanded, tossing the paper and the folder onto the floor. "You're made, you're done. It's a miracle you're even still alive."

"Why *am* I still alive?"

He swore, bending down to collect the papers and stuff them back into the desk drawer. "Because I didn't take the job." He sighed, sitting down at the foot of the bed and grasping my ankle. "I've never killed a woman before, and I'm sure not planning start with my favorite one."

"Well… thanks."

"But I am incredibly mad at you."

"Oh. Right. I guess that makes sense."

"Tell me what you were doing in Colorado. The truth this time, please."

"You know what I do. You know I can't tell you that."

"Okay, let me put this into perspective for you," he said briskly, moving from the foot of the bed to sit next to me. "There's a target on your back, and the man who put it there trusts me implicitly. He thinks the last time I saw you was six months ago in New Mexico, and that the only reason I turned down the job to kill you is because I don't like the idea of killing a woman. He doesn't know we're together, but he knows you're in London. He—"

"How does he know I'm in London?"

"We'll get to that. For now, just accept it. He knows where you live, and your roommate may already be a victim of whoever took the job that I turned down."

"Don't you know who?"

"Why the heck would I know that? Stop interrupting. You don't have anywhere to go. The way I see it, the only thing keeping you alive is my beneficence. If you lose that, you're dead."

I glared at him, refusing the invitation to interrupt again.

"So, tell me what you're up to. Maybe I can help. The worst that can happen is you'll get fired, which is a lot better than being dead."

"Fired? This stuff's classified, I could be prosecuted."

"Still better than being dead. And can't you share it with people who need to know?"

"You *don't* need to know. Even if you did, I'm pretty sure you don't have a clearance. I can't just hand classified out like free samples."

I could see his frustration mounting. He clenched his jaw for a moment, then asked, "So what's your plan? You're just going to carry on with your mission until you get killed?"

"You make it sound so noble…"

"It's asinine." He stood again, agitated. "You work for this Camposanto guy, right?"

"No."

"Is he the one who sent you to Colorado? Who told you my real name?"

"No."

"So the dossier I got is wrong?"

"… No."

"Enough, Abigail, Anna, Tegan, whatever your name is!" he exploded, making me jump. He sat down on the bed again, took me by the shoulders, and shook me. "I'm trying to help you!"

"And you're being very scary about it," I said with forced calm. "But no matter how much you want to help, or why, I can't give you details about an ongoing operation, not even to save my own life."

"That's—I'm not interested in the operation. I've got my own problems. I just want to know how I fit into it, that's all."

"I can't tell you that." His hands tightened around my shoulders, foretelling another outburst. I hurried to add, "However. The cat's pretty much out of the bag that I need information from you. I can't gain your confidence through chicanery and subterfuge anymore, but I can still ask you flat out."

"Then ask," he snapped.

"Okay. Did you kill Thomas Holladay on February fifteenth in Houston?"

"I don't know who that is."

"Were you in Houston on February fifteenth?" I asked.

"Sure. But you already know that, I assume."

"Did you kill anyone?"

He studied my face, perhaps wondering how much harm it would do to answer me honestly. His low answer of, "Francisco Lira. Money guy for a Colombian cartel" sure sounded true to me.

"Which cartel?"

"You tell me."

I took a deep breath, wrestling against an angry outburst of my own. It seemed to me that the rules for this conversation had been plainly established, and he was testing me. I asked slowly, "Why did you kill a Tres Islas Cartel money guy?"

"Because I was paid to."

"Okay. So you're a hitman. Now we're getting somewhere. Do you know who killed Thomas? Did you see it happen?"

"I told you, I don't know who that is."

"You probably wouldn't have heard his name, but he was an odd man out. He went there to meet Lira. Maybe they mentioned a Mick, or a Spanish pejorative for an Irishman?"

"I remember seeing a white kid, yeah, but it wasn't like I was going around chatting with the Narcos. Shaved head, about your height?"

I nodded. "You saw him? Did you see what happened to him?"

"No. It had to have been one of the TIC guys, though. No one else was there that night."

"I was," I sighed, abandoning the pretense of a one-way exchange of information.

"You're kidding me."

"We were undercover. He was my partner."

He shook his head, saying, "I didn't see you there."

"I got out," I said, hoping he wouldn't ask how. "Tommy didn't. Philip—the guy Jim is investigating—he was our boss. We suspect he gave Tommy and me to the cartel in exchange for something, but we don't know what."

"And you were married to this Philip guy, to your boss?"

"What? No, that was a complete fabrication."

"But in Colorado, he called you his wife. I distinctly remember that."

"Yeah, I don't know what he was playing at. He knew my cover story, and he decided not to blow it. I haven't gotten a chance to ask him why. He tried to shoot me the last time I saw him." I gasped, remembering the date it happened, and asked, "Maybe your boss asked Philip to kill me when you said no!"

"That's not how it works. I'm not saying this is the case, but *if* Philip was in his pocket at the FBI, that's all he'd be good for. Killing you would tend to interfere with his usefulness in that regard, don't you think?"

"If?" I asked, visibly disappointed.

"Sorry, I can't help you there."

"You can ask your boss…" I suggested.

"That would be dangerous. I thought your theory was Philip was working with the TIC."

"Is your boss not TIC…?"

"Nope, not answering that," he said, standing up yet again. "So this Campo guy tracked me down in Colorado and sent you there, all alone, to pump me for information so you can link Philip, who is your ex-boss and not your ex-husband, to the Tres Islas Cartel?"

"Not answering that."

"Why not arrest me? Bring me in, try to make a deal?"

"If anything you had just said were true, then obviously we wouldn't want you to know what we were doing."

"Your boss has a very high opinion of your skillset."

"I almost had you," I said.

"I don't know anything about Philip or this Thomas guy, so the whole thing was pointless."

"You don't know who sold us out?"

"I was there to kill Lira. That's the extent of it. I'm not part of the cartel, I'm not privy to their information streams, and I sure didn't know there were a couple of feds there. If you came all the way to London to keep trying to get information out of me, you wasted your time."

"Well… back to the drawing board, then."

"No, no way. We need to get you back to the States, and you need to lay low. Probably forever. You have a way to contact your boss, right? Just call him and tell him you need to be… extracted, or whatever you call it."

"He knew when he sent me here that whoever was pulling Philip's strings wanted me dead. Nothing has changed."

"Except someone else wants you dead now too, and he's hot on your trail."

I frowned up at him. "You still haven't explained that."

He sighed, looking evasive. Sensing we'd reached his limit, at least for now, I asked, "Maybe you can let me out of these handcuffs? This is very uncomfortable."

"Probably going to regret this," he mused, fishing a pair of handcuff keys out of his pocket. He sat down and unlocked the cuff around the headboard, pausing when he got to the one around my wrist. He gave me a quizzical look, asking, "You're still not afraid of me, are you?"

I rolled over to stretch my right hand toward my left, clasping them together, and whispered, "Should I be?"

He laughed, shaking his head as though he simply couldn't comprehend me. "You trust me a lot more than you should."

"I like you a lot more than I should."

He brushed my hair away from my shoulder, inviting, "Tell me about these French brothers."

"Hm?"

"The stalkers. Tell me about them."

"Oh, them… They were kind of short, about five eight. One of them had short hair, and the other's was longish, curly. Mousy brown. They were stocky, not fat." I thought back to the cathedral and added, "The one with longer hair had green eyes."

"Anything else?"

"Yeah, they dress nice and favor a Märzen. Will you uncuff

me, please?"

"You don't know their names?"

"I haven't had the pleasure yet." I studied his expression and asked, "Do you?"

"Giles and David Marchand. Younger brothers to Marcel Marchand, the person who signs my paychecks."

37

Saturday, December 26, 2020

Marcel, Giles, and David Marchand certainly didn't sound like members of a Colombian cartel. I hadn't heard of them or read their names anywhere, let alone associated with the TIC. I deflated, finally accepting that Luke might be right: I might have two different targets on my back.

I perked back up right away, asking, "Wait, if you turned down the job, why do you exist?"

He caught my meaning after a moment's confused pause. "I got a different one."

"Who are you supposed to kill?"

"Come on. I'm not gonna tell you that."

"So you're still on good terms with the brothers?" I asked.

"We go way back, they didn't take it personally."

"Are they Frères Enterprises?"

He frowned. "Yes, how do you know that?"

"I mean… Frères? It's not exactly code."

"Is that how you found me?"

"Yep."

"And have you reported that back to this Jim guy?"

"No," I lied, too easily. After all my recent honesty, Luke accepted it without question. I still had about four and a half hours until the extra check-in Jim had insisted on. I was going to have to conjure up some privacy.

Luke mused, "Well… if you figured it out, he probably has, too. How did he find me in Colorado?"

"Sorry, that's classified. Also, I have no idea." I jiggled my left hand, which was still cuffed, and said, "I'm taking another shower. Where can I find some clothes that actually fit me?"

"In a pile in the bathroom. Slob."

"No, clean clothes. Everything I own was part of a crime scene last time I checked."

While he unlocked the cuff, he asked, "You know you can't go back there, right?"

"I'm not an idiot."

"Just making sure."

"But I have to find out what happened to Alice."

"So, do that voodoo you do. You found me, you can find her."

"Good idea." I stood up and headed to the bathroom, calling over my shoulder, "I wouldn't say no to another grilled cheese!"

Once I was alone in the shower, no longer distracted by Luke, I started to think about Alice again. I had to at least turn on the TV and start digging through news sites to try to get a handle on what had happened. The part of me that didn't want to know, that childishly believed no news was good news, would have to be overruled.

Newly resolute, I finished up in the shower and wandered downstairs. The requested grilled cheese was waiting for me in the kitchen, and Luke was flipping through news channels on TV.

"Anything yet?" I asked.

"Nothing. I'm thinking either it wasn't newsworthy, or they're not ready to broadcast it."

"Probably the latter."

"Don't get carried away. We don't know anything yet."

While Luke continued cycling through channels, I surfed their respective websites, and any other news site I could find, for any mention of a crime yesterday in my neighborhood. In vain I searched for records at the Met, knowing they hadn't released anything newer than two years old, let alone a report from less than twenty-four hours ago.

Finally, desperate, I considered finding a payphone and calling the police to see if they'd tell me. I ran this idea by Luke, who unsurprisingly talked me down.

"I know you're new to the UK, so trust me: You step outside, you're on CCTV. Certainly at a public phone."

"So I'll cover my face. It's cold."

"What if they track you back here?"

I narrowed my eyes at him, asking, "Can they really do that, or are you just trying to freak me out?"

"Both."

"Well—come up with a better idea," I begged.

Luke's idea was for him to go alone tonight to the pub where Alice and I worked to see if she was there. If she was, end of mystery. If not, we'd figure out where to go from there. He had me halfway convinced, until I found a hiccup in the plan.

"And if the brothers Marchand are there again, looking for me?" I asked. "They'll recognize you and that's that."

"Oh yeah. Wait. No, they won't be there. They'll know you're not dumb enough to go back there."

"Maybe they're keeping an eye on the pub in case I am dumb enough."

"All right, fine. Let's hear your next great idea."

I stared into space for a few moments and then snapped my fingers. "Duh! I'm such an idiot. I'll ask Jim to find out what happened to her."

"Whoa, what?" Luke protested as I found my coat and started digging my mangled phone out of the pocket. "You're calling the FBI?"

"Not the whole FBI. Just Jim. And not right this instant. I have to get this stupid thing plugged in and see if it even still works."

"I'm not crazy about you reporting back to him now that we're together."

I paused in my study of the cracked surface of my phone to look up at him. "You think I'm gonna tell him I'm with you?"

"I have no idea."

"Even if I did, what could he do about it? He doesn't have any authority here."

"I'm sure he could work something out with MI5," Luke argued.

"To do what, arrest you?"

"I don't know, maybe."

"I thought we established that's not the FBI's objective."

"You said that, yes."

"But you don't believe me."

He shrugged.

"This is all irrelevant," I concluded. "If I don't call him at three o'clock today, he'll send in the cavalry. Since I already told him about what happened yesterday—*before* I ran into you," I interjected in response to his raised eyebrows, "he's probably already got some info for me about Alice. All we have to do is wait until this afternoon."

I plugged my phone into the laptop and tried to turn it on, but either it was fully drained of power or I'd permanently broken it by dropping it onto frozen concrete. I left it alone for half an hour, busying myself with internet sleuthing once more, and then tried again. With relief I felt the phone buzz feebly and begin to power up, but I was soon disappointed. The entire top half of the screen was useless, a chaotic patchwork of colors and bright, white cracks. I stared at it, wondering if I could convince Luke to buy me a new phone, until a notification appeared on the phone app in the crack-free, lower righthand corner. I opened the app.

"Hey, I have a voicemail," I announced.

"From who?"

"I can't tell… the top half of the screen is too mangled to

make anything out."

Luke came to look over my shoulder. He studied the screen for a few seconds and then carefully pressed on a green square of pixels near the top.

"What was that?" I asked.

"The speakerphone button, I think. You go through a lot of phones, don't you?"

Interrupting my retort was a scratching, wordless noise issuing from the speaker. I turned up the volume in time to hear the first words of the message.

"Tegan… It's Alice. You've got to go to the Parthenon exhibit at the British Museum at noon tomorrow. I'm—I'm supposed to tell you not to bring anyone with you, and not to tell the police. I think they're—"

The message ended abruptly.

I met Luke's eyes and saw my own confusion and shock mirrored in his expression. He found his voice first and asked, "Was that really her?"

"It sounded like her."

"She didn't sound scared."

"When is tomorrow? Is tomorrow today?" I asked him, staring at the ruined screen and willing it to show me when the voicemail had been left.

"If it's today, you need to book it. It's already eleven."

"What are you gonna do?"

"I'm gonna find out where they're keeping her," he said, his tone precluding any argument.

38

Saturday, December 26, 2020

Alice's brief message was stuck on repeat in my head for the entire journey on the Tube from Luke's house to the British Museum. The Saturday crowd was swollen due to the holidays. I could hardly squeeze my way into the Parthenon exhibit, let alone stand still and scan the crowd for familiar or otherwise notable faces.

The more I played her words over in my mind, the more fear was injected into her voice. I was at once thrilled to know she was alive and terrified I might not be able to save her. I doubted seriously whether I'd be able to comply with the demands of whoever had her.

My only hope, and hers, was that Luke would be able to track her down and snatch her away while the Marchand brothers—and we were both convinced that's who we were dealing with—were distracted with me.

So, I milled around the exhibit, colliding with other tourists every few seconds, perpetually in someone's way. Around ten minutes after noon, I saw a spot open up at the southern end of the room in the tiny space between a replica column and the wall, a perfect place to stand still without being pushed this way and that. I gained the spot ahead of another woman heading straight for it, shrugging apologetically at her as I leaned against the column. From my new vantage point, I could see the length of the room and was finally able to start people watching.

Another fifteen minutes passed uneventfully. Every person who paid me more than passing attention was carefully scrutinized, but I never spotted the brothers from the pub, and no one approached me. I'd been lost in the store enough as a child to know the best way to be found is to stand still, so I resisted the urge to wander around the exhibit.

The crowd began to thin at the bottom of the hour, but having fewer faces to scan didn't help me at all. I was beginning to think I'd have to shell out another Tube fare to come back tomorrow when a tiny voice behind me made me jump.

"Etes-vous Anna?"

I turned, forgetting I was supposed to be Tegan now, and saw a boy about nine years old on the other side of the column. Before I could answer, he pushed a piece of paper into my hand and dashed away, grinning triumphantly.

It was a carefully folded museum map, and tucked inside one of the folds was a key with the number 35 etched into it, presumably corresponding to a locker I'd have to find. Someone had drawn a line in pencil from the Cloak Room, around the Great Court, and into a grayed out area that was almost certainly off limits to the likes of me.

"Great, a scavenger hunt," I muttered to myself, stuffing the key into my pocket and setting out for the Cloak Room.

I found locker 35 and opened it to find a black shopping bag containing a blue blazer and an ID badge belonging to someone named Marge Henry, an Administrative Assistant. Hoping against hope that she was alive and I wasn't about to make myself a suspect in her murder, I threw the blazer over my arm and pocketed the badge.

I followed the map as far as I could without the badge, which turned out to be a Staff Admittance Only door beyond which the penciled-in line continued into the bowels of the museum's administrative area.

On went the blazer, which was way too big for me. The door unlocked at a swipe from my stolen badge. Without the benefit of walls and doors marked on the map, I had to take my best guess at where to go from there. This led me to an exterior door labeled Receiving Bay B. No badge-swipe was needed to open it, so I let myself in and closed the door behind me.

I found myself at the top of a short flight of metal stairs overlooking a two-bay garage. Yellow emergency lights illuminated the space enough for me to make out another staircase leading to a matching door on the other side of the far bay. Even though this area was obviously not for tourists, it was clean and tidy. It was also completely devoid of life.

In each corner of the room facing the closed garage doors was a sleek, black security camera. I leaned back to look into the nearest one, wondering if anyone was looking back at me.

"Hello?" I called, my voice echoing back to me from the far wall. "Is anyone here?"

The only part of the room I couldn't see was directly beneath my feet. In the opposite corner, I could see a space about five feet tall underneath the landing in front of the door. I assumed the same space was underneath my staircase. The stairs were treads only, no risers, which meant anyone standing in that space would be able to grab my feet as I walked down the stairs. The thought gave me a thrill of fear that nearly sent me scurrying back through the door; but, reminding myself I'd tumbled down a staircase before, and a much longer one at that, and lived to laugh about it, I steeled myself and stepped onto the first stair.

Nothing happened, and I reached the concrete floor of the bay without incident, tension stiffening my movements. At least I'd been half-right: As soon as I turned to look under the stairs, a man emerged from beneath them gun-first, pointing his weapon at my head. The light reflected off the barrel of a suppressor attached to a large handgun, but it was too dim for me to discern any more detail. I didn't need any more light to recognize the man.

"Who was the candle for?" I asked in French, slowly raising my hands to show they were empty.

"My brother. Your little girlfriend stabbed him in the neck with a steak knife, and I had to leave him there."

I couldn't suppress a smile. "She is a handful. Where is she, by the way?"

"Shut up. Turn around."

I half-obeyed, asking as I turned, "Can you at least tell me if she's okay?"

For that I received a heavy blow to the back of the head. Though I held on to consciousness, I was completely disoriented, sinking to my knees to keep from falling. He kicked me over the rest of the way, pressing his knee into my back while he zip tied my hands together.

A moment later, sunlight flooded into the bay as the garage door opened. I was hauled to my feet only to be tossed into the back of a van that pulled into the bay. My assailant climbed in after me, and I began to roll nauseatingly back and forth across the floor of the van as we sped away.

I labored onto my back and sat up, fighting to keep my grilled cheese down. From my angle, pressed against the driver's side of the van, I couldn't see who was at the wheel. I could, however, see the occupant of the passenger seat.

Though my vision was a bit blurry from the blow to the head, and he was studiously gazing through the windshield, there was no mistaking Luke's profile.

Thanks for reading! If you hate cliffhangers, don't forget to read the bonus content at the end of this book: the first chapter of the sequel, *House on Fire*. If you enjoyed *Enemy Closer*, please take a couple minutes to leave a review or rating. Reviews help readers decide whether to buy my books, and every single review helps so much—even the bad ones.

Want to be the first to know when new stories come out? You can sign up for my mailing list on my website, akweller.com. You'll get my occasional newsletter, and you'll receive a link to download a free short story

▼

About the Author

AK Weller was born and raised in Texas, moved to New Mexico, and now lives in Montana with her husband, four cats, and three dogs. She mostly enjoyed brief careers as a technical writer, private investigator, social worker, and pet sitter before finding her calling as a semi-employed writer. AK writes mysteries and thrillers while running her own graphic design business. Her favorite books to read over and over again were written by JRR Tolkien, Stieg Larsson, Sue Grafton, Michael Crichton, and JK Rowling.

▼

Also available from AK Weller

The Anna Bowman Thrillers: a 5-Book Thriller Epic

Book 1: Enemy Closer

On the run from her ex-husband, a powerful federal agent, Abigail takes shelter in a cabin in rural southwest Colorado with her trusty German Shepherd, Dude. When she learns someone else has been using the cabin to hide out too, she'll find herself stuck with a shady, surprise roommate for the summer. While they figure out how to get along, they'll learn their stories were intertwined long before they met. *Enemy Closer* is a suspense thriller that allows you to experience each new piece of information along with the characters right to the end, when you realize everything you thought you knew was a lie. A deeper story has only just begun to unfold.

Book 2: House on Fire

Thanks to her boss, shady FBI Agent Jim Camposanto, Analyst Anna Bowman finds herself the target of two different international criminal cabals. With no obvious way out of the mess she's just beginning to understand, she'll have to drag the truth out of her secretive boss and a hitman who just can't seem to shake her. Will Anna ever get to relax and feel safe with her beloved German Shepherd, Dude, or will she become addicted to Camposanto's dangerous games? Anna Bowman's misadventures continue in *House on Fire*.

Book 3: Bigger Fish

Home from her unlikely triumph in Argentina, Anna thinks her life is getting back to normal until a surprise visit from David Marchand sets her on a collision course with Luke Jackson once again. With a little help from two people straight out of Anna's past, they'll unravel a mystery that takes them out of the frying pan and into the fire.

Book 4: No Port in a Storm

After unraveling a murderous family feud, FBI castoffs Anna and Jim travel to Italy to deliver a final peace offering. Amidst their fraught romance, they find no shortage of ways to make new trouble. While fostering unlikely friendships against an idyllic Mediterranean backdrop, they provoke dangerous enemies closer to home. Emily, Luke, and Dude were supposed to be safe in Texas, but suddenly they're in the crosshairs again. As tensions escalate, Jim's clever schemes are put to the test. When generations of hostility erupt into all-out war, will Jim's cunning save them, or will Anna's fighting spirit be their only way out?

▼

Coming soon from AK Weller

<u>2.15.2020</u>

In the prequel to *Enemy Closer*, Anna Bowman escapes her boring hometown and joins the FBI. After a few years as a quiet but efficient cog in the machine, she tries to achieve her childhood dream of becoming an FBI Agent, only to be rejected and bewildered. Ensnared instead in the intrigues of Agent James Camposanto, Anna will embark on an unexpected assignment in Houston, Texas with her protégé, Thomas Holladay. What really happened on February 15, 2020, in Houston, and how in the world did a divorced art historian from Manchester, Texas end up there?

<u>Friday the 14th</u>

Anna Bowman and her older sister, Emily, just wanted a fun night out to celebrate Anna's twenty-fifth birthday. While enjoying some much-needed time away from their significant others, the sisters accidentally pick up a new friend at a casino in Oklahoma. When a tongue-in-cheek plan to burn down each other's houses and collect the insurance money falls into the wrong hands, Anna and Emily will have to band together to stop an arsonist… if they decide they want to. Find out who's left standing on *Friday the 14th*.

<u>A Last Time for Everything</u>

A Last Time for Everything tells the tragic and unbelievable origin story of 17-year-old Anna Bowman and the events that set her on the path to joining the FBI.

Sam Walsh, PI Mysteries

<u>Prequel - Tiger by the Tail</u>

Private Investigator Samantha Walsh has been in denial about her true identity for 25 years. When a terrifying figure from her past explodes back into her life, Sam will have to decide how much she's willing to sacrifice to stop running from her father's killers in *Tiger by the Tail*.

<u>#1 - Sam vs. the Black Hat</u>

Newly independent PI Sam Walsh needs clients, and she can't afford to be picky. When her old boss sends a prospective client her way, Sam takes the case - a classic cheating spouse - against her better judgment. Caught between a dishonest client and a dangerous, shadowy foe, Sam will either solve her first case or die trying. Sue Grafton's iconic Kinsey Millhone is catapulted into twenty-first century Texas suburbia in book one of the Sam Walsh, PI Mysteries.

Underworld: A Short Suspense Thriller

Underworld follows mystery woman Seffy Nix as she moves into a 140-year-old mansion that seems to be haunted by a slovenly, inconsiderate ghost bent on distracting her from the mission that brought her to small-town Helena, Montana.

The Beast and the Books: A Short Monster Story

All alone one night, Rodney is clearing out a storage unit. His biggest problem is his wife's massive book collection, at least until the lights go out and he realizes he's not alone. Something is living deep in the bowels of the storage facility, and it's about to make a break for freedom. Unfortunately for Rodney, he's right in the creature's path.

Anywhere But Home: A Memoir

A short memoir about budding author AK Weller's increasingly nonsensical attempts to fill a void in her life caused by an abusive relationship. From Oklahoma to Texas to Colorado, she hops from one distraction to another until she realizes the answer to her problem is starting over.

<u>The Institute: A Short Story</u>

High school junior Miguel thought getting an underage drinking charge would derail his life at New Mexico Military Institute in Roswell, but when his new friends draw him into their world of pranks and mischief, he'll discover there's a lot more going on at NMMI than he ever imagined. Will Miguel maintain his hard-won GPA and graduate with a diploma that will open doors for him to wherever he wants to go, all while learning how to mix a little fun into his busy life? Will his new friends have his back when things start to get spooky?

▼

Keep turning for a sneak peak at the next
chapter of Anna's story: *House on Fire.*

1

Saturday, December 26, 2020

I struggled to my knees on the ribbed metal floor of the cargo van. My arms, zip tied at the wrist behind me, were no help. The van turned sharply to the right, throwing me against exposed metal wall behind the driver while I stared stupidly at the man in the passenger seat.

Luke.

I turned away from him far too late to hide my recognition, and I locked eyes with the man riding it out in the empty cargo area with me.

"A familiar face, eh?" he taunted, English with a thick French accent.

Lacking any coherent or helpful response to that, I settled for kicking him in the jaw as hard as I could. While he recovered, I struggled on my knees toward the rear of the van in a wild bid for freedom, but he tackled me from behind. Gripping me by the hair, he swung my head toward the bulging wheel well.

The impact knocked me senseless, but only for a moment. I could tell very little time had passed because the Frenchman was still breathing heavily, swearing at me under his breath, as I came to. I remained motionless, wondering if he'd kill me if I kept fighting.

"What're you trying to do, kill her?" Luke complained, echoing my thoughts.

His voice sounded too far away, as though my hearing had been impaired. He was speaking French, and to my ears it was indistinguishable from any native French-speaker. He spoke better French than I did.

"She kicked me! She nearly broke my jaw!" the man whined.

"Well, maybe next time you won't forget about her feet," Luke shot back.

I rolled onto my back as the Frenchman began patting himself down, searching his pockets for more zip ties. The driver remained silent, only his right ear visible to me. Luke was again absorbed in the windshield, his jaw set.

Rage surged through me and I screamed, "You lying scumbag! Where is Alice? *Where is she?*"

I caught a flash of the driver's profile as he turned sharply, silently, to Luke. A hand closed over my right ankle, distracting me. I met the Frenchman's eyes and saw a satisfying gleam of apprehension. He tightened his grip, and I jerked my knee toward my chest, dragging him forward by the hand. He toppled forward onto my stomach.

As I tightened my thighs around his neck, thinking I might be angry enough to actually kill the guy, the driver finally spoke.

"For God's sake, Giles," he sighed. "Luke, do something about her."

With a grunt, Luke climbed into the back and knelt beside me. He and I watched Giles' face turning purple for a moment before Luke pried my knees apart and allowed him to slither backward, gasping for air.

Luke leaned over me to mutter in English, "Anna, stop it. Please."

Giles hacked, coughed, and snapped, "You do it, then."

A thick, black zip tie flew at Luke's face. He caught it, then met my eyes again. My brain had caught up enough to keep my most pressing questions to myself: Why are you helping them? Why aren't you rescuing Alice like you said you would? Why did you let me go to the museum if you knew this was going to happen?

As Luke formed the tie into a loop to secure my ankles together, I considered what would happen if I attacked him. I knew enough jujitsu now to grapple most people into submission, but I'd learned it from Luke. And it was two against one. And my arms were still tied together. Luke and Giles would put a quick end to my struggles, and I'd end up taking a nap. I didn't want to lose consciousness. I'd heard on TV that it's bad for you.

Luke rolled me over onto my stomach, bent my knees toward him, and slipped the zip tie over my shoes. I let him do it, telling myself I was waiting my turn rather than letting my last chance slip away because I was too afraid to fight a superior opponent.

Where had I gone wrong? What was it my Krav Maga teacher always said? "Don't go stupid places to do stupid things with stupid people." Something like that. Well, I didn't know any particularly stupid people, and I'd never understood what he meant by "stupid places." It wasn't like I made a habit of visiting bad neighborhoods at midnight. So that left doing stupid things. What one stupid thing had I done to start the chain reaction of events that ended in London in this van with these three men?

After a too-quick mental review—sometimes known as one's life flashing before one's eyes—I had to conclude I'd made a serious mistake when I fell in love with fireworks as a child. That was the beginning of the end. Had I not become obsessed with fireworks, I'd have skipped out on the Independence Day show when I was 17 and no one else in my family wanted to go with me. Then I never would have met my high school boyfriend; gotten pregnant; been effectively spayed by said boyfriend; become a barren social cast off in my tiny, backward hometown of Manchester, Texas; and ended up desperate enough to marry Aaron Oakley when I was only 19.

Then I never would have fled to an internship with the FBI in Washington, DC to get away from Manchester and my violently abusive husband. Without the FBI, there would certainly be no Agent James (Jim) Camposanto in my life.

Jim never would have picked me out of a stack of wannabe agents (for God only knew what reason) to be his mole inside the undercover operation of his nemesis, Agent Philip Levin. Wherever I might have ended up on February 15, 2020, it wouldn't have been a warehouse in Houston where my partner,

Tommy, was killed and Luke Jackson assassinated a Tres Islas Cartel (TIC) money guy named Francisco Lira.

Had I not been involved in that ill-fated operation, I never would have been sent to Colorado to find Luke and question him about what happened that night. I wouldn't have built between us the bond of affection and attraction that goaded Luke to tell me he was coming to London. He wouldn't have invited me to come find him here, so I wouldn't have. I never would have been sucked into Luke's world where these wretched creatures dwelt.

Contrary to an earlier assumption that Luke was involved with the TIC, he appeared to be working for a totally unrelated criminal syndicate represented by the two Frenchmen in the van with us. The only one missing was their brother, who was recovering in the hospital after being stabbed by my roommate, Alice Murphy, who may or may not be dead.

Oh, God, Alice…

Lost in thought, I was jerked back to reality by something cold and hard pressing into my knee. I realized the Frenchman was about to put a retaliatory bullet into my knee cap, and terror erupted inside me.

Luke noticed, too, because he snarled, "Put that away, you petty little idiot."

"What do you care, it's just her knee."

"Giles I will tear you apart if you hurt her."

At least Luke was partially on my side. The pressure disappeared from my leg, the roar of the axle beneath me drowning out my sob of relief.

Into the relative silence that followed Luke's threat, the driver of the van spoke again.

"Luke."

He conveyed a lot with that one word. I felt tension swell, tightening Luke's voice as he answered, "You said she wouldn't get hurt."

Disregarding this, the driver asked, "Did anyone see you at the museum, Giles?"

"No."

"You're sure?"

"Positive."

Luke climbed back into the passenger seat. I wormed around on the floor, ignoring the Frenchman's smirk, until I was seated with my legs stretched toward him and my back against the wall. I hoped to hear more crosstalk, but all three men were silent for the remainder of the ride. Through the windshield, I saw nothing but overcast skies.

I reviewed what I knew about the Frenchmen so far: Luke had told me the three Marchand brothers were named Marcel, Giles, and David. Marcel was the eldest, the one in charge. I couldn't remember if Luke had explicitly said that, or if I'd inferred it, but I felt it was true. Giles and David were the two who'd been casing the pub where Alice and I worked, so David must be the one out of commission thanks to Alice's impressively gritty stab to the neck. David was either dead or receiving medical treatment somewhere. Marcel, then, was the driver. The three of them represented the shady import-export company Frères Enterprises.

Jim. That *liar.* He was the real reason I was tied up in the back of a van. Hadn't he told me to look for Luke in locations associated with import-export companies? He definitely had not told me about Frères Enterprises specifically, no more than Luke had. I'd worked that out on my own, and it hadn't been easy. Could Jim have known that the eponymous frères were the Marchand brothers, the very people who sent Luke to kill Francisco Lira in Houston in the first place? Would it have killed him to give me a heads up?

Before I'd left for the museum, Luke had told me he would find Alice. He was supposed to rescue her while I was at the museum doing my best impression of a worm on a hook. Either that was still in the works, his plan had taken a left turn, or that had never been his plan at all.

I lost track of time. By my best guess, I had about two hours until I was supposed to check in with Jim. The chances of that happening were remote enough to be counted as impossible. Even if I could get to a phone, it would only be to sound the S-O-S. An hour after the missed call, Jim would put the wheels in motion to track me down and send someone to my aid. How long that would take, if anyone could even find me, I had no clue.

When I judged we'd been driving for about an hour, the van took a right turn and slowed considerably. Fifteen minutes later, another right turn put us on a gravel road. Through the windshield, I could see trees arching over us. The already dim, grey light became dimmer still. I stopped hearing other cars around us.

A long, slow left turn, possibly around a circular driveway, finally brought the trip to an end. The van lurched to a stop, and Marcel instructed, "Luke, I'd like to speak to you inside. Giles, see to our guest."

Evidently Giles wasn't that keen on taking orders. He opened the side door and climbed out without a word or a glance, slamming the door shut and leaving me alone in the van. I heard an indistinguishable shout from Giles, an answering bark from Luke.

I peered around the dark interior of the van, looking for a weapon of any sort. Tie-down straps, a packing blanket, and a ripped corner of a cardboard box comprised the entire contents of the van. The heavy hook at the end of the straps would have made a handy bludgeon, but that required hands. I inched my way toward the passenger seat, saw the face of a large, grey stone house to the right of the van, and was eyeing the glove compartment when the side door slid open again.

"Oh, no you don't," Luke cried, grabbing me by the tail of my sweater and hauling me backward. I grunted my annoyance as he threw me over his shoulder and headed towards the house. He asked, "Are you an idiot, or are you trying to let her get away?"

I realized he wasn't talking to me when Giles answered, "She's too heavy."

"It's no wonder you two needed my help. Couldn't even handle a tiny little pub wench."

"Ah, shut up."

Up a short flight of stairs, through a tall doorway, and

across a marble foyer, Luke carried me, finally depositing me onto a hard, narrow couch in an old-fashioned sitting room. Marcel and Giles were there, the latter getting a fire going while the former stared motionlessly through a picture window that looked out over the driveway and front lawn.

Like his brothers, Marcel was of average height and stocky build, his short hair slightly darker and peppered with white at the temples. Luke interrupted my study by stepping between us and helping me into a sitting position. I watched his face, trying to pick up on some kind of clue about how I should be reacting to him while he cut away the zip tie around my ankles. He left my wrists bound, shot me one totally indecipherable glance, and left to help Giles with the fire.

Marcel turned around, and I found myself staring up at the type of face for which the paradoxical 'nondescript' had been coined. If one could create a mental picture of dark brown hair, matching eyes, exactly one nose, one mouth, and two ears, they'd have as good a grasp on Marcel as I did in that moment. Even his expression was hypotonic, and as he stared at me I couldn't decide whether he was planning to make me a sandwich or put a bullet between my eyes. I figured after all the cloak-and-dagger nonsense to get me here, an immediate execution probably wasn't anything to worry about.

"Hello, Anna," he said in French with neither a friendly nor a threatening tone. His voice was soft, as though he were unwilling to expend the energy required to speak at a normal volume. He sat down in an armchair across from the sofa. "I'm Marcel, and this is my brother, Giles. Luke you already know. I hope

Giles wasn't too hard on you. He has a capricious nature."

"He's standing right here," Giles grumbled. I glanced from Marcel to Giles, outwardly confused.

"Sorry, I don't understand French," I lied, so badly I was impressed at Marcel for not laughing.

Marcel's eyes drifted to Luke, who was watching the exchange from his post next to the fireplace. "You told me she was a good liar," he said in English, making it an accusation.

Luke said, "She is. She's sandbagging you."

I scowled at him. "Don't act like you know me."

I hoped I wasn't imagining the glimmer of approval in Luke's eyes as he frowned down at me. He crossed his arms but didn't respond.

Marcel said, "You should be nicer to my friend, Miss Bowman. It's his unexpectedly soft heart you have to thank for being alive today."

"Thanks, softie," I mumbled, not looking at either of them.

I already knew what Marcel meant. Luke had gone back to Marcel after leaving me in New Mexico back in July, and Marcel had asked him to kill me. Luke had refused. I assumed Marcel had hit pause on my contract murder, because there I sat, stubbornly alive and so confused I was forgetting to be mad or scared.

"Marcel," Giles said.

Marcel's gaze sharpened warily as he glanced at his brother. "What now?" he asked.

"I'm sick of her attitude. Just give me half an hour with her. Upstairs. I won't kill her, I promise."

Marcel shrugged. "If you must. I need to rest anyway. Bring her back here when you're done, please. Luke, we still need to talk."

Luke argued, "I'm not leaving her alone with Giles. You promised me she wouldn't get hurt."

"You tendered certain promises as well, if you recall."

Marcel's calm, even tone was deeply unsettling. I stared at Luke, silently begging him to drop it. Whatever was going on here, I could see Luke's position was nearly as precarious as my own. With my feet free, I was pretty sure I could handle Giles. Maybe I could even convince him to untie my hands. I'd take care of him, then come back down here and help Luke—

"I told you, I don't give a crap about her," Luke said, cutting across my conniving thoughts. "That FBI lackey she's working for does. You wanted her here, and she's here. Who cares about her attitude?"

Marcel weighed Luke's words for a long minute, gazing at me all the while. I tried not to look too hurt by Luke's assertion that he didn't give a crap about me, but it stung all the same.

"Giles, go feed the dogs," Marcel finally said. "Luke, get her something to eat."

www.ingramcontent.com/pod-product-compliance
Lightning Source LLC
Chambersburg PA
CBHW011316310726
48973CB00011B/2947

9798991630863